Praise for *Gruel and Unusual Punishment*

"Snappy descriptions . . . humorous shenanigans."
—*Pittsburgh Tribune-Review*

"Think *Mayberry R.F.D.* with Mennonites. Think *Murder, She Wrote* with a Pennsylvania Dutch accent. Instead of Jessica Fletcher, think Magdalena Yoder, a plain-dressing, blunt speaking, middle-aged innkeeper who frequently rescues the incompetent chief of police by solving his cases. . . . The series' popularity is rising like sticky dough. . . . [The] key to Myers's success is her main character."
—*The Morning Call* (Allentown, PA)

"Very funny . . . colorful . . . rings true . . . endearing . . . a tasty culinary mystery." —*Midwest Book Review*

"With her sassy wit and odd habits . . . Magdalena is a delightful main character."
—*The Champion Newspaper* (Atlanta, GA)

"Deadly games, food, and fun. . . . Fast-paced, tongue-in-cheek . . . zany humor . . . a funny and entertaining read . . . [by] a wise and perceptive writer."
—*The Rocky Mount Telegram* (North Carolina)

"Satiric humor intermingled with quirky, likable characters . . . a very tasty story. Magdalena Yoder's adventures always make for nicely nutty reading and the ending will delight."
—*Romantic Times*

"Had me constantly laughing. . . . Life would never be dull with [Magdalena] around. . . . A wonderful book with skillful writing and I highly recommend it to everyone."
—*I Love a Mystery*

continued . . .

GRUEL AND UNUSUAL PUNISHMENT

A PENNSYLVANIA DUTCH MYSTERY WITH RECIPES

Tamar Myers

A SIGNET BOOK

01072 6213 A

SIGNET
Published by New American Library, a division of
Penguin Putnam Inc., 375 Hudson Street,
New York, New York 10014, U.S.A.
Penguin Books Ltd, 80 Strand,
London WC2R 0RL, England
Penguin Books Australia Ltd, 250 Camberwell Road,
Camberwell, Victoria 3124, Australia
Penguin Books Canada Ltd, 10 Alcorn Avenue,
Toronto, Ontario, Canada M4V 3B2
Penguin Books (N.Z.) Ltd, 182–190 Wairau Road,
Auckland 10, New Zealand

Penguin Books Ltd, Registered Offices:
Harmondsworth, Middlesex, England

Published by Signet, an imprint of New American Library,
a division of Penguin Putnam Inc.
Previously published in a New American Library hardcover edition.

First New American Library Hardcover Printing, February 2002
First Signet Printing, January 2003
10 9 8 7 6 5 4 3 2 1

For the best in-laws in the world,
Robert and Vonnie Root

AUTHOR'S NOTE

1

I killed Clarence Webber just three days after he bought my sinfully red BMW. It was an inadvertent killing, to be sure. If anything, I killed him with kindness.

You see, my name is Magdalena Yoder, and I own the PennDutch Inn, a full-board establishment in Hernia, Pennsylvania. Although quite charming, Hernia is only a tad larger than a gnat's navel, and there are no restaurants in town. So when the county jail over in Bedford ran out of space, they starting housing their overflow of lawbreakers at our lockup, and guess who got to cook for them?

Well, not me exactly, but my double second cousin once removed, Freni Hostetler, a surprisingly cantankerous Amish woman in her mid-seventies. Freni has worked for me—a mellow Mennonite in her mid-forties—since the day my parents died, squished to death in a tunnel when the car they were driving got caught between a milk tanker and a semitrailer filled to the gills with state-of-the-art running shoes. Although Freni cooked for the Hernia prisoners, she was under my employ, and besides, it was I who chose the menu that fateful day.

"You idiot, Yoder!" the Chief of Police yelled. "Didn't you know Mr. Webber was allergic to shrimp?"

I glared at the man, although I tried not to actually see him. Melvin has bulging eyes that move independently of each other, and virtually no lips. In short, he looks like a praying mantis.

I'm not judging the man by his looks, mind you, because I'm no picnic to look at myself. Generous folks have described me as being somewhat horsy in my appearance, and they're right—if they're referring to a very skinny mare, one with virtually no curves. I have a long narrow face, and a nose that deserves its own zip code. I wear my faded brown mane in a bun atop my head. I cover the bun with a white organza prayer cap and I wear solid-color dresses with elbow-length sleeves and knee-length skirts. My shoes have often been referred to as clodhoppers. So you see, physical beauty means very little to me.

Character is what counts, but alas, Melvin seems sadly lacking in that department. The man has always been my nemesis, and will always be so. The fact that he is now married to my sister, Susannah, has done little, if anything, to change the way Melvin and I feel about each other. I know, it isn't Christian to harbor these negative thoughts—I wouldn't quite call them hate—and I pray daily for a change of heart. That prayer, like so many others of mine, has gone unanswered. The best I can do is hold my tongue.

"He didn't have to eat the shrimp," I said evenly. "It's not like they were hidden in the sauce."

"That's why you're an idiot, Yoder. If they were in the sauce, that's all that mattered. And anyway, you had no business serving him gruel. I hired you to serve food. *Real* food."

"It wasn't gruel, it was shrimp and grits. I picked up the recipe on my vacation in Charleston, South Carolina."

I peeked at Melvin just long enough to see that his right eye was fixed on me, his left on the phone. "Meat and potatoes, Yoder, that's what we like to eat."

"Mantises eat their mates," I said wickedly, and then wondered for a second if my sister, Susannah, was in danger. She wasn't, thank heavens. It's the female mantis that eats her mate.

"Very funny, Yoder. Unfortunately I can't arrest you until I get the lab results, but I'm expecting the phone to ring any minute."

I prayed for a charitable tongue. I really did.

"You're crazy, Melvin," I said kindly. "You're as nutty as a jar of Jiff. If you arrest me, you'll have to arrest Freni. She's the one who actually made the meal. I simply supplied the menu."

That shut him up. In addition to being my cook, Freni is Melvin's mother's best friend. They are also some sort of cousins, which—and I shudder to say this—makes Melvin kin to me.

Oh what a tangled web they weave, when Amish-Mennonites conceive. Both Melvin and I are Mennonites of Amish derivation, which puts us squarely in that category. My blood lines are so tangled that I am, in fact, my own cousin. All I need is a sandwich in order to qualify as a family picnic.

I willed myself to look at Melvin. "Melvin, if you need my help solving this case, just ask. Threats, however, will get you nowhere."

"I don't need your help, Yoder," he said vehemently. Of course we both knew that was a lie. Melvin couldn't pass an I.Q. test for blondes. The story goes that Melvin's lack of mental acuity is the result of having been kicked in the head by a bull—one he was trying to milk.

You might ask, then, how is it Melvin came to be our Chief of Police? The answer is simple. No one else in Hernia wanted such a low-paying, thankless job.

"In that case," I said calmly, "I'm outta here." I turned on my heels—which are quite narrow by the way—and strode to the door of his small, stuffy office.

"No, Yoder, wait!"

"Give me one reason."

"Because—uh—well—"

"Spit it out, Melvin."

"Because sometimes you have a pretty good head on your shoulders."

Of course he was right. It may be a horsy head, but it's actually quite bright.

"Flattery will get you everywhere, dear, but you need to be a little more profuse."

"Damn it, Yoder, don't make me do that." Melvin is a lapsed Mennonite, which explains his foul language. I'm sure it doesn't help either that he's married to Susannah, who is, of all things, a Presbyterian. In her case, the apple not only fell far from the tree, it rolled out of the orchard altogether.

"Ah, ah, ah," I said. "No swearing."

"Okay," he grunted through clenched mandibles. "I rely on you a lot. But part of that has to do with the fact that I'm running for the state legislature. I can't do two things at once, you know."

The phone rang before I could respond with a clever quip. I waited patiently while he carried on an interminable mumbled conversation into what has to be the world's last remaining rotary phone.

Finally he turned to me. "It wasn't the shrimp, Yoder. It was the gruel itself. Somebody put arsenic in it."

2

I felt like I'd been hit on the soft spots behind both knees. Fortunately, my bony bottom found the cold hard seat of a metal folding chair, sparing me a nasty fall to the floor.

"What did you say?"

There was a faint, triumphant glimmer in his wandering eyes. "You heard me. Arsenic. Now, I wonder how that happened."

"Don't even go there, Melvin. Not if you want my help with this case." As much as we dislike each other, we both know the other is incapable of cold-blooded murder.

The glimmer died. "You got to help me with this one, Yoder. If word gets out that I've been poisoning my prisoners, I'll never make it to the legislature. That means the U.S. Senate is out, not to mention the presidency. Then where will America be?"

I bit my tongue so hard, it was a wonder I didn't swallow it. As it was, my poor lingua was so punctured, I could have strained soup with it.

"Before you cancel your plans to redecorate the Oval Office," I lisped, "I suggest we have ourselves a little tête-à-tête."

"Yoder, I'm married! And you call yourself a good Mennonite."

I gasped at his twisted interpretation. "In your dreams, buster. I wouldn't do that with you if you were the last arthropod on earth. I simply meant that we need to get our heads together and figure out some things."

"Ah," he said, sounding slightly disappointed. "You want to tête now?"

"The sooner the better." I pulled my chair closer. "Start at the beginning, Melvin."

His left eye blinked. "You were there, Yoder."

"Yes, I know, I sold my BMW to Clarence Webber. But I had no idea at the time that he was wanted for credit-card fraud. After all, he paid me cash."

"Money cash, or check cash?"

"Money. Nice, crisp, one-hundred-dollar bills." I could still feel them between my fingertips. The sound of Clarence snapping them as he peeled them from his wad, and the sound of me snapping them as I counted them aloud—even Mozart didn't write music that sweet.

"How many of these bills, Yoder?"

I bristled at the question, but it was a matter of public record. I'd advertised in both the *Hernia Herald* and the *Bedford Daily News*.

"Two hundred of them. The car was out of warranty and needed a little work."

Melvin was drooling like a teething baby. He knew I'd bought the car for cash, and therefore the twenty grand had gone straight into my bank account. That much money was more than he ever hoped to see in one lump sum—well, without me in the picture, at any rate. Perhaps if Melvin and Susannah stuck it out, and perhaps if Susannah showed a smidgen of responsibility, I might leave her more than I currently plan to.

There's no law that says I have to leave my sister my

money. I love her dearly, but moolah slips through her mitts like sand through a bottomless bucket. I, on the other hand—with the exception of that sinfully red BMW—pinch a penny until it screams. I work hard for every cent, while my sister lolls around on her divan eating chocolate-covered bonbons and watching trash TV. But I digress.

"So, Yoder, you had no idea he was a con man?"

"None whatsoever."

"And those bills, you sure they're real?"

"I'm a businesswoman, Melvin, not a fool. They were real."

"But it didn't strike you as strange that a sleazeball like that would have so much cash on him?"

"Look, I know what you're getting at, and I'm not going to fall for it. That money stays right where it is."

Melvin leaned forward, his head bobbling on a neck far too scrawny to give it adequate support. "What if that money belongs to his victims?"

"I've already prayed about that. I told the Good Lord that He was free to take from my money market account any dough that didn't rightfully belong there. Last time I checked, I was already earning interest."

"You're kidding, right?"

"I never joke about spiritual matters. Now, let's move this discussion along, shall we? As I understand it, Clarence Webber was arrested in Bedford when he tried to use a stolen Visa card at the liquor store. Is that correct?"

"Yeah. You'd think they'd build a bigger jail in Bedford."

"So the Bedford police asked you to keep him here until his arraignment, but then since he couldn't even make bail—"

"Because you had all his money."

My glares mean nothing to Melvin, but I gave him

one on principle. "I didn't have all his money. He's apparently quite loaded. You know as well as I do that his assets were frozen on account of the fraud charge. And anyway, my point is, he had to stay in jail, at least for a few days, and since you're not exactly equipped for guests, you asked me to feed him."

"But not gruel," he growled. "And not arsenic."

I drummed on Melvin's desk impatiently. Both Mennonites and Amish are peace-loving denominations, and if it were not for five hundred years of pacifist inbreeding, I would have drummed on Melvin.

"The *facts*, Melvin. We're trying to sort through the facts here. Did Clarence Webber have any visitors?"

Even a blindfolded person, facing the other way, would have seen the lightbulb go on in Melvin's head. No doubt all that emptiness magnified the light, because I didn't think the man had that many watts in him.

"Are you trying to say, Yoder, that one of his visitors may have killed him?"

"Bingo."

"Yeah, maybe you're on to something, Yoder."

"I take it you have a record of these visitors."

It must have been a three-way bulb, because it clicked to a lower setting. "That's Zelda's job."

I nodded. Zelda Root is Hernia's only other police officer and functions as Melvin's right arm. She's a short thing with broad shoulders, huge bosoms, and no hips. She has no chin, rabbit teeth, and a nose like Karl Malden's. I'm not being unkind, merely observant here. Besides, these less than perfect features could be offset somewhat by creative grooming. But Zelda chooses to wear her hair in a man's haircut—what folks used to call a buzz—and she doesn't just put her makeup on with a putty knife; she uses a garden trowel. Still, like I said, she's indispensable and highly organized. I should have thought to ask her in the first place.

"She's off now, right?"

"Need you ask?"

Melvin is forever griping that the Hernia police force needs a larger staff, but the truth is, in a town of just under two thousand—1,999½ now that Agnes Stucky is five months pregnant—there's not a whole lot for them to do as it is. We have no bars, there's very little worth stealing, folks generally drive slowly because of all the Amish buggies, and with the majority of us being pacifists, violence against one's person is a rarity—unless you want to count murder. We have had our share of those, but most of these cases have involved persons from the outside.

"Right," I said, "I'll swing by Zelda's place. Any messages you want me to deliver?"

"Very funny, Yoder." Zelda carries a torch for Melvin. Why she does is one of life's great mysteries, along with why it is we park our cars in driveways, but drive them on parkways.

"Well, see you later, alligator," I said cheerfully. The truth be known, I rather enjoy these investigative ventures I undertake on Melvin's behalf. Even if my inn's reputation was not at stake, I would probably snoop around just for the fun of it.

Melvin didn't respond. In a rare instance of ocular coordination, both eyes were focused on the ceiling, which has been graced by a single footprint for as long as I can remember.

I let daydreaming mantises lie, and sneaked off to examine Clarence's empty cell for clues. I found Susannah's phone number written on the wall—it's been there for years—and a girlie magazine under the pitiful excuse for a mattress, but nothing suspicious. A quick look around the reception area was fruitless as well. I hadn't really expected to find anything, but now I knew for certain that my investigation would have to focus elsewhere.

*   *   *

Welcome to Hernia. We are located just twelve miles from the city of Bedford in the mountains of south-central Pennsylvania. We are not—and I repeat *not*—at all like Lancaster County. Tourists occasionally find us, but they have yet to descend upon us in droves. While some of us eke out our livings from the soil, or have related occupations, the majority of us drive into Bedford, where we are engaged in occupations that represent a cross section of that community.

Even though our town limits generously include a good deal of arable land, Amish comprise less than one fifth of our population. Their presence appears to be greater, however, because of their distinctive garb. Roughly half of us are Mennonites, which makes us the largest single group, although, to be totally honest, we are divided amongst several branches of this denomination, and don't always get along as well as the Good Lord intended. Methodists rank number two in sheer numbers, followed by United Presbyterians. Baptists are a distinct, if vocal, minority, but the smallest congregation is the First and Only True Church of the One and Only Living God of the Tabernacle of Supreme Holiness and Healing and Keeper of the Consecrated Righteousness of the Eternal Flame of Jehovah. Last I heard it had one member for each word in its title. Oddly, we have no Roman Catholics or Episcopalians, but last summer we finally got our first Jew. He, of course, does not constitute a congregation.

In the older part of town the houses are mostly built of wood, many in the Victorian style. On the fringes, and in our one official suburb, one sees brick and vinyl ranch homes. My sinfully red BMW was the flashiest car in town, and the only reason I drove it was to tweak the noses of those folks who condemned me as a harlot for having inadvertently married a bigamist. But that's another story.

After leaving Melvin to stare at the ceiling, I followed North Main almost to the edge of town, where it intersects with Meadow Lark Lane. I turned left into Zelda Root's driveway.

She lives in a 1950s-style brick bungalow with green and white striped aluminum awnings over every window and door, and all badly in need of new paint. A lone silver maple towers over the back of the small house, and, with the exception of two ubiquitous Japanese yews on either side of the front entrance, is the only concession to landscaping. It was already the middle of June, but the weed-choked grass did not appear to have been cut once that year. Clearly Zelda had other priorities.

The driveway was empty, and I didn't bother to peer through the dusty garage windows. Therefore it came as a bit of a surprise when the door swung open the second I rang the bell.

She smiled warmly when she saw me. "Hey! Come on in!"

I smiled back. It is hard not to like people who perpetually—well, how should I phrase this—kiss up to me. I know, some folks don't like groveling, but I'd rather deal with a groveler who knows her place than an alpha female who doesn't.

Zelda suffers from the mistaken notion that I have it in my power to break up Susannah and Melvin's marriage and return the miserable mantis to her heaving, oversized bosom. Even if that were true, I would never do such a thing. I don't believe in divorce—not unless at least one of the parties has been unfaithful, and as far as I can determine, my baby sister and her irritating hubby have been as faithful to each other as Ruth and Billy Graham.

"Hi, Zelda. I just stopped by to ask you a few questions. I hope this is a good time."

"No time like the present," she said as she ushered me into the 1970s. "Have a seat."

Instead of a proper couch, Zelda has six orange bean-bag chairs arranged in a circle around a zebra-skin drum. This percussion instrument serves as a miniature coffee table, although there is very little room for coffee cups thanks to the largest lava lamp I've ever seen. A brightly colored Mexican serape functions as an area rug, and completes this montage. The walls are decorated with large, beige macramé pieces that hang suspended, like giant spiderwebs. Since Zelda is not the most fastidious of housekeepers, real spiderwebs connect several of these monstrosities.

I picked the least dusty beanbag chair and arranged my lanky frame in as modest a pose as possible. Even the most conservative Mennonite skirts were not designed for beanbag chairs. Zelda, on the other hand, was wearing a black T-shirt and black stretch pants, and she literally threw herself on the chair opposite me.

"So what's up, Magdalena? Is this about Melvin?"

"Well, indirectly. He—"

"He's leaving Susannah, isn't he?" She hopped nimbly to her feet. "I knew it! I knew that marriage wouldn't last. No offense, Magdalena, but your sister doesn't have what it takes to please a man like Melvin."

I was tempted to derail the conversation right there, but curiosity got the better of me. "What does it take?" I asked stupidly.

"These!" She thrust out her chest, which, even clad in black as it was, appeared impossibly large.

On the other hand, Susannah, like myself, suffers from MDS—mammary deficiency syndrome. Susannah is so flat, she carries her little dog, Shnookums, in her bra just to keep the garment from riding up on her. But Melvin has always been crazy about Susannah. As far as I know, her breasts, or the lack thereof, have never been an issue.

"It has nothing to do with Susannah," I said. "It has to do with Clarence Webber."

"Oh, him." Zelda threw herself back down on the bright orange bag. "What about him?"

"Melvin just got a call from the coroner. The autopsy report is in. Apparently Mr. Webber died from an overdose of arsenic."

Zelda popped up again and virtually leaped across the room. In the process she knocked the lava lamp to the floor, but didn't seem to mind. Her mission was to comfort me.

"I'm so sorry." She threw her stubby arms around me, nearly smothering me in the process.

I struggled free. "There's no reason to be sorry for me, dear. I sold him my car, delivered a few meals, but it's not like we were close."

"Magdalena, you don't need to pretend with me. I know you came here to confess. But before you say anything else, I should advise you of your rights. You have the right to remain silent, and every word—"

"Don't be an idiot," I cried, my Christian charity having worn thin. "I didn't kill Clarence Webber. I am, however, working on the case."

A frown creased her spackled forehead. As a matter of fact, a little piece of the makeup actually chipped off and landed on the black shirt. There are those in town who believe Jimmy Hoffa may be hiding behind that mask, but I'm not one of them.

"Melvin asked you to?" Her voice was suddenly an octave higher.

"Yes. I understand that there's been a parade of visitors through the jail—"

Zelda waved a plump little hand. Her nails were painted as black as the coal that riddles our mountains.

"Not what you'd call a parade, Magdalena. Just four people, that's all."

"Do you have the list here, or is it back at the office?"

"No list," she said defensively, "but I can tell you exactly who they were."

I scrabbled in my pocketbook until I found last Sunday's church bulletin and the much-bitten remains of a pen. Incidentally, those were not my teeth marks on the pen. The culprit was Shnookums, Susannah's pitiful petite pooch, who enjoys a good romp in a purse as much as he does in a bra.

"Okay, dear, shoot."

3

Zelda flicked the bit of makeup on to the floor. "Well, first there was Emma Kauffman."

"Which one?" That was a solid Mennonite and Amish name. I knew of at least six Emma Kauffmans in the area.

"The artist. You know, the one who lives up on Buffalo Mountain."

"Ah, that one."

"She brought Mr. Webber a bag of cookies. Of course I had to confiscate them."

"Why? Was there a weapon in the bag?"

"No, but there were raisins."

"What's wrong with raisins?"

"They're dried grapes, Magdalena. They can be fermented and turned into wine. The last thing we need is a drunken riot in Hernia jail."

"A lone prisoner can hardly riot, dear."

She sniffed. "Maybe. Just to be on the safe side I plucked out all the raisins before handing the cookies over. Some were embedded too deep and the cookies crumbled. I'm afraid Mr. Webber ended up getting only half a bag."

I smiled patiently. "Who else stopped by?"

"Agnes Schlabach. She's the piano teacher over in Bedford who was written up in last week's issue of *The Broad Top Bulletin*. You know, in the Meet Your Neighbor section."

"The woman with thirty-two cats?"

"That's her. She brought Mr. Webber a little flute."

"A *flute*?"

"Yeah, you know, the musical instrument."

"Did you confiscate that as well?"

She threw herself yet a third time into the much-abused chair. "Why would I do that?"

"Well, if it was made of metal—"

"It was wood."

It was becoming apparent that I had to tread carefully if I wanted Zelda to salivate every time she saw me. It was time to throw her a bone.

"Susannah and Melvin had a little spat last week," I said wickedly. "Something about her spending habits."

Zelda beamed, her eyes gleaming like coals from behind that Kabuki mask. "Do tell!"

"Maybe later, dear. First, tell me about visitors number three and four."

"Ah!"

"Work before play," I said, dangling that Mennonite motto like a carrot. Zelda, a nominal Methodist, needed a big sister to instruct her.

"If you insist." She sighed. "Dorcas Yutzy stopped by a couple of times. Stayed longer than the rest."

"Was she too bearing gifts?"

Zelda shrugged. "You know Dorcas. I just waved her right on through."

I knew Dorcas all right. She's the girls' gym teacher at Hernia High. I know all the teachers, because I'm on the school board. And no, I don't have any children. But I am the town's wealthiest citizen, and therefore entitled to some privileges.

I'd have waved Dorcas through as well. The woman is a chatterbox. Perhaps it's because she spends her days with sweating teenagers and her evenings with an aged mother who is stone deaf, but if you as much as make eye contact with the gym teacher—fortunately not a casual occurrence, since she wears bottle-thick glasses—she latches on to you like a leech. As much as I hate to say it about any woman, this particular one needs to marry. Unfortunately, there are few prospects in Hernia for a myopic six-foot-five-inch woman with widely spaced teeth, not unlike those of a jack-o'-lantern, and who wears her mousy brown hair pulled back with pink barrettes, making her look for all the world like an overgrown twelve-year-old.

"So, who's the fourth?" I asked.

Zelda made a face, thereby dotting her black T-shirt with a shower of dried makeup. "The so-called Reverend Richard Nixon."

"Surely that wasn't his minister!" Reverend Richard Nixon (his real name, I kid you not) is the pastor of that church out by the Interstate, the one with thirty-two words in its name.

"Who knows? Whenever I saw him coming I ducked into the restroom. He talks as much as Dorcas, only it's all about religion."

I nodded knowingly. The Good Lord created Sundays for long boring sermons. Folks who drone on and on about their faith during the week are not being considerate. There's nothing wrong with sharing the gospel, don't misunderstand me. It's just that one should share it by example or, at the very least, by brief snippets. No one was ever saved while asleep.

"I don't suppose you happened to notice if he brought anything with him."

She shook her head. "No, wait—his Bible. I'm sure he brought that. You never see him anywhere without that."

"Right. One last question. Did any of these visitors come during mealtime?"

All the makeup in the world couldn't hide the expression on Zelda's face. She swallowed hard, precipitating a few more fissures in her furrowed façade.

"How was I supposed to know someone would try to kill Clarence Webber? In the three years I've been on the force, we've only ever had three other prisoners. And that's counting Farney Kimloch and his Saturday-night drinking sprees. We always let him out the next morning, but he never wants anything to eat. That leaves just Susannah and you."

"Don't even go there!" I wailed.

Susannah was twenty-three at the time of our parents' tragic death, but that was only her chronological age. Thanks to Papa, who had doted on her as if she were the only living child in the world, her emotional age was more like sixteen. Papa's demise, rather than thrusting my sister into adulthood, knocked a few more years off her maturity level. In the ten years since that awful day, I've been trying to get my sister out of her teens, so to speak.

But how does one go about raising a twenty-three-year-old woman? You can't spank her—believe me, I've tried. And you can't ground her and send her to her room. The last time I tried that, Susannah sneaked out the window, stole my car keys—and car, of course—and headed for Alaska. There was a surplus of men up there, she'd heard, and reckoned that there were at least a few she had yet to sleep with.

Although I didn't press charges that time, my sister has had so many run-ins with the law that the Hernia jail has been decorated to suit her taste. After all, that is where she and Melvin Stoltzfus fell in love.

My brief incarceration was a matter of principle, and I will not go into details here. All you need to know is that I am not the criminal type, and have never consciously broken the law—okay, so I sometimes have a heavy foot. Let he who has never had a speeding ticket be the one to cast the first stone.

"So you see," Zelda said, "I don't have a lot of experience with prisoners. It isn't my fault. When Susannah was locked up, it was always Melvin who fed her, and believe you me, he kept any visitors away. At *any* hour. And of course I never had to worry about Melvin poisoning your sister." Her voice dropped to a whisper. "But sometimes I wish he had."

"I heard that!"

Zelda popped to her feet again. She has the strongest leg muscles of any woman I've ever known. No doubt about it, if there was an Olympic event for beanbag chair emergence, Hernia's woman in blue would have a gold medal to suspend from her stupendous bosom.

"Well, it's the truth! Magdalena, you *know* Melvin and I belong together. Susannah can have any man she pleases—heaven knows she already has—so why does she want Melvin?"

"Why do you?" I asked calmly. If Zelda could answer that question to my satisfaction, she belonged on a mountaintop, dispensing bits of wisdom to ardent truth-seekers.

"Because he's so cute!"

"Gag me with a spoon, dear!" That is not a typical Mennonite expression, but the by-product of trying to rear a Presbyterian.

My ejaculation didn't seem to faze Zelda. "You don't like Melvin—in fact you hate him. So—"

"I hate no one!" Well, I try not to, at any rate. The Bible commands us to love our neighbors as well as we love ourselves. Having tried mightily to love Melvin over the years—and failed miserably—my new strategy is to try to love myself a little less. If I can get really good at that, then maybe things will even out a little bit.

Black nails flashed as Zelda waved away my protest. "It would be in your own best interest to help me snag Melvin. Then maybe Susannah would grow up a bit. Who knows, she might decide to go back to college. She might even marry a Mennonite."

"Get behind me, Satan!" I cried.

"Just some thoughts," Zelda said. Her wicked smile was making a shambles of her face.

I struggled to my feet. It was time for me to go, before I changed my name to Judas. Or would that be Judy? Judy Yoder had a nice sound to it. And oh, what a relief it would be to bust up the marriage before the two could spawn! A swarm of mini-mantises was the last thing Hernia needed.

"So far," I said, trying to keep my mind busy, "the suspect list includes Emma Kauffman, our reclusive local artist, Agnes Schlabach, the piano teacher from Bedford, and Dorcas Yutzy. One might even add Reverend Nixon to the list—if one were cynical enough to believe a man of the cloth could actually commit murder."

"There's still another suspect."

"There is?"

Zelda nodded. "Rachel Blank."

"Our illustrious mayor?"

"Yup. Of course she stops by a lot. Then again, Melvin basically works for her."

That had to stick in Melvin's craw. Rachel Blank is a beautiful, impeccably groomed woman who looks like she could anchor any of the morning television news shows—not that I watch TV, mind you. In fact, Rachel's previous job, before winning her landslide victory as mayor, was to work as the weather girl at a Philadelphia station.

But until she went away to college, no one in Hernia would have pegged Rachel for success. Shy to the point of muteness, and as plain as unvarnished pine, the little

Blank girl lived up to the family name. Melvin, who was one of Rachel's classmates, taunted her mercilessly, as did virtually every other kid. Thank heavens I was a good ten years older, or I might have done the same.

What exactly happened at that fancy girls' college in the East to transform a Mennonite farm girl into a poised pseudo-celebrity is anybody's guess. But happen, something did. When Rachel finally returned to her roots, the citizens of Hernia rolled out the red carpet. They even had the existing mayor declare her birthday Rachel Blank Day. Frankly, I thought all the hoopla a bit too much, but then who am I to complain? I'm just a hardworking innkeeper who has always contributed to my community, and who is still a Mennonite in good standing (Rachel became an agnostic at that fancy-shmancy school).

However, it seems that being mayor was not enough for our Rachel Blank. The day we all learned that Congressman Whipple had been found dead in a Mrs. Nora Maynard's bed—all the way up in Pittsburgh—our new mayor threw her little pillbox hat into the ring. Melvin, who is always a day late and a dollar short, didn't file his intention until a week later. Never mind that our mumbling mantis maintains it was always his plan to run for political office.

I would have thought it illegal for a mayor and her police chief to both run for the same congressional seat, but it isn't. And while it has to irk Melvin no end that his boss is by far the more popular candidate, I derive very little pleasure from the situation. At least Melvin has paid his dues, by staying put all these years. What I mean is, anybody can run off and become famous. But *you* try living in Hernia from the day you're born until the miserable day you die. Enough said—well, except for one last thing. I am *not*, as some have suggested, envious of our glamour gal mayor.

"Zelda," I said, as an awful thought popped into my

mean little mind, "you don't think Mayor Blank has designs on Melvin, do you?"

When the stout woman stopped laughing, it was finally plain that Jimmy Hoffa had not been hiding under that makeup. Tammy Faye Bakker, however, was still a possibility.

"I don't know what's so funny," I sniffed.

"Oh, Magdalena, sometimes you're so—uh—how should I say this?"

"Spit it out!"

"Simple."

"Moi?"

"Rachel Blank is not interested in Melvin. Take my word for it."

"How can you be so sure?"

Despite her build, Zelda's feet are barely larger than goat hooves. She tapped one impatiently.

"Because the mayor is gay, Magdalena. Her excuse is that she's been coming by to see Melvin, but she's really been coming to see me. I can feel her vibes."

That was certainly a surprise. I'd never felt the slightest vibes from Rachel Blank, and I'm no less attractive than Zelda. Which is not to say that gay folks come on to everyone of their gender, but surely I would have picked up something. I have a lot of personality, for crying out loud! Why should I be left out?

"Are you sure about this?"

Zelda's freer face allowed her to smirk. "I know more about the world than you do, Magdalena. Like I said, trust me on this one."

"Well—"

"Maybe I can help you two get together. In exchange for your help getting Melvin, of course."

"But I'm not gay!" I wailed. I'm really not. Yes, I waited until I was forty-five to get married, and yes, that marriage didn't work out, but those facts have absolutely nothing to do with my sexual orientation. If Zelda was any good at her job as a policewoman, she would know that I've been dating Dr. Gabriel Rosen, a fairly recent immigrant from New York.

And please don't get me wrong. I do not judge gay people by their sexual habits. My personal take on the matter is that I agree with every word Jesus had to say on the subject—which is nothing. What people do behind closed doors is none of my business, unless of course they're guests at my inn and their behavior damages my property.

Alas, my protest meant nothing to Zelda. "So, you'll help me with Melvin?"

"When pigs fly," I said breezily, and skedaddled before I yielded to temptation.

It's less than five miles from Zelda's bungalow to the PennDutch Inn, but I dawdled. I do my best thinking while driving, or in the shower, and I had a lot to mull over. Besides, I was in no hurry on that fine, late spring day to get back to my real job—that of proprietress.

Contrary to what most folks think, it isn't fun running a full-board inn. And yes, I know, I'm extremely fortunate that, thanks to a good review early on, my establishment has hosted the rich and famous. The infamous as well. But if I once equated money with good manners, I no longer do.

Food fights, broken furniture, and burned sheets are bad enough. These I have come to expect, and believe you me, I make the hooligans pay. But I have a fancy new barn, and copulating in the cupola is completely out of the question. The couple who tried that got a nice little jab with the tines of my pitchfork. The Secret Service agents standing guard got a good tongue-lashing.

So it was with some trepidation that I finally turned

off Hertzler Road and pulled up the long gravel drive. The white clapboard inn is a rebuilt farmhouse—the original having been destroyed by a tornado—and sits off to the right under the shade of ancient maple trees. To the left is the barn—also white, as is our local custom. Between the two sits my henhouse, home to my prized flock of Rhode Island Reds.

I parked my new (it was second-hand, but new to me), conservative gray Buick under a maple next to the chicken coop and hoofed it to the back door. This is the kitchen, and as it is the domain of Freni, my faithful friend but fickle cook, I am less likely to encounter annoying guests there than elsewhere about the inn. Freni Hostetler is Amish, and therefore also a pacifist, but she has the temper of an NBA star. Although she would never actually hit anybody with it, she has been known to wield a spatula in a threatening manner.

It's no secret that the source of Freni's irritation is her daughter-in-law. Don't get me wrong, Barbara Hostetler is a peach of a gal, and recently supplied Freni with three grandchildren in one fell swoop. The triplets are adorable, and you would think that the elder Mrs. Hostetler would feel kindly toward the younger, but alas, that is not the case. Try as she might, Freni cannot forgive the woman for having claimed the affection of Jonathan Hostetler, Freni's only son. This ill feeling is, of course, a sin, and Freni knows that. This is what makes her so cross.

When I opened the screen door, Freni, who was at the sink, whirled. "Ach, Magdalena, where have you been?"

"To see Melvin. Then Zelda. That prisoner we were feeding—Clarence Webber—well, according to the coroner, he died of arsenic poisoning."

Freni dried her hands on her white starched apron. "So, who gives him this poison?"

"That's what I'm supposed to find out. Apparently it was in the shrimp and grits I had you make."

Freni's normally somewhat florid face turned the color of bleached cake flour. She flapped her stubby arms, like a cock about to crow.

"Ach, I told you, Magdalena. It says in the Bible not to eat these shrimp."

"That's in the Old Testament, Freni. That doesn't apply to us. But I'll read my Bible again just to make sure it doesn't warn us about eating shellfish purchased in Bedford. We're not exactly near any large bodies of water."

Freni frowned. "Enough with the jokes, Magdalena. There is something important I must tell you."

"Yes, dear, in a minute. I just want to make sure you understand that it wasn't the shrimp that killed him, but the arsenic. And you're not to worry about that, because I've already got a nice little list of suspects drawn up."

Freni flapped again. Perhaps she was hoping to get airborne.

"This list will have to wait, yah? Because now you are a mama!"

"Oh, Freni, you didn't take the babies away from Barbara, did you? I know you think I'd make a better mother, but—"

"Ach, such nonsense, Magdalena. There is your baby!" She pointed to the far corner of the kitchen, and I noticed for the first time that we were not alone.

4

A teenage girl sat slouched on one of the tall kitchen stools. I vigorously discourage children as guests—if you think celebrities are the most destructive humans, think again—so I knew the child was not in residence. She did, however, have a punk look about her, one that I've come to associate with the world of entertainment.

Her hair was an impossible shade of black, with hints of maroon, and had been sculpted into spikes about four inches long that stood straight out from her head in all directions. Her ears had been pierced an obscene amount of times and resembled more the spines of spiral notebooks than auditory appendages. Even her eyebrows had been pierced, and from a ring on the left one hung a small silver skull on a chain.

Moving down, a plump body, not yet in the full throes of adolescent development, was clad in only a tube top and black spandex shorts. The latter barely covered the region Eve made famous with her fig leaf. But Eve went barefoot, I'm sure of it, whereas this girl was wearing black platform shoes with leather straps that snaked their way about chunky calves and tied just below the knee.

The child stood when she saw me scrutinizing her. "Hey lady," she said in a flat, midwestern accent, "give those eyeballs of yours a rest."

I strode over to confront her. "Who are you?" I demanded.

The girl's pale blue eyes regarded me calmly. "What's the matter, Mom? You have trouble hearing, or something? I'm your daughter."

"Not even in my worst nightmare, dear. Tell me who you really are, or I'm calling the police."

The P word made her blink. "Ain't ya the famous Magdalena Yoder?"

I'm a sucker for flattery. "Well, I guess I'm famous. I mean, Mel Gibson once referred to me—hey, let's stick with the program here! Either you identify yourself, or I dial."

"Alison Miller," she said, enunciating with such exaggeration that I could see the metal stud in her tongue. "But call me Allie."

"Thank you. So, Alison, what are you doing in my kitchen?"

"Sheesh! You are deaf, ain't ya? How many times do I have to tell you that I'm your daughter?"

I turned helplessly to Freni. "You let her in, maybe you should explain."

Freni is seventy-three years old and has a figure that attests to her firm belief that green tomato pie counts as a vegetable. But when she wants to, that woman can move like greased lightning. One minute she was there, flapping about like a rooster, and the next thing I knew I felt the breeze on my face as the door to the dining room swung closed behind her.

"Uptight old lady, ain't she?"

I glared at the girl. "A good look at you would spook the horses, dear."

"I ain't your dear. Hey, what's with that old lady's

getup, anyway? And what's with that funny little hat you got on? Youse actors of some kind?"

"Not hardly. She's an Amish lady, and I'm a Mennonite. I wear this funny little hat because I believe a woman should keep her head covered when she prays."

"You ain't praying now."

"That's what you think. Unfortunately my prayers aren't being answered."

She laughed, and I could see a second stud on her tongue. I wanted to gag.

"I haven't given up on calling the police," I said.

"Hey, come on, take a chill pill. I told you I'm your daughter, and I guess I am, because my dad is Aaron Miller. You know, the one who used to live across the road from you?"

"Aaron Miller?" If it hadn't been for the resistance offered by my thick cotton hosiery, I would have collapsed to the floor. As it was, I swayed. Like a tall, skinny tower of Pisa.

"You and him was married, right?"

"Yes, but—"

"Then you're my mother."

"But I never gave birth!" I wailed.

"You sure?"

"I ought to be. I mean, fathers can sometimes be surprised years after the fact, but we women—"

"Hey, spare me the sex talk, lady. I know how it happens. Anyway, that don't change a thing. If you were married to my dad, then you're my mom. It's as simple as that."

"Says who?"

"Says me." There was desperation in her voice, and her face was turning red. Curiously, those areas surrounding metal were the color of cottage cheese.

"How did you get here?"

"My parents brought me."

"They're *here*?" I staggered to the nearest empty stool. It was almost too much effort to sit.

"Nah, not here—not at this dump, but in that little town up the road."

"Dump? Well, I'll have you know—" I caught myself. There are more important things than defending one's business, even if it is also one's residence. "Alison, are you saying that your parents are in Hernia? Where?"

"Not Hernia." She laughed. "Or Hemorrhoid, either. The other little town. The one that starts with a B."

"Bedford!"

"Uh-huh. They swung by and dropped me off. Now they're at the motel waiting for you to call. I got the number right here in my pocket."

If my blood had run any colder, I could have damaged my heart with ice crystals. It was hard to breathe.

"Hey lady, you all right?"

"I'm fine," I gasped.

Of course I wasn't. Aaron Miller—Alison's father—had been my Pooky Bear. We grew up together. Then at age eighteen, Aaron committed the ultimate act of Mennonite teenage rebellion by joining the army during the height of the Vietnam war. The moment he signed that paper the ground in Hernia shook, thanks to hundreds of pacifist ancestors turning over in their graves.

After the war Aaron didn't feel comfortable returning to Hernia, so he bummed around the country a bit, eventually settling in Minnesota. It wasn't until twenty-odd years later, and only when his aging, widowed father really needed him, that Aaron returned to stay. Shortly after his homecoming, I met him in the cow pasture across the road, on his farm, and promptly fell in love.

You would have too. Aaron is tall, with black hair and eyes the color of sapphires. His teeth are so white that when he smiles you have to look away or risk being blinded. His lips are like lush, ripe strawberries bursting with flavor. But more importantly, he was the most decent, kindest person I'd ever met.

I married Aaron in front of God and half of Hernia right here in my barn. We would have married in Beechy Grove Mennonite Church, but a bodacious storm blew in the night before, knocking a tree into the roof of the sanctuary. They say that what you don't know won't hurt you, but that isn't always the case. I had no idea what a naked man looked like until our wedding night, and then to suddenly see the male appendage—in all its unbridled glory—was traumatic. I still have nightmares, and Thanksgiving is forever ruined for me. I can't even look at a turkey neck now without feeling embarrassed.

But enough of that. It isn't your business anyhow. What's important for you to know is that I had absolutely no idea—not even an inkling of a hint—that my Pooky Bear had not only been married before, but was, in fact, *still* married. The woman—and she shall forever remain nameless as far as I am concerned—befriended him when he first moved to Minnesota. Shortly after they were married things went sour, but the marriage was never ended.

All this I learned after I'd given the man my maidenhood, making him a bigamist in the eyes of God, the law, and my neighbors. I thought then I'd heard—and seen—everything. I never dreamed there would be another shoe to drop. But apparently there was, and it was a doozy. The old woman and her kids, plus half of Hernia, could comfortably live in this one.

"Why does your father want me to call him?" My voice sounded tinny, and I wasn't sure at first I was actually speaking. I felt my lips; they were moving.

"You need to sign a consent form, that's why."

"Consent for what? He's not getting a cent of alimony. It was a phony marriage."

She laughed, treating me to yet another view of her lingual jewelry. There were actually three studs.

"You're funny, just like Dad said."

"He said that?" I shook my head vigorously to dislodge any thoughts of reconciliation. "This consent form, dear, what's it for?"

"Hey, lady, like I said, I ain't your dear. And the stupid form is about me. You gotta agree to let me stay here."

"I do? For how long?"

She shrugged.

"How long? A week? A month?"

"A year," she said quietly. "Maybe more."

"Come again?"

"They can't handle me. It was either you or the girls' detention center. You get to pick."

I felt like fainting. I needed to faint. With any luck I would hit my head on the corner of the kitchen table and knock myself utterly and permanently senseless. But alas, a good fainting spell was not to be had.

"Give me the number," I finally said. "I'll give your dad a call."

Aaron answered on the first ring. In fact, it wasn't even a full ring. He must have had his hand on the receiver.

"Mags, is that you?"

"Don't you call me Mags! Only folks I love get away with that."

"Sorry. So how are you, Magdalena?"

"Apparently doing better than you." I was calling from the privacy of my bedroom, and could have said anything I wanted. "There's a multi-pierced urchin sitting in my kitchen who claims to be your daughter. Is this true?"

I could hear Aaron swallow. "I should have told you when you found out about my wife—I mean my other wife—but hey, you know me, Mags—I mean, Magdalena. I'm a coward."

"You got that right." I took a deep breath. "So what's this child doing in my kitchen? Is she really asking for asylum?"

"Well, it's a long story—"

"Then talk fast."

"She's fourteen, Magdalena. Well, almost. Her birthday's next month. Anyway, she hasn't adjusted at all to my moving back in with her mother. Started acting out about a year ago. At first it was small things like shoplifting candy bars and hair doodads. Then she started smoking dope. Drinking too. Last month she went all out and stole a car—a 1988 Ford Festiva! A banged-up one at that."

"For pity's sake."

"The hearing was the day before yesterday. The judge said she was reluctant to put someone that young into the system, but her hands would be tied if there was one more incident. She suggested we switch to a new family therapist—we've been going to one, you know—but I had a better idea."

"And that would be?" I knew what was coming. I only *look* stupid.

"You, of course. There is only one person on the face of this earth who could put the fear of God—and I mean that literally—into someone like my Alison."

"I'll take that as a compliment."

"And that's how it's meant." He paused, and I could hear the shrill voice of what's-her-name in the background. "So, will you?"

"For a *year*?"

"Or less, if that's all it takes."

I wanted to ask him why. What, if anything, was in it for me? But I already knew the answer, and it might not be the same as his.

The spiked, pierced, and studded child in my inn's kitchen was both my first and second chance. It was my first chance to raise a child who was chronologically under the age of twenty-one, and it was a chance for me to make up for the way I'd failed Susannah. Yes, I know, a baby would have been ideal. A baby I could raise to near perfection, I'm sure of that. But the Good Lord apparently wanted me to remain as barren as the Gobi Desert, and I would go to my grave with the fruit of my loins unplucked.

At the same time, He is a God of mercy. Had not a child just fallen into my lap—so to speak? Was this not a Heaven-sent opportunity to preach those things I know I should be practicing? And really, what did I have to lose? I know, I complain about my guests pilfering and destroying my property, but to be honest, I am heavily insured. Besides, the girl was a relative of sorts. And I'm not just talking about her sarcastic reference to me as her mom, either. You see, Aaron and I are distantly related—but not so close we couldn't have been legally married, mind you—which made this child also a relation.

"Six months," I heard myself say. "That's what I'll aim for. But if I can't handle the job, I'm sending her right back. And you pay any damages she incurs. You got that?"

I could feel his sigh of relief wafting through the tiny holes on my receiver. "Magdalena, you're a real peach, you know that?" He lowered his voice to a whisper. "Sometimes I wish you and I—"

"Stop right there!"

"Sorry." He paused. "Look, I've got all her stuff here, and the papers you need to sign. Do you want me to drop them off, or do you want to swing by here?"

That was a hard choice. Did I want to see my ex–Pooky Bear at my house, where I'd been blissfully, although unlawfully, married for a month, or did I want to visit the motel where he was holed up with his real wife? It was a choice I couldn't make.

"You know where Susannah and Melvin live?"

He didn't. I gave him directions and told him to drop everything pertaining to Alison at my sister's house. Then, rather than giving him my best pithy parting shot, I simply hung up.

I confess. For the next couple of minutes I stayed in my room, replaying in my mind some of the highlights of being Mrs. Aaron Miller—albeit a bogus one. They say beauty is only skin deep, but if that's the case, then Aaron has the epidermis of an elephant. Unfortunately, he has the soul of a snake, and I really was better off without him. Still, it was fun to imagine what might have been, and what could still be, if I had remained married to that magnificent Miller.

I was planning our twenty-fifth wedding anniversary party when my reverie was interrupted by a loud knock on the bedroom door. Knuckles that hard could only belong to Freni.

"I'll be out in a minute, dear."

"Yoder!"

I put my pillow over my head. I should have known that praying mantises had hard knuckles too. The door was locked, thank heavens. Perhaps if I ignored him, he'd eventually wander off in search of other prey.

"Yoder, I need to speak to you."

"Go away," I yelled. "I'm indecent."

That should have been enough to put off any man, but of course not Melvin. "Yoder, this is very important. I have to speak to you right away."

"In that case I'll have to open the door naked," I said, just to make sure he'd understood.

"I don't give a damn what you're wearing, Yoder. Just open the door."

I sighed. I was, of course, fully clothed. And of course I would never allow a man to see me naked. Only God,

Aaron, and my doctor have had that privilege. So far God's made no comment. Aaron, of course, bolted. As for Dr. Simonson, he announced his retirement a month after my last visit.

Reluctantly I opened the door. Melvin looked worse than I'd ever seen him. Both eyes were focused right on me, and he was trembling.

"What's wrong, dear?"

That's when Melvin began to cry.

5

The Lethal Gruel (Shrimp 'n Grits)
Freni Served

1½ cups peeled raw
   shrimp
½ lemon
salt and cayenne
   pepper to taste
1 cup chicken or
   vegetable broth
   (canned will do)
2 tablespoons flour
1 tablespoon
   ketchup

1 teaspoon
   Worcestershire
   sauce
1 small onion finely
   chopped
2 teaspoons chopped
   green bell pepper
3 tablespoons bacon
   grease
Basic Boiled Grits
*arsenic to taste

Season raw shrimp with lemon juice, salt, and cayenne pepper and set aside. Add broth to flour in small bowl, a few drops at a time, stirring constantly until a smooth paste is formed. Continue to stir in remaining broth, ketchup, and Worcestershire sauce and set aside.

Sauté onion and chopped bell pepper in bacon grease until onion begins to turn translucent. Add shrimp and cook two more minutes. Slowly add flour mixture until desired amount and consistency of sauce is reached.

Immediately serve over Basic Boiled Grits (see the recipe in Chapter 10), or grits that have been cooked according to package directions.

SERVES 4

*Omit the arsenic if you like your guests.

6

I was astounded. I honestly didn't think Melvin had it in him to cry, and I'm not referring to all my jibes about him being an insect, either. As long as I've known him, the man—and I still use that term loosely—has never exhibited a vulnerable side. Sure, he's been needy, but that's not the same as vulnerable. Melvin has begged for my help on occasions too numerous to mention, but I always had the impression that if I turned him down, he would somehow survive. Of course, I'd pay dearly for my decision. That was a given. This time, however, was different.

Hugging him was out of the question. For both of us. Instead, I pointed to the simple maple chair beside my vanity.

"Have a seat."

Vulnerable or not, Melvin sat on the bed. "Yoder, I know you're a practicing Mennonite—deeply religious—so you can't take an oath. But I still need you to swear to something."

"Consider it done," I said. I'm sure you'll agree that's not the same as actually swearing.

"Thanks, Yoder. You got a tissue?"

I handed him a box of the generic type I buy at the I.G.A. over in Bedford. You can't hang on to your wealth if you're addicted to brand names, you know.

Melvin honked like a Canada goose. "God, this stuff is rough!"

"No taking the Lord's name in vain, Melvin," I said evenly. "I don't care what your problem is, I won't stand for it in my house."

"Who said I had a problem?" He blew again.

Melvin always does this. He begs for my help, and then as soon as I agree, he gets cocky. However, I was surprised at how fast he rebounded in this instance. Perhaps I'd misread him.

"You've been bawling like a baby," I said, not unkindly. "Your nose is red and your eyes look like peppermint hard candies—only not as big, of course. So, either you have a problem and I help you, or you're out of here. You can't have it both ways."

The gates to Niagara opened again. This time he blubbered aloud. He was truly devastated about something. I thought of at least patting him on the back, but twenty-five generations of inbred Swiss ancestors made that an impossibility. Besides, Melvin was Swiss too. What he needed was a little direction.

"Move to the chair, dear. You're staining my bedspread."

Melvin gratefully moved.

"Now, honk again a few times, and tell Auntie Magdalena what this is all about."

If his nose had been the three little pigs' house, there would be nothing left of it today. He went through half a box of tissues, which even at generic prices is rather extravagant for something that just gets thrown away.

Finally he got it together enough to speak. "You see, Yoder, the Clarence Webber case is a little more complicated than I let on."

"Oh, my stars! You killed him, didn't you?"

Melvin recovered just long enough to give me a snotty sneer. "No."

"Then what is it?" I would have shaken the daylights out of him, but his eyes were welling up again.

"You know that call I got from the coroner?"

"Yes. Go on."

"Well, that arsenic part—"

"Wasn't true?" Never mind stains on my dress, I was going to shake the mantis like a can of paint at Home Depot.

"Yes, it's true!" he cried before my knobby fingers could close around his bony neck. "But there's more."

I backed off. "Tell me *everything* this time."

"Well, you see, Yoder, the coroner just called back claiming to have some evidence that Clarence Webber was—uh—I don't know how else to say this—tortured."

"Tortured?"

"He was whipped. With something thin, and probably metal."

"Like a wire coat hanger?"

"Thinner than that. Like maybe a guitar string. Anyway, his back and even his legs were covered with scars, and a whole lot of marks that were pretty fresh."

"How fresh?"

"Maybe less than a week old. But you got to believe me, Magdalena, I didn't do it."

I believed him. The mantis is as irritating as sand in a wet bathing suit, but cruelty is not his shtick. I've known the man since he was born. While some little boys I knew would deliberately pull the wings off flies, Melvin would affix the appendages back on with super glue. Then he'd try to have the boys arrested.

"Zelda?" I didn't know her as well. I couldn't imagine her doing such a thing, but I didn't want to be one of those people who said about the mass murderer living next door, "He seemed like such a nice young fellow."

Melvin emitted a low moan. "I don't know, Yoder. Sure, she was alone with him a lot, but the coroner said that most of the marks were healed. Old scars."

"That's using your noggin," I said encouragingly. "Zelda told me Clarence had four regular visitors. Maybe one of them is responsible for those scars. But what I don't get is, why would he have those scars in the first place? Why would one person whip another with a guitar string?"

Melvin gave me the same look half my seventh-grade health class gave me when I read my paper on human reproduction aloud. I knew where babies came from, I was just a little confused about how they got there. In her mother-to-daughter talk with me, Mama had gone on and on about how fathers gave mothers seeds, that then magically—well, at least in my eyes—grew into babies. I still think it was logical for me to assume that Papa bought his seed at Miller's Feed Store. That's where we got our best planting corn and onion sets.

"Yoder," Melvin said, with just a hint of superiority, "it's a sexual thing."

"Get out of town!" I was incredulous. The mere act is torture enough, without having to involve guitar strings.

Melvin nodded, no doubt enjoying my discomfort. "It's called S and M. Some people find pain stimulating." Then, probably remembering he was married to my sister, he quickly added, "But not me, of course."

I was shocked into silence.

"So you see, Yoder, I can't let something like this get out. Especially not if any of it happened in my jail. Dave—that's the coroner—has promised to sit on this for a while, but it will eventually leak out. When it does, Yoder, unless I can prove, without a shadow of a doubt, that it didn't happen on my turf—well, there goes the election."

He was right, of course. Hernia is the buckle on the belt of American conservatism.

"My lips are sealed, and I'll certainly do what I can to help."

"That's good, Yoder, because if I lose the election, Susannah and I will have to move in here with you."

"You most certainly will not!"

Melvin's left eye spun as if it were in a Bingo tumbler. "I'm running against the mayor who gave me my job, remember? Win or lose, Hernia P.D. is behind me."

"Maybe, but your mother's farm is in front of you. She could use your help, and she has lots more room than I."

"Yoder, she's eighty-three. I can't be imposing on her."

It was useless to argue. He'd made his point. Unless I cleared him of any suspicion in the death of Clarence Webber, my life was going to change yet again. As if becoming a mama overnight wasn't enough.

I stood. "Don't worry, I'll get to the bottom of this. In the meantime, you campaign like crazy."

"Thanks, Yoder." He stood, and then, in a gesture that shocked me more than anything yet that day, gave me a hug.

Imagine, if you will, being hugged by a five-foot-eight-inch lobster. When Melvin pressed me to his bony carapace, it was all I could do to keep from screaming. Of course I was touched emotionally, don't get me wrong, but the "ick factor," as Susannah would say, was way off the charts.

What if you detested liver, and then found yourself licking a giant, liver-flavored ice-cream cone? You'd be grossed out too. After Melvin left—all smiles by the way—I consoled myself by playing with my pussy.

My pussy is a purebred chocolate-point Siamese, a

gift from Gabe the Babe across the road. When Dr. Gabriel Rosen first gave the cat to me, she was a tiny kitten, small enough to curl up in the cozy confines of my bra. But Little Freni grew at warp speed, and soon even the biggest bra I could find at the Wal-Mart over in Bedford was not large enough to hold the three of us, if you get my drift. Besides, I didn't have the heart to declaw her.

Lately my sweet pussy has taken to spending her days sleeping under my quilt, next to my pillow. She'd been in the room all along, and during Melvin's impromptu visit had not uttered as much as a muffled meow. But as soon as the door closed behind my brother-in-law, dear Little Freni crawled from beneath the covers, stretched, yawned, and climbed onto my lap.

"You know," I said, as I stroked her sleek short fur, "I really should think about retiring. I have all the money I'll ever need. I should sell this place—maybe even just give it to Susannah and Melvin—and move somewhere far away. Sarasota, Florida, has a large Mennonite community. If I move all the way down there . . ." I stopped. Unless Gabe moved to Florida as well, I didn't want to go. What use was Eden without an Adam to enjoy it with?

Little Freni purred contentedly.

"Besides," I said, "I'm a mother now. I can't just—"

The door to my room slammed open, and Little Freni sprang from my lap like a jack-in-the-box and dived under the bed. I shrieked with pain. The little beast could disembowel an antelope just as easily as a lion could.

"Hey lady, you got anything to eat in this house?"

I glared at the girl. "You may not enter without knocking. And then only when I tell you it's all right. Is that clear?"

She glared back, but said nothing.

"Look, Alison, if we're going to get along, you need to understand that I'm the boss here. This is my house. If you can't follow my rules, this whole thing isn't going to work. But just so you know, living here will be a piece of cake compared to any girls' detention center."

She rolled her eyes until both irises disappeared. "Hey, no need to get so bent out of shape. I get the picture. So, you got anything to eat around here, or not?"

"There's plenty of food in the kitchen." I glanced at my watch. It was ten-thirty. At the PennDutch, breakfast is served promptly at seven, lunch at noon, and supper at six. Snacks in between are discouraged, although I do keep fresh fruit and vegetables for dipping on hand at all times. Freni, who has a weakness for baking, stocks a huge molasses jar with cookies, as those guests who are in favor with her are eventually informed. "Did you check with Mrs. Hostetler?"

"Man, she tried to give me some stupid old cookies. And milk! Don't you have any nachos? Or at least any chips?"

I couldn't help but smile. Rearing a child this young was going to be a breeze. For shame on Aaron Miller and his floozy of a wife for giving up so easily. Chips? Nachos? Was that all the hoopla was about? Teenage rebellion, indeed.

"I'm going into Bedford this afternoon, dear. I'll bring you back a variety of snacks. And pop. What sort of soda pop do you prefer?"

Alison made a face. "Pop is for kids. Get me some beer."

I laughed politely at the joke. "In your dreams, dear."

"None of that cheap stuff, either. I like Budweiser."

I gently propelled the child from my room, and locked the door behind us. "Now be a good girl and go scrub off that makeup. Lose the tongue jewelry too. And the eyebrow ring. In fact, lose it all, except for two of the earrings. That's being plenty generous if you ask me. A girl your age doesn't need to adorn herself."

Quite frankly, I've never understood the public's penchant for piercing. The Good Lord gave the human body more than enough openings, for crying out loud. Why anyone would intentionally add more is beyond me.

Apparently it was my turn to shock Alison, because she looked at me much the way I must have looked at Granny Yoder's ghost the day I saw her standing on the stairs. I gave Alison a slight push toward the kitchen.

"Tell Mrs. Hostetler I said you could have a cookie or two after you've cleaned up. Now, if you'll excuse me, dear, I have to go put my John Hancock on those papers your parents want me to sign."

I left her standing in the hall with her mouth open wide enough to catch a swarm of bees.

Susannah and Melvin live in a modest aluminum house on the south side of Hernia, as far away from me as one can get and still reside within the town limits. This is a new neighborhood of blue-collar folks, and bears the lofty but nonsensical name of Foxcroft. In my dictionary a croft is either a small enclosed field adjoining a house, or a small farm worked by tenants. It has nothing to do with rows of identical homes on postage-stamp lots.

As usual, it took me forever to find the right house. All the streets have foxy names, and her number, 66, is so small one needs a pair of good binoculars to spot it from the street. Alas, I'd neglected to bring my pair with me. I made two complete circuits each of Foxhaven, Foxmoor, and Foxmoss before spotting a telltale strip of red at one of the windows. Susannah's living room drapes are the color of fresh blood, and the neighborhood association made her line them with white. But Susannah, being who she is, keeps one edge turned outward, so that a sliver of red shows—*if* you are approaching from the right direction. This is not just an act of defiance, but helps Melvin and Susannah find their home as well.

I parked on the still unstained concrete driveway beside a maple not large enough to shade a grasshopper. Before I could even get my seat belt unbuckled, my sister was beside the car and rapping sharply at the window. I pressed the automatic button and nearly got a fist in my face.

"Easy, girl. I'm getting out as fast as I can."

"Oh, Mags," she cried, "you're not going to believe what just happened!"

7

I grabbed my sister by her bony shoulders. "What happened?"

"Your studmuffins was just here!"

"Aaron's not my studmuffins! Gabriel Rosen is my—oh, never mind. Is that it?"

"Isn't that enough? Man, is he ever dreamy. He hasn't changed one bit."

I clamped both hands over my ears, and in the process hit myself on the chin with my pocketbook. "I don't want to hear it!" I wailed.

Susannah forced my left elbow down and steered me into the house. "*He* may be dreamy, but you should see *her*. Ugh, what a dog."

I put my right hand down voluntarily. "Do tell."

Susannah does not wear dresses as we know them. She wraps herself in fifteen feet of filmy fuchsia fabric in free-form fashion, sort of like a messy sari. Because of the loose fit it is impossible to tell that she carries a dinky dog around in her bra. The mongrel mutt's name is Shnookums, a nasty beast that is sixty percent sphincter muscle and forty percent teeth. It is hard to say which is worse, his bark—a high-pitched yip that can shatter wineglasses—or his bite.

At any rate, when lowering my right hand I accidentally grazed the front of my sister's getup, setting that insidious creature off like the antitheft device on a car. It was a good thing we were inside, or half the folks on the block would have been peeking out their windows. In Hernia, spying on one's neighbors is *de rigueur*.

"Shnookums, your auntie Magdalena didn't mean to hurt you," my sister said in baby talk.

Of course the rat didn't listen. I would have stuck the canine alarm in a closet until he piped down or his lungs wore out, whichever came first. But Susannah pampers that pathetic pooch excessively, and began crooning doggy nursery rhymes. Meanwhile I tapped one of my size-eleven brogans impatiently.

"*Please*," I finally begged over the din, "can't you just put him out in the backyard or something?"

Susannah gave me the look pit bulls reserve for mailmen. "My bundle of joy's been going through a lot of stress, Mags."

"This is no picnic at the beach for me either, dear."

"I know it's because his daddy's been neglecting him. But how do I explain that to him?"

"Tell him his daddy was a stray dog that roamed from yard to yard, and he shouldn't take it personally."

To my great happiness, my remark about Shnookums' paternity shut him up. Perhaps it gave him something to ponder. No doubt he already knew he was the son of a bitch, but having a pooch for a pop was food for thought.

"Shhh!" Susannah peeked into the flimsy folds of her pseudo-frock. "Not that daddy," she whispered. "Melvin."

I nodded. Who knew how much, if anything, Melvin had told his wife about the Clarence Webber case. But as far as I was concerned, the less Susannah knew, the better.

"Okay, I won't disparage his lineage if we can get back to Aaron and that woman. Is she really that homely?"

Susannah made the same face she makes when she accidentally eats a vegetable. "Remember Eunice Zook?"

I nodded. Eunice was a year ahead of me in school, and the homeliest woman I'd ever seen. Too poor to afford plastic surgery, she put a ski mask over her head and turned to a life of crime. Eventually she robbed enough gas stations and small-town banks to pay for the operation, but decided she rather liked the stocking cap. When she was finally arrested in New Jersey she was a wealthy woman, and had long since put her life of crime behind her. But she'd been unable to part with the ski mask, and that's what tipped off authorities that torrid day in July.

"Well, Eunice was a beauty queen compared to this woman. And jeez, talk about rotten dispositions. Even you're nicer than her."

"Thanks, dear. So she's a real witch, huh?"

"I don't know what Aaron sees in her."

"Maybe she's rich." I doubted the woman had more money than I.

"Mags, I don't think he likes her all that much."

"How do you mean?"

"Well, he kept sneaking peeks at that photo of you on the TV, and whenever he said your name, it was like he was in church or something."

I'm only human, and can't be blamed for the thoughts that pop into my head. Acting on them is another thing, however.

"Get behind me, Satan," I said. That seemed to do the trick.

"Hey," Susannah said, almost as if it was an afterthought. "They left this wad of papers for you. What's it all about?"

"I've decided to become a mother."

"*What?* Aaron and that—that—woman are going to be surrogate parents for my niece?"

I smiled broadly. "How did you know it was a girl? Actually, dear, they're not the surrogate parents, but the biological ones. I've agreed to look after their daughter for a while."

Susannah's eyes widened to the point that I worried they might literally pop out. All that eye-rolling she does can only mean that they're not anchored very well.

"Holy shoot!" She used a more vulgar term, of course.

I filled her in on the details, signed the papers, and left them in her care. Before leaving I made her promise that she wouldn't try to set up an "accidental meeting" between Aaron and me. Even without my bifocals I can read my sister's mind, and that's exactly what she would have done.

When I pulled out of the driveway she was cooing into the creases of her clingy costume. The sound of my engine had startled the mangy menace and she was doing her best to mollify him. I said a quick prayer that Susannah wouldn't become a real mother anytime soon. As I well know, there are limitations to even the most spacious brassieres, and I sure as shooting didn't want my niece or nephew to share real estate with the hound from Hell.

It was time to roll up my broadcloth sleeves and get to work. Who killed Clarence Webber, and who on earth—and this still made me shudder—whipped him repeatedly with a guitar string? The culprits could have been one and the same, but not necessarily. Undoubtedly the use of wire was a sexual thing. One thing amateur sleuthing has taught me is that there is no end to the bizarre behavior folks are capable of, and sex is the largest category on that ever-expanding list. If only people did *it* as the Good Lord intended—strictly within the confines of marriage, face to face, once a month, and for three minutes at a time—the world would be such a better place. There would be no teenage pregnancies, no so-called social diseases, and a marked improvement in the economy, thanks to all that effort redirected. But oh no, the devil has turned our heads and we—and I mean society in general—engage in things that would make the Whore of Babylon blush.

You know, we wouldn't have all these perverse practices to contend with if it weren't for dancing. All that gyrating is poison for the soul. It's worse than sex. In her birds-and-the-bees talk, Mama warned me never to let my future husband pass me his seed in a standing position, lest it lead to dancing. Whenever we drove by the Arthur Murray Dance Studio in Bedford, Mama would waggle a bony finger and hiss, "That's the den of iniquity, Magdalena. That's where the devil lollygags about, waiting to seduce young girls like you. Don't you ever go near that place. Or your school gym either."

I listened to Mama, of course. While my liberal Methodist and Presbyterian friends attended sock hops (in Bedford, *not* Hernia) where they did the Twist, the Freddie, and the Funky Chicken, I stayed home and did the laundry. But Mama forgot to warn me that the devil only *worked* at Arthur Murray's. His real home was our 1957 Maytag with the unbalanced legs. The first time I sat on the machine to hold it in place, well—I better not go there, as I've become fond of saying. My point is, even that incident, in a roundabout way, was related to dancing. At least it didn't involve guitar strings.

Based on what I knew about sex and its relationship to dancing, I decided to begin my investigation with Dorcas Yutzy. Last year she had raised quite a ruckus by attempting to teach square dancing in her high school girls' gym classes. Granted, it would have been girls dancing with girls, but in this day and age that can be problematic as well. The irony is that the students really liked it, and even the Mennonite girls weren't about to squeal, until one mother finally figured out that the Virginia Reel her daughter was raving about wasn't a transfer student.

Believe me, I'm not ascribing evil intentions to Dorcas Yutzy for her choice of curriculum. Although she has Mennonite and Amish ancestors, Dorcas is a second-generation Presbyterian with a Catholic grandfather. The woman can't be expected to know better. All I'm trying to say is that Dorcas, more than any other of the suspects on my list, seemed to have a connection with sex. At least it was a place to start.

I parked my newly modest means of transportation under a sweet gum tree on Briarcliff and hoofed it the two blocks to Main. I wasn't trying to sneak up on Dorcas; this is the oldest section of Hernia, and by far the most attractive. The majority of the houses are two-story Victorians with enough gingerbread to keep Hansel and Gretel fat for life. I'll take any excuse to walk in this part of town, and on pleasant evenings Gabe and I often drive in for a stroll.

Romantic that I am, I pretended Gabe was with me now as I walked. "You see that yellow one there with the gray trim? That's where Wilmer and Henrietta Augsberger used to live. They never had children—at least not officially—but folks were always seeing little faces pressed to the glass on that third-story gable over there. Ah, and that house, the one with the huge blue spruce in the front yard, that's where Otto and Lovinia Petersheim live. They have sixteen children, and all but one of them moved away. He still lives at home, and he's the reason you see those cardboard boxes piled up at the side door. Booze boxes. Vodka, I think they say." I turned right on Main. "I know I told you about the crazy pastor's wife, the one who locked me in a burning outhouse. That's her house over there, only she no longer lives in it, of course. Some rich retirees from the Big Apple snapped it up." I stopped. "Well, this is it. This little white dollhouse that looks totally out of place belongs to Dorcas Yutzy. She lives with her elderly mother, who's as deaf as a fence post. It's what folks hereabouts call a Grossdawdi hause. Back when Hernia was just a couple of Amish farms, this house was built on one of them as a place for grandparents to live. Rumor has it that it was connected by a tunnel to the main farmhouse, so the elderly couple could attend family dinners in inclement weather. That original house burned down a hundred years ago or so. If memory serves me right, Dorcas was born in this cute little cottage."

Leaving Gabe behind, I strode up a walk so clean I wouldn't hesitate to lick gravy off it with my tongue. On either side early plantings of periwinkles had already filled into a solid border. Pairs of glazed pickle crocks bearing bright red geraniums crowned each step. At the windows hung snow-white lace curtains.

The front door opened as I reached for the bell. "Magdalena Yoder!"

"That's my name, dear. Don't wear it out."

Dorcas giggled. "You here to see me? Oh, I hope you are. Mother's napping, so this happens to be a perfect time for a visit. Although you're welcome to come—"

"Actually I'm here to visit the little troll who lives under your porch."

Take it from me, sometimes it's not wise to tease a six-foot-five-inch gym teacher. In her haste to look under the porch, the gangly gal nearly trampled me.

"I was just kidding," I gasped, as she tried to prop me up against a wooden railing.

"Well, I have been hearing noises under there. I thought maybe it was a cat, or a raccoon, but then when you said—never mind. Would you like to come in and have tea?"

"That would be lovely, dear."

Dorcas led me into an immaculate, if minuscule, sitting room. A Victorian settee, two matching side chairs, and a marble-topped coffee table were crammed into a space barely larger than my closet at home, which, by the way, is not of the walk-in variety.

I sat on the chair nearest the door, so I wouldn't feel claustrophobic. While Dorcas clomped about in the kitchen, I studied the cubicle closely. Other than an oil painting of reed-boat fishermen on Lake Titicaca, there were no adornments. Not even a single photo graced the walls or table. I will say, however, that Dorcas Yutzy doesn't suffer dust bunnies. I could have licked those floors as well.

"Well, here we are," she said, as she entered carrying a bamboo tray with two ceramic mugs—one from Disney World, one from Busch Gardens. Both mugs, by the way, had more chips than a New Jersey casino. "I didn't know if you took lemon or cream, so I put in both."

"Isn't that how one makes cottage cheese, dear?"

She giggled again. "Not both in the same cup, of course. I drink it both ways, so you get to choose."

I chose the lemon. They're *supposed* to be sour. Having been raised on a farm, and owning two Holstein cows of my own, I'm very picky about my dairy products. There are few things worse than being forced to down a glass of milk that has just turned.

Without spilling a drop of her own tea, Dorcas managed to fold her body into a zigzag that could be accommodated by the other chair. Her knees nearly touched her chin.

"So, to what do I owe the honor?" she asked.

I took a sip of tea. It was surprisingly good.

"Well, dear, I understand you knew the late Clarence Webber."

The milky tea sloshed over the edge of Dorcas's cup. It's a good thing she was wearing a man's thick sweat suit, or she might well have been burned.

"Oh, so that's what this is about. Magdalena, you're working for Melvin Stoltzfus again, aren't you?"

There was no use in denying it. "It's not like I get paid, dear. I consider it my civic duty."

She stared at me for a moment, her eyes as big as boulders behind the thick lenses. "In that case, Magdalena, you might as well know everything."

"Spill it, dear," I said blithely.

"Clarence Webber was my husband."

8

"Get out of town!" I cried, as lemony tea found my lap. Fortunately, by then it was no longer scalding.

The huge irises registered surprise.

"It's just an expression," I said, dabbing at my lap with a useless paper napkin. "I picked it up from my sister. Did I just hear you say Clarence Webber was your husband?"

She nodded. "We were married on Valentine's Day."

"But your name—you're still a Yutzy, aren't you?"

" 'Klutzy Yutzy,' that's what my students call me. That's what everyone's been calling me since I was a kid. But yes, in answer to your question, I kept my maiden name. A girl doesn't have to give everything away when she marries."

I couldn't have agreed more. If only I hadn't given my most precious possession to that bigamist Aaron on our wedding night. And to think that all I got in return was a nasty little prick. I should have known that the hat pin I was wrapping—which I intended as a tie tack for Aaron—was sharp enough to draw blood. But how was I to know that the cheap rhinestone pin I had found hidden in Mama's dresser drawer after she died was really solid gold, and that the so-called rhinestone was a VSI diamond of good color?

"So, you kept your maiden name, dear, good for you! But the two of you didn't live together. Not in this house. Isn't that a bit more unusual?"

She blinked, her lashes magnified to the point where they resembled licorice sticks. "How do you know we didn't live together?"

I smiled kindly. "This is Hernia, dear. We're one big family. In fact, you and I are second or third cousins, I think."

"Second cousins twice removed on my father's side," she said. "Fifth cousins on my mother's side in both the Weaver and Miller branches. Say, don't you have a bit of Berkey blood as well?"

"Yes, dear. Anyway, the town was named after a rupture my great-great-great-great-grandfather, and founding father, Amos Stucky, suffered when he was building that very first log cabin up by Settler's Cemetery. There hasn't been a secret kept since then."

"Well, you didn't know I was married," she said defensively.

"*Didn't.* That's the operative word, dear. But tell me something—why were you married, if you weren't going to live together?"

Dorcas grinned, displaying her jack-o'-lantern teeth. It wasn't that she didn't have a full contingent—although I didn't count them—but the simple fact that her mouth was so large that an even spread was sure to cause gaps.

"Because of another secret. One you *don't* know."

I'm not psychic, because I don't believe in that stuff. I do, however, have good instincts. And ever since the gangly gym teacher had revealed that she was married, a stubborn thought had been kicking around in my brain. Yes, Dorcas had Mennonite and Amish ancestors, but that didn't make her a paragon of virtue. Besides, like I said, she was a second-generation Presbyterian with a Catholic grandfather. That made her capable of virtually anything.

I gave her the quick once-over. Yup, just as I suspected, the woman was pregnant. While my womb may be as fruitful as the Kalahari in drought, I've seen enough women in her condition to recognize the signs.

Although Dorcas was a big enough gal that she could carry a baby elephant to full term and still not show a stomach, she had that certain glow every expectant mother I've ever known has exhibited. In Dorcas's case, if the glow got any brighter, someone was likely to swipe her head and save it for Halloween.

I cupped my left hand to the corresponding ear. "I hear the potential patter of little feet," I said. "Am I right?"

I wouldn't have thought it possible, but Dorcas's grin widened. "Does it show?"

There are times when the Good Lord doesn't mind a white lie or two if it will make someone happy. Of that I'm sure.

"You're enormous, dear." She could take that as she wished.

She tugged at her sweats, and for the first time I saw the barest hint of a belly. "You really think so?"

"Immense. So where were you married, dear?" I study the marriage license list on a weekly basis, and had not seen her name. Believe me, I'd have remembered it.

"Cumberland."

"Maryland?" I shuddered. It had to be. Cumberland is only thirty-two miles south of Hernia, but because it is across the state line, it offers an anonymity Bedford can't. It may as well be on the other side of the world.

I'm not saying anything against Cumberland, mind you, but it's where serious sinners from Hernia go to misbehave. "If you have to do it in Cumberland," Mama used to say, "you better get down on your knees and have a talk with the Good Lord." So far, thank Heaven and knock on wood, I've never *had* to go to Cumberland.

Dorcas nodded vigorously, a wiener-sized finger holding the heavy glasses in place. "We found this justice of the peace who lives in this great big old house on top of a hill. It's higher up there, you know, and some of the rhododendrons were still in bloom. The justice of the peace's wife—her name was Bonita—cut a couple flowers and made a really nice bouquet for me. She even served us coffee and doughnuts. Not on paper plates and cups either, but real china—well, maybe it was only ironstone, but it had a really nice pattern. Wisteria, I think. Anyway, when we left, she threw birdseed at us."

"That's nice, dear, but why didn't you just marry here?"

Dorcas flinched. It was only a slight tensing of the muscles, but I could see it plain as day. When you're that big, the smallest movement is magnified.

"Well, Clarence thought it would be romantic if we went somewhere. We stayed in a really nice motel afterward with a view of I-70. It was right next to the new Cracker Barrel too."

"A honeymooner's dream." I wasn't being sarcastic. I spent my own honeymoon, if I may be permitted to call it that, at my inn, which was at that point crowded with oversized relatives of Aaron's who called themselves the Beeftrust. A view of an interstate, without family, would have been delightful. After all, Cracker Barrel has great shopping, comfortable rocking chairs, and aside from Freni's famous chicken and dumplings, the best food on the planet.

Dorcas peeked at me over horn-rims, and finding no

smirk on my face, continued. "Even Mama had a good time. She especially likes the breakfast menu at Cracker Barrel."

I gasped. "You took her with you?"

"I couldn't exactly leave her here, could I? Besides, she had her own bed. And as you know, she can't hear anything." Dorcas glanced at a closed door along the short hall to her left, and giggled before continuing. "It isn't like we'd never done it before."

"TMI!" I cried.

"I beg your pardon?"

"Too much information. It's something else I picked up from Susannah."

She nodded, her face suddenly grim. "But still, Magdalena, *it* wasn't an issue—if you know what I mean. In fact, it hasn't been since—well, ever since I found out I was pregnant."

I didn't know which to do, clap my hands over my ears or start taking notes. Never one to waste space, I withdrew a little green spiral-bound notebook and ballpoint pen from the cup Little Freni used to call home.

"So tell me, dear, how did you meet your late husband?"

More giggles followed yet another glance at the closed door. "At a dance," she whispered needlessly.

"I knew it!"

Freckled furrows framed the bottle-thick lenses. "What is that supposed to mean?"

"Dancing. Didn't you know it's the root of all evil?" I was only half kidding.

"I thought that was supposed to be money."

"I'm sure that's a mistranslation, dear. Why, just look at what happened when the daughter of Herodias danced for King Herod. John the Baptist lost his head! You'll find that story, by the way, in the gospels of Matthew, Mark, *and* Luke."

A smug smile made Dorcas look twelve years old again. "That's true, Magdalena, but in Psalm one hundred forty-nine, verse three, it says, 'Let them praise his name with dancing.'"

I swallowed. I don't normally run across people who know as many scripture verses by heart as I do. Who would have suspected that a gal of mixed ancestry—Presbyterian and Catholic, no less—would know her Bible?

"Okay, dear, but what about Exodus, chapter thirty-two, verse nineteen? 'When Moses approached the camp and saw the calf and the *dancing*, his anger burned and he threw the tablets out of his hands, breaking them to pieces at the foot of the mountains.' Just think, Dorcas, if it hadn't been for all that sinful gyration, it would be the *real* Ten Commandments the Supreme Court outlawed in schools."

"Ecclesiastes, three, four," she shot back. " 'A time to weep and a time to laugh, a time to mourn and a time to dance.' The dancing you just quoted wasn't at the right time."

There is also a time to keep one's mug firmly shut. Especially if one has met her match.

The smug smile widened until it threatened to split the big gal's head in two. "It was only a square dance in Bedford, Magdalena. It wasn't at all sexy, if that's what you're thinking."

"I only—"

"Besides, I wanted to get pregnant."

"You *did*?"

"It was my intention from the very beginning. In fact, it was me who first asked Clarence for a dance. Then we went out for some fast food and—well, the burgers weren't the only thing fast that night."

"TMI!" I wailed again.

"Sorry, I keep forgetting. But isn't this how best girlfriends are supposed to talk?"

There is no point, ever, in telling someone that they are not your best friend. Lydia Bontrager dissuaded me of that notion when I was in third grade. For weeks she trotted after me like a little puppy, even giving me her favorite doll. I was flattered, of course, but not so flattered that I didn't turn on her when Catherine Hershberger—the most popular girl in school—asked me to be her best friend. I can still see Lydia's eyes well up with tears when I told her the news. Unfortunately for me, Catherine and her crowd soon found me "icky," leaving me virtually friendless for the rest of the term.

"Just tell me this," I said, shaking my head to clear it of residual guilt. "Why did you want a baby so bad?"

Dorcas leaned forward in her chair, and I saw my reflection grow in the huge spectacles until, finally, I had to look away. A distorted view of my mug is not an especially pretty sight.

"Magdalena, why do you insist on being so difficult?"

"Me?"

"You of all people should know why I want a baby."

I set my little green notebook and pen on the bamboo tray with the tea things. "I do?"

"Because I'm lonely, of course. Just like you. But I have a lot of love to give, and—"

"I'm not lonely," I said evenly. "I have a boyfriend."

"Ah yes, that cute Jewish doctor. But Magdalena, is he really your boyfriend, or is this just wishful thinking?"

It was time to change the subject. "Why did you bother visiting Clarence Webber in jail? I mean, you'd already gotten what you wanted from the man, which was his seed, right? And clearly, that's already sprouted."

Dorcas's dissecting grin had shrunk to a small, tight smile. "Right."

"Oh," I said, as light penetrated my thick Yoder skull.

"You got more than you bargained for. You fell in love with the man!"

She turned so that she appeared to be studying the painting of Lake Titicaca. "Is that so bad?"

I shook my head. Who was I to condemn another woman for her choice of heartthrobs? Unless, of course, the woman was Susannah and the man in question was that mantis, Melvin Stoltzfus. I hadn't exactly scored a home run with Aaron, had I?

"How often did you visit him?" I asked softly.

"As much as they let me, which was twice a day. Six times altogether."

"Did you ever take him food?"

"I'm a terrible cook. I can barely boil water. Besides, he was getting plenty to eat from your inn."

"And all of it perfectly safe and nutritious," I said quickly. I stood. Dorcas unfolded her lanky frame and stood as well. "Well, I really must be going."

"It was good seeing you again, Magdalena. Maybe we can drive into Bedford together some time and have lunch."

I shrugged.

"Or if it's more convenient, we could just meet there someplace."

I shrugged again.

"How about next Wednesday? I have to take Mama in to the audiologist at eleven. We should be done by noon. You don't mind if Mama joins us, do you? She won't be able to hear a word we say." Her voice had risen an octave. "Oh let's! It will be fun. We can have ourselves another girl talk. Maybe even pick out some baby clothes afterwards."

Since I would rather have a root canal without anesthesia than eat lunch with Dorcas and her mother, I had no choice but to resort to a white lie. The Good Lord, I'm sure, understands these things.

"I just remembered I left a pot on the stove," I said, and made a beeline for the front door.

Dorcas tried to block me, but she only coaches sports, she doesn't actually play them. The big gal was no match for me. I was halfway to my car before I realized I'd left my notebook and pen behind.

9

I would have turned around and marched right back to the house, had I anything important written in that little notebook. But it had been blank when I pulled it out for Dorcas, and the few silly comments I'd entered weren't worth the hassle. Instead, I'd bill Melvin sixty-nine cents plus tax for a new one. As for the pen, there were oodles of them waiting for me back at the inn, each with the name of my establishment stamped in gold.

A prudent Magdalena would have headed straight back to the PennDutch, not just to get a new pen, but to check up on things. My guests book by the week, and I had a full house. But most important, now that I was a mom, there was that mite with the motor mouth to monitor. Was she getting along with Freni? Had she, as instructed, washed her face and shed that gruesome jewelry?

Alas, I'm about as prudent as those chocoholics who spend their vacations in Hershey, instead of Hernia, Pennsylvania. I pointed that modest gray Buick toward my next victim's house, although given the area's undulating topography, it was anything but a straight line.

In fact, Emma Kauffman lives at the very top of Buffalo Mountain, one of the highest spots in the county. To
get there you follow Route 96 as if going to Bedford, but
turn right on Baughman Lane. For the first mile and a
half the road is paved, and the twists and turns are no
problem, even for a leadfoot like me. Just past Henry
Baughman's house it becomes little more than a dirt
track that climbs at an alarming grade. Since we get our
fair share of snow and ice hereabouts, I imagine that Ms.
Kauffman—a woman I know only by reputation—finds
herself stranded from time to time during the winter.

Having already confessed that I did not know the
aforementioned woman personally, I will add that it
wasn't for lack of trying. Twice before, I'd been up the
mountain to see her—one can never have too many rich
and famous friends—but had not found her at home.
Perhaps she'd been out in the woods getting inspired or,
more likely, she'd been hiding from the droves of reporters that descended on—or more correctly, ascended
to—her home following an article that appeared in
American Artist magazine last year.

The article, I'm told, referred to Emma Kauffman as
"this century's most talented landscape painter," and
dubbed her "the mother of simplicity." I didn't read the
piece, of course; neither did I watch Emma's subsequent
interviews on the *Today Show* and *Good Morning
America*, and a host of other television talk shows. But
from what I've been told, Ms. Kauffman handled herself
very well—even mentioned Bedford County several
times—and managed to cement her position as an artist
of national renown.

What makes this story remarkable—because surely
there are a number of simple landscape painters—is the
fact that Emma Marie Kauffman was born and raised
Amish. I don't know all the details—Freni can be remarkably tight-lipped when it comes to her people—

but I do know that Emma left the sect approximately twenty years ago, when she was in her early twenties.

I also know that Emma had been officially banned by her church for not following the Ordnung, the Amish code of behavior. The bishop had forbidden her to paint—it was considered too worldly—and she had persisted in secret, hiding her canvases in the hayloft of the family barn. In the end somebody, perhaps a nosy neighbor, ratted her out.

The ban, based on 1 Corinthians, chapter five, verse eleven, meant she was completely excluded from the community until she repented. Even her parents and siblings were forbidden to talk to her. They couldn't even eat at the same table. This pressure was designed to make her cave in, to repent of her sin. But Emma Kauffman undoubtedly had some Yoder blood coursing through her veins, because she stubbornly refused to submit. Critics of Emma would say she had condemned herself to a life of solitude.

As I finally pulled into the clearing in front of the banned woman's log cabin, I felt a sudden wave of guilt. Who was I to interrupt this solitude? If I had forsaken family and friends, even if it was to develop a God-given talent, and had sought refuge atop a mountain, I can assure you I would not take kindly to trespassing strangers. Having left my pacifist traditions behind, I might well take to greeting interlopers with the barrel of a shotgun.

Still, I had only five suspects in the death of Clarence Webber, and the famous, albeit reclusive, Miss Kauffman was one of them. Not only that, but, in my considerable opinion, she was the most likely of the group to have committed murder. After all, a woman who would leave behind everyone she loved in order to pursue a career was capable of anything.

*   *   *

Emma Kauffman obviously possessed a gentler soul than I. She didn't even come out waving a broom, something I *have* done on several occasions. In fact, she didn't come out at all. Nevertheless, I knew she was there, because of the late-model Ford bearing the vanity plate EMMAK parked in the shade of a towering sycamore.

I turned off the engine and hustled my bustle to the front door. It is important in my job to appear confident, if not competent. Finding no doorbell, I gave the post frame a rap with diamond-hard knuckles. There was no answer. I continued to rap until those babies were sore, but still no answer.

In Hernia and environs, folks with clear consciences don't lock their doors. And trust me, those who do lock doors have something to hide. "Magdalena, open that door!" Mama used to scream with regularity. Now I'm glad she did, because Lodema Schrock, our pastor's wife, has knuckles even harder than mine. And lungs to match. Thanks to Mama, I'm almost immune to the shrieking Schrock. It's when Lodema tries to use a hairpin to jimmy the lock that I get really irritated.

So, you see then, I had no compunctions about trying Emma's door, just as long as I didn't use a hairpin. Fortunately, the knob turned easily.

"Hello," I called. "Miss Kauffman, are you in?"

Again, there was silence, but that didn't necessarily mean I was unwelcome. Perhaps the woman was gravely ill, and was at that very moment praying mightily for help. On the off chance that I was an instrument of the Lord, I stepped across the threshold. Then, because the Good Lord eschews darkness, I opened the blinds that covered the picture window, and switched on a floor lamp.

It was only then that I noticed her sitting on a small

sofa that faced the window. I don't mind sharing the fact that this revelation briefly parted me from my size elevens. I may even have vocalized a bit.

"Shame on you!" I cried, just as soon as I was capable of forming words. "I could have had a heart attack."

"Who are you?"

"Who are *you*?" The woman on the couch was enormous. She must have weighed over three hundred pounds. She was wearing a lime green dress that gapped down the front and had more wrinkles than the city of Sarasota. Instead of shoes, she had on purple thongs. Her mousy brown hair—my exact shade—was completely disheveled, and she wore not a smidgen of makeup. In short, she did not look like a rich and famous artist, even one of Amish derivation.

"Ah," she said with a knowing sigh. "With that attitude, and that nose, you have got to be the infamous Magdalena Yoder."

I didn't know whether to feel insulted or exulted. My nose may be deserving of its own zip code, but it is not the largest in the county. I certainly don't have the most attitude; Freni takes the cake for that. Still, being called "infamous" by a perfect stranger was quite an honor. If indeed the woman was Emma Kauffman, I was flattered to the core.

"You answer first," I said. "After all, you were here first."

"That's because I live here."

"So you are Emma Kauffman!"

"I am."

As much as I despise hand-shaking—all those germs to worry about—I was eager to pump this woman's hand. I've had a lot of celebrities stay at my inn, but none, to my knowledge, have been even distant relatives. Not so with Emma. I have more Kauffmans in my family tree than there are peaches in Georgia. Although physically we had about as much in common as Jack Spratt and his wife, the odds were that Emma and I had at least four sets of great-great-grandparents in common. Who knows? In some weird genetic twist of fate, Emma and I might actually be sisters. We were, I reckoned, approximately the same age.

Emma must have felt about germs the way I normally do, because she kept her hands buried in the folds of her ample lap. I tried fumbling for one, but she slapped my probing hand away.

"You know," she said, "technically, I could have you arrested for breaking and entering. Maybe even molestation."

" 'Breaking and entering' is such an ugly phrase. Besides, this is police business."

"Do you have a search warrant?" The woman had only the slightest Pennsylvania Dutch accent, much less than that of most Amish women her age. It wasn't until the W in "warrant" that I picked up on it.

"I just came to ask you a few questions, dear. I'm not here to steal one of your precious paintings. Speaking of which, where are they?"

"In my studio."

"May I see them?" I asked, momentarily forgetting my mission.

Emma sighed, and with a great deal of grunting managed to hoist herself out of the sofa. Then, panting with each step, she led me through the darkened house, pausing every now and then to rest or turn on a small table lamp. The artist used annoyingly low-wattage bulbs, but because she moved so slowly, I was still able to get a good gander at the furnishings.

The media had been right to call her the mother of simplicity. Sturdy furniture, bare floors, no wall adornments—if it hadn't been for her lime green dress (which was shockingly sleeveless, by the way) and purple thongs, I could easily have imagined that Emma was a stout Amish woman leading the way.

It was a much larger house than I'd expected, based on its log exterior. Emma led me down a long paneled hallway lined with tightly closed doors. A small frosted globe overhead barely illuminated that portion of the tour, and I briefly entertained fearful thoughts. What if Emma Kauffman wasn't an ex-Amish artist at all, but a eunuch, working for the Sultan of Brunei? What if her plan was to capture me and ship me off to the sultan's harem? It was quite possible, I assure you. I'd read someplace that tall, thin, horsy women with mousy brown hair were all the rage in neighboring Malaysia. Who knows, I might even be made a princess.

Of course the title would come with strings attached. I mean, would I just have to know the man—in the Biblical sense—or would I be expected to do more? Like belly dance, for instance. But even more distressing than the aforementioned sins was the possibility that I might never be chosen to perform when he made his nightly pick. Could I endure the shame? It was bad enough being the last one chosen in gym class, but it would be just too much to bear if the potent potentate perpetually preferred pretty petite princesses over plain but prosperous proprietresses.

"Don't I at least get the chance to audition?" I wailed. "And I want to choose my own outfits. Baby blue for that silk pajama thing, with matching chiffon for the veil. That color really accents my eyes, and they're my best feature. But no bare navel; that's just wrong."

"Magdalena—"

"Oh, I'll get my own tambourine, won't I? Because I want to name it Booty. 'Shake your booty, shake your booty.' That's what my sister, Susannah, says, although I haven't the foggiest idea what she's talking about. And castanets. I want my own too. Or is that Spanish?"

10

Basic Boiled Grits

Authentic grits are coarse in texture and require thorough cooking. Because the oily germ of the kernel is preserved under the cool grind of the stone, these grits must be consumed very soon after purchase or they will turn rancid. Luckily you can hold these grits in the freezer for up to six months.

Old recipes always direct you to first "wash" the grits. Even today most modern stone-ground grits need rinsing to separate the last remains of the hull or chaff from the kernel. Simply cover the grits with cold water. The meal will sink to the bottom and the chaff will float to the surface, where it can be skimmed off with a kitchen strainer.

1 cup stone-ground grits
4 cups water

½ teaspoon salt, or to taste
2 tablespoons unsalted butter

Pour grits into a large bowl and cover with cold water. Skim off the chaff as it floats to the surface. Stir the grits and skim again until all the chaff has been removed. Drain the grits in a sieve.

Bring 4 cups water to a boil in a medium-size saucepan. Add the salt and slowly stir in the grits. Cook at a simmer, stirring frequently, until the grits are done—they should be quite thick and creamy—about 40 minutes.

Remove grits from heat and stir in butter.

SERVES 4

Note: Most grits in the grocery store are called "quick." The corn is ground very fine and then quickly steamed. Quick grits cook in much less time than coarsely ground traditional grits, and they definitely come in handy.

Basically the proportion of liquid to dry grits is the same (4 to 1) no matter how the grits are milled. Only the cooking time varies, and the manufacturer's directions should be followed up to a point. All instant and quick-cooking grits are improved with longer, gentler cooking than the directions indicate. Or, at the end of cooking, you can just cover the pot and let the grits swell over very low heat for 5 minutes.

11

―――◆―――

It took at least a minute for my eyes to adjust, and as they did, it became apparent that the hallway opened onto a large room that was enclosed mostly by glass. There were five easels, each with its own painting, and dozens of other paintings leaning against the clear walls.

"Wow! This is really neat! How come I didn't see it from outside?"

"That big sycamore blocks most of it. But that's okay. It's the north light that counts. I keep the drapes on the east and west sides pulled most of the time anyway."

I stopped paying so much attention to the room and began to focus on the paintings. The one on the nearest easel was on stretched canvas and measured probably eighteen inches by twenty. I'm not a painter, but I guessed the medium to be oils. The subject matter was what interested me.

"An Amish buggy wheel," I said. "Just a simple buggy wheel in a snowdrift. But it's really good. There's something powerful about those spoke shadows against all that white."

"That's what the critics said. That's my first painting, and it's not for sale. Most of the others are, except for those that aren't finished, of course."

I trotted over to the next easel. "I like the way this hand pump drips water on the dead leaves around it. It's sort of life and death all in one."

"The critics said that too. This, incidentally, is just a signed print. I've sold over two thousand of them."

I went from easel to easel and then started pawing through the paintings on the periphery of the room. The paintings were really wonderful, and I was prepared to shell out a few bucks to get a couple for my parlor walls back at the inn. Maybe even a few for the guest rooms upstairs.

"How much are they, dear?"

"That depends. The prices are written on little stickers on the back."

I turned over a particularly appealing painting, one of a plow in an overgrown field. Tawny grasses grew up through the rusting disks. The colors would go beautifully with the earth tones in the guest room in which I planned to install Alison.

"There aren't any price tags, dear. Just these long identification numbers."

"Those are the prices."

"Five *thousand* dollars? For a painting?"

Emma was still breathing heavily, even though she'd taken a seat. Her ample buttocks completely enveloped the round black-leather-topped stool, and she appeared to be propped up by three rather spindly sticks of wood. I prayed that the tripod would hold.

"My painting of fence posts at sunset," she wheezed, "sold for ten thousand. Of course it was a bit larger."

"Maybe I should take up painting!"

That seemed to startle her. "Do you have talent?"

"No. I was just kidding, dear. The sad truth is, I have

no talents of which I am aware—except for jumping to conclusions. If that were an Olympic event, I'd win a gold medal every four years."

By the look on Emma's face, I gathered she was not amused. "I didn't become a painter on a whim, you know. I was born with the urge to create, and with a hand that could reproduce what my eyes saw." She sighed heavily. "That's why I had to leave the faith."

I nodded. "I know Amish aren't supposed to have graven images in their homes, and they extend that prohibition to include photographs, but your paintings don't even have people in them."

"Yes, but as a purely decorative art form, they're considered prideful."

"There is nothing wrong with a little pride," I said. I meant it in the best Christian way. I, for one, am proud of my humility.

She rubbed her eyes with the balls of her hands. "I had to choose, Magdalena. I had to choose between the Ordnung and the gifts God gave me. It's a decision I still wrestle with."

"If you don't mind my saying so, I think you made the right choice."

She looked straight ahead, to the north, and in that perfect light, she was almost pretty. "It cost me my family," she said quietly.

"I'm sorry, dear."

"Thanks. But you didn't come here to listen to my problems, or to buy paintings. Why did you come, Magdalena?"

I looked for a place to sit, and finding none, leaned against the nearest easel. "It's about Clarence Webber."

She blinked. "What about him?"

It occurred to me that she might not have heard about his death. "Well, uh—do you listen to the news, Miss Kauffman?"

"Sometimes. I haven't lately."

"I see. You read the paper?"

"Magdalena, if I share something personal with you, will you stop playing games with me?"

I'm all for buying time. "Sure. Share away—but this isn't going to be anything of a sexual nature, is it? I mean, I've had all the surprises I can handle in that department."

She turned to face me, a faint smile playing at the corners of her wide mouth. "It has nothing to do with sex. At least not as far as I know. You see, I suffer from depression."

"I get the blues every now and then myself, dear. It's nothing to be ashamed of."

"This isn't the blues, Magdalena. It's clinical depression. When it hits, all the energy just drains out of me. Every step is like walking under water. Sometimes I get so I can't even lift a brush."

Suddenly it clicked. "Ah, so that's why you were sitting there in the dark when I arrived."

"Yes, that's why."

"But you seem okay now."

"It's easier to respond at some times than at others. Okay, so now you know my little secret. Tell me why you're here, and what it has to do with Clarence."

"Clarence Webber is dead," I said softly.

Emma swayed wildly, and for a second I thought I was going to have to catch her. I may be strong, but not that strong. One or both of us would go down. I could even be crushed to death. On the other hand, if one has to go by this method, having the crusher be a celebrity is a nice way to do it.

Thank heavens I didn't have to meet my maker while shaped like a crepe. Emma stabilized herself quite nicely. She even made a futile attempt at smoothing away some of the wrinkles on that lime green dress before speaking.

"When did this happen?"

"Three days ago. Don't you read the paper? Watch the news?"

She shook her head. "Not when I've hit a low."

"Aren't you going to ask how it happened?"

"I was just getting there. So, tell me."

"It was poison."

"Arsenic?"

My pulse raced. "Why did you guess that?"

"Well, it was obvious Zelda didn't like him."

"What makes you say that?"

"You wouldn't believe the sarcasm that woman used. 'Mr. Webber, you have a guest,' she'd say. 'Shall I show her in? Mr. Webber, will the two of you be having tea?' That sort of thing. She was always mocking him. Making faces even."

"I wouldn't take those faces to heart, dear. Five pounds of makeup tends to have a life of its own. It could have just been her foundation shifting."

"Very funny, Magdalena." Emma didn't sound at all amused. "As an artist, I'm first and foremost an observer. That makes me a fairly good judge of people. Zelda hated Clarence."

It is, of course, always easier to mollify someone than to convince that person that she is dead wrong. I prayed for a patient tongue.

"Zelda can come on a little strong. But tell me, dear, what's with the cookies?"

"I beg your pardon?"

"You took Clarence a bag of cookies—"

"Wait just one damn minute! I'm one of your suspects, right?"

I reeled at her use of the D word, almost knocking over my easel. As in Susannah's case, Emma's apple had rolled out of the orchard altogether.

"Well?" she demanded. "I'm one of your suspects, aren't I?"

I leaned back against the easel. The gig was up. It was time to confess.

"Yes, but you're not the only one. You are, however, the only one who brought him food."

She stiffened, the stool beneath her wobbling precariously. Again I feared for her safety.

"I wouldn't have had to take him a care package, if the food provided had been at all palatable."

That did it. That hiked my hackles.

"There is nothing wrong with Freni Hostetler's cooking! Why, once she even won a blue ribbon at the county fair for her bread-and-butter pickles."

Emma regarded me stone-faced. "Then maybe she should have sent over her pickles. What she sent instead made Clarence sick just to look at it. And as if that wasn't bad enough, the place in general was a pigsty. I'm sure that toilet hadn't been cleaned in years, and that mattress! How is someone supposed to sleep on just an inch of foam?"

"What was Clarence Webber to you?" I cried. "You sound like his mother!"

"I was his wife!" She spat the words like a string of firecrackers. "He was the love of my life. The only man I'll ever love. The only man who will ever love *me*!"

The shock of her emotional outburst was too much for me to bear standing up. That's the only way I can explain it. My spindly legs simply gave out, and I fell over backwards, taking the easel with me.

It is a fact that I have a long pointed nose, and I've been accused of having a sharp tongue, but who knew my elbows were capable of so much damage? Especially the right one, of which I've always been inordinately fond? It penetrated the fallen canvas like a steak knife through an angel food cake.

Rest assured, I was not hurt. The painting was, of course, ruined, and the easel was a shambles. As was my pride.

*   *   *

Emma Kauffman was livid. Not only did she charge me sixty-five hundred dollars for the painting, she hustled my bustle to the nearest door. Most important, she absolutely refused to say another word about her relationship with the deceased. There was nothing I could do to change her mind. Even my offer to double the price on the damaged painting—for a little more info, of course—fell on deaf ears.

Well, like they say, when the going gets tough, the tough get going, and that's exactly what I did. I pressed the pedal to the metal until I reached the bottom of Buffalo Mountain, then I squashed that accelerator right into the floor. I know, the Good Lord expects us to be law-abiding citizens, but He also gave us plenty of examples in the Bible of folks who like to speed. Maybe they didn't have cars back then, but fast is fast. Even the angels zipped around so quickly no one was ever quite sure where they came from.

At any rate, what would normally take me a good twenty minutes to cover, took me just over ten. I might even have shaved off another minute or two if I'd bothered to look up Agnes Schlabach's address. Unfortunately I had to stop once to ask where the piano teacher with thirty-two cats lived. I might as well have announced that I had plans to date O.J. Simpson. The fierce father of four frowned as he gave me a lecture on the follies of frolicking with a floozy famous for her feline fixation. The air for blocks around was fetid and foul, he fumed. Did I want to ruin both frock and Ford? I told him it was an old dress and I was driving a Buick.

The truth is, I couldn't smell the cats until I was on the front porch reaching for the bell. But when Agnes opened the door, the rank odor nearly knocked me off my feet. I'd fallen one too many times that day, and was not in a good mood.

"Thirty-two cats is too many," I managed to say kindly.

She was a slight woman, perhaps nearly seventy, with a face as pale as cake flour, and yellow-gray hair piled in a formless mass atop a long narrow head. The unattractive do was held in place by enough bobby pins to build a scaffold around the Washington Monument, where they would have undoubtedly done more good.

Her watery gray eyes searched my face. "Who are you? Are you the lady from animal control?"

"No. My name is Magdalena Yoder, and I'm from picturesque Hernia. I'd like to have a few minutes of your time, if I may."

"I already belong to the Methodist church," she said, sounding wistful, but started to close the door.

There are advantages to having feet as long and narrow as mine. I was able to literally get a toe in the door before it closed. Unfortunately, Agnes was pretty strong for a woman her age, and I could well lose that nail.

"I'm not here to convert you!" I cried.

The door opened just wide enough for me to retract my flattened tootsie. "Then what do you want?"

I can smell a lonely woman, even one who's been living with thirty-two cats. "I just want to chat."

"Oh? What about?" The door opened wide enough for me to push my way in, had I the desire.

"This and that. Look, dear, could we possibly conduct our little chat outside? It's such a nice day and—well—I'm allergic to cats." Like I said before, there is nothing in the big Ten about lying—not when it comes to telling tales on oneself. Read the book of Exodus if you don't believe me.

She stepped halfway out and scanned the sky beyond her porch. "Well, I suppose we could visit in the grape arbor. I've been looking for an excuse to do that all spring. Sit in there, I mean. Would you care for some lemonade?"

"Do cookies come with that?"

"Peanut butter. Just made them this morning."

"With the crisscross fork marks?"

She smiled. "Of course, is there any other kind?"

I said a plate of those sounded fine. She excused herself and returned in a very few minutes bearing a mahogany tray with ivory handles. It was loaded with a large pitcher of lemonade, a plate piled high with cookies, two tall frosted glasses, and neatly folded napkins. I had the feeling she'd been expecting company.

"This way," she said gaily.

I followed her around to the side of the big white Victorian house. We squeezed past a Colorado blue spruce planted far too close to the foundation, and entered a secret garden. I couldn't believe what I saw.

12

The intimate space was barely larger than my boudoir at the PennDutch. The old spruce, in fact, formed an entire wall of this natural courtyard. Lilac trees and the house formed the other three sides.

In the middle of this outdoor room was a white wooden arbor with built-in seats. The rickety structure was peeling, and looked as if it might well fall apart were it not for the lush grapevines over it. In fact, the thick, woody vines had so intertwined themselves throughout the lattice that the arbor had long since become superfluous.

"Sit," Agnes directed.

I picked the seat with the least amount of bird droppings, and gave it a thorough scrubbing with a twig before plunking my bony bottom down. Agnes sat without so much as a downward glance. She placed the mahogany tray beside her and poured the lemonade.

I thanked her for my glass, but stopped just short of putting it to my lips. There were enough cat hairs floating on the surface to make a fur coat. A small coat, mind you, but still, a festive one of many colors.

"Cookie?" she asked.

I chose what appeared to be a furless cookie. One bite, however, had me pulling hair from between my teeth.

"Is anything the matter?" she asked.

"Nothing, dear. I just hadn't planned to floss again until bedtime."

"I beg your pardon?"

"Nice place you have here." Changing the subject with a compliment is a surefire dodge.

She took a long draft of her lemonade. "Daddy built this arbor for Mama for their first wedding anniversary. Mama planted the grapes herself. Every summer this thing used to be covered with fruit, but not anymore. It's gotten too shady." She giggled. "It's cozy though, don't you think?"

"Until Tarzan gets back. Then it will be crowded."

She giggled again. "You're funny. What did you say your name was again?"

"Magdalena Yoder. I own the PennDutch Inn in Hernia. Surely you've heard of me."

"I'm afraid not. Where is this inn?"

"Hernia," I snapped. "I just told you that."

"Ah, yes. Hernia. I think my parents may have taken me there as a young girl. Isn't that where the chocolate factory is?"

"That's Hershey! This is Hernia. We're named after a rupture."

"Oh, dear. I don't think my parents took me there. Daddy particularly loved chocolate—Mama was partial to butterscotch cremes—but neither of them cared for ruptures."

"Never mind your parents," I cried. "You took yourself to Hernia just last week."

She looked genuinely surprised. "Why ever would I do that?"

"To visit Clarence Webber."

She blinked. "I don't believe I know anyone by that name."

"Oh, but you do."

"I do?"

"You bet your bippy you do. Now stop playing games with me, Miss Schlabach, and tell me about your visit to Clarence Webber."

"Clarence Webber," she said slowly, as if trying to put face to name. "I suppose it's possible I know someone by that name. It sounds very familiar. Did I see him in your Hershey?"

"My Hernia!" I bellowed. "You visited him in the city jail."

"Jail? You must forgive me, Miss—uh—"

"Yoder."

"I have these little lapses of memory, you see."

"And I'm just a wee bit short of patience, dear." I clapped a bony hand to my mouth. "Oops, silly me. I forgot to mention that I'm here on police business."

That helped her focus. "Did you say *police*?"

"I did indeed, dear. I'm not a policewoman, mind you, but I am acting on behalf of Melvin Stoltzfus, Hernia's Chief of Police. You might say I'm his special assistant." The truth is, I had no official moniker, even though I'd been begging Melvin for a title for years. At the very least, I wanted a badge to pin over my meager bosom. So far all I'd gotten was an official mandate to stick my big nose into places it didn't belong.

Agnes gulped some more of her drink. "What do the police want with me?"

"You are aware, aren't you, that Clarence Webber is dead?"

She looked like the deer I'd once seen, caught in the headlights of my car. It had taken some expensive body work to get that deer removed from the headlights. I fervently prayed Agnes Schlabach would be less trouble.

"Uh—yes, I think there was something about that in the newspaper."

"So you do know the man?"

"Yes," she said softly, "but like I said, what does this have to do with me?"

"Well, according to the register of visitors, you were a regular. And although the newspaper account doesn't mention it, we have reason to suspect foul play."

"Oh, dear, it's coming back to me now. Clarence *was* in jail when I saw him last."

"Did you take him cookies?" Maybe the coroner had been wrong. A hairball can be just as lethal as arsenic if you ask me.

Agnes Schlabach took her sweet time answering my question. "I don't recall taking him any cookies," she finally said. "But I did take him something."

"A flute."

Again the look of genuine surprise. "How did you know?"

"Zelda Root, the police officer on duty, made a record of it."

Agnes fumbled with a cookie. "Well, the flute I brought him wasn't a proper flute. Not like you'd find in a symphony. It was a wooden shepherd's flute. One that I bought in a museum gift shop years ago. In Chicago, I think. Yes, that's it. The Field Museum of Natural History. I had no use for it anymore. I thought it might help Clarence pass the time."

Funny how her memory was improving by the second. It was time to strike while her iron was still hot. Well, at least warm to the touch.

"There was a big write-up on you in the paper recently. It said you teach piano." I let my voice rise, turning it into a question.

"Oh, my, that was some years ago. Reporters always seem to get at least one thing wrong."

"Truer words were never spoken, dear." I knew exactly what she meant. According to one misguided member of the press—the legitimate press, I might add—I was a sharp-tongued harpy who gouged tourists in my quest for the almighty dollar. Oh, and I wailed a lot. The tabloids were almost as bad. One went so far as to claim that I was the love child of Hitler and a female Martian.

My hostess took a bite of her cookie. "I once had as many as forty students. Then one by one they started canceling their lessons and—well, this year I had just the one."

"Clarence Webber?" A sharp-tongued Magdalena would have suggested a correlation between the dropout rate of Agnes's students and the birthrate of her cats.

"Yes. How did you know?"

"Just a lucky guess, dear. How did you meet Clarence? Did you advertise?"

"Oh, no, I would never do something like that!"

"Don't most piano teachers advertise?"

"Yes, but for piano students. Not for husbands. I met Clarence at a church potluck.

"It's funny, you know. When I was a girl I believed in love at first sight, and then when it never happened to me—falling in love, I mean—I slowly became convinced that it was all a myth. Then I met Clarence, and suddenly I was young again."

"Whoa! Back up a minute. Did you say Clarence was your husband?"

She took another draft, draining the glass. "Yes, Clarence was my husband—if you can call it that. He was never very faithful."

"You're telling me!"

Watery eyes regarded me warily over the empty glass. "What is that supposed to mean?"

Who was I to break the news that the man under discussion was a bigamist? Or would that be a trigamist? No, I'd be much better off letting the women involved make that connection for themselves. It's human nature to want to kill the bearer of bad news, and I had only a life or two yet to go.

"Nothing really, dear. I was just being agreeable. Although I will say, I find it pretty strange that just a minute ago you barely remembered the man, and now you tell me he was your husband."

She poured herself a refill. "I did confess, Miss Yoder, that I have these memory lapses. Senior moments, I think they call them."

"Senator Strom Thurmond has senior moments, dear. Yours are more like centuries."

Her response was merely to guzzle more lemonade.

"You don't seem particularly sad that your husband is dead," I offered.

She swallowed and shrugged. "You ever make a big mistake, Miss Yoder? Regarding men, I mean?"

"Well—"

"Because that's what Clarence was. Nothing but a big mistake. You'd think a woman my age would know better. But oh no, Agnes Shlabach had to fall for the only man at the church potluck who actually brought a dish. Swedish meatballs, they were. Not very good, the truth be told, but that didn't matter. Clarence had this way about him. He was incredibly charming."

"I know," I grunted. "I sold him my car for thousands of dollars under the Blue Book price. I even threw in a mini-vac and some perfectly good maps."

She drained her second glass with a loud slurping

sound and set it on the tray beside her. "Then you know just how persuasive he could be."

"You're not the only one to have been snookered by a man, dear."

"You too?"

"Not Clarence—not on a personal level. But I was married to the slime on the ooze that clings to the sludge of the bottom of the pond. Turns out he was still married to someone else."

Her rheumy eyes widened. "Oh, you're *that* Magdalena Yoder." She glanced around the arbor as if the tiny space might possibly be harboring an eavesdropper. "You're the famous bigamist," she hissed.

"Look Miss Pot, don't you be calling this kettle black."

"What on earth is that supposed to mean?"

"That meant nothing, dear. I suffer from Tourette's syndrome."

She nodded. "Well, that does explain a lot."

I bit my tongue lightly, trying my best to match teeth with existing holes. "Look, dear, can you think of any reason someone would want Clarence dead?"

"No. I mean, just because a man is unfaithful—well, that's no reason to poison him."

"Poison? Who said anything about poison, dear?"

"You did. You even asked if I brought him cookies."

I tried, but failed, to stop a triumphant smile. "I did ask about the cookies, but I never mentioned the P word."

She struggled to her feet. "Miss Yoder, I'd like you to leave."

"But I haven't had my lemonade yet." I blew the cat hair to one side of the glass and took a tiny sip. It tasted so bad, I took a second sip just to make sure I'd gotten the first one right. Perhaps I'd damaged my taste buds with all that tongue-biting I'd been forced to do lately.

But if indeed that were the case, it might take three or four sips to get an accurate taste reading. Maybe even five.

As I—one who likes to keep an open mind—did my little taste test, Agnes Schlabach's expression changed from one of defensiveness to pride. She bent and picked up the half-empty pitcher, ready to give me a refill.

"It's my mother's secret recipe," she said. "Do you like it?"

I took a sixth sip—something I was incapable of saying just then—and it hit me. I'd encountered a similar sharp undertaste when I'd unwittingly drank half a pitcher of mimosas while trying to solve a different murder. This stuff, however, was a good deal stronger. Aware that jumping to conclusions is one of my worst faults, I took a seventh sip to confirm my findings.

"Your secret mother's recipe contains booth."

"I beg your pardon!"

I willed myself to concentrate. "I meant to say booze. Your mother's recipe contains alcohol."

"It most certainly does not!"

"I'm no expert, mind you, but I'd say gin." That was indeed just a guess. The only thing I know about the various types of alcohol—those champagne mimosas excluded—is that the consumption thereof is tantamount to purchasing a first-class ticket on the train to Hell. Read any Bible to see for yourself.

Agnes Schlabach recoiled in shock. The sudden movement caused several clumps of yellow-gray hair to slip loose from their underpinnings and cascade down the sides of that narrow head.

"Gin?" she gasped. "Why, that's for martinis. Mother's recipe calls for the finest vodka."

"Aha!" I stood. I was able to do it in one try, although I must admit I had a newfound appreciation for day-old colts. "You planned to get me drunk, didn't you?"

"I did no such thing. I was simply being gracious."

I waggled a warning finger in her approximate direction. "You're not off the hook, missy. And don't even think about leaving town!" Then, taking great care to maintain as straight a line as possible, I placed one hoof—I mean, foot—in front of the other, squeezed past the blue spruce, and tottered to my car.

Folks who sneak up on you deserve to be shot—not with bullets, of course, but with acorns. Good slingshots, by the way, are not that hard to make. I know those are strong words coming from a cradle pacifist, but there is nothing worse than being scared out of one's wits in broad daylight.

I was bending to insert the key into my car door—alas, it doesn't have that automatic gizmo my Beamer had—when someone tapped me on the shoulder. I whirled, keys ready to rake my attacker's face. (I would have led with my purse, which is a bit more benign, but I'd been holding it between my knees and it fell to the street.)

"Well, well," a male voice said, "look who we have here."

Fortunately for him, I recognized the man. However, that was just barely in his favor.

"Aaron!"

"I thought that was you, Mags. 'Course I wasn't sure at first. I thought what are the odds that I'd be driving down some little side street in Bedford, and the one and only, incomparable, beautiful Magdalena Yoder would just happen to be bending over to unlock her car."

I would have given all four of my eyeteeth for a snappy rejoinder. "Uh—what *are* you doing on this street?"

"My wife—I mean, Lucinda—needed some feminine

products in a hurry, and this is the quickest way from the motel to the store. Now tell me what you're doing here."

Lucinda? Lucinda was a floozy's name if I'd ever heard one. How could someone I once loved have married a Lucinda? While we were dating, if Aaron had as much as hinted that he liked the name Lucinda, I would have dropped him like a hot potato.

Clearly Lucinda represented the wild side of Aaron Miller, no doubt acquired overseas in the jungles of Asia. I, on the other hand, was the sensible, down-to-earth woman he would have married, had there been no Vietnam war. So in the final analysis, the reason for my angst was LBJ. If Lyndon Baines Johnson had kept his promise to get us out of the war, I would today be Mrs. Aaron Miller, and he would be on his way to the store to buy *my* feminine products.

Aaron snapped his fingers. "Hey, a penny for your thoughts."

"I wasn't thinking anything."

"Yes, you were. Your pretty blue eyes looked like marbles."

"I was lost in thought," I wailed, "and it was unfamiliar territory. So give me a break."

He grinned, displaying teeth so white they'd blind polar bears. "You look stressed."

"I am."

"Well, sorry about what just happened."

"That's okay." It's impossible to look at the man and stay angry. "But someone your age should know better than to sneak up on people."

"Sorry about that too, but I meant what just happened with Alison. I'm sure it was just a matter of her acting out because of the move. You know, new place, new faces, it's got to be a little upsetting."

The hair on my arms was standing up at that moment.

If the hair on my head hadn't been secured into a tight, modest bun, it might well have stood on end too.

"*What* just happened with Alison?"

The broad, handsome brow puckered. "Didn't Freni track you down?"

"What happened?" I shrieked.

Aaron took a step back. "Maybe you better get back to the inn, Magdalena."

13

Scientists claim to have exceeded the speed of light in laboratory tests. This raises the interesting question of whether or not the light reached its destination *before* leaving its starting point. I feel pretty sure that I traveled faster than the speed of light that day, but I know for sure I didn't arrive before I'd left. Had that been the case, I would have put a stop to things before they got so far out of hand.

I didn't even need to speak to Freni to see what the problem was. Lying on a towel in the middle of my front yard was my new charge, Alison. She was sunbathing. This situation would have been problematic enough if the girl had been wearing a conservative one-piece bathing suit. Maybe something with a skirt. Definitely black. After all, most of the people who use Hertzler Road are of the Amish or Mennonite persuasion.

But Alison was not wearing a sensible suit. The itsy-bitsy, teenie-weenie bikini she sported contained less fabric than one of my handkerchiefs. As for the color, it was the shade known hereabouts (perhaps in part due to my ex-BMW) as "harlot scarlet."

"Alison," I said sharply. "This is simply not acceptable. Either put something else on, or go back inside."

She was lying on her stomach, her face turned in my direction. She opened one eye lazily.

"Hey, you ain't gonna get all bent out of shape too, are ya?"

"Alison, you heard me. Now get inside."

She closed the eye. "Make me."

"No problem, dear." I took a step forward. My intent was to pick her up and throw her over my shoulder like a skinny bag of bikini-wearing potatoes.

"You lay one hand one me and I'll press charges."

"What?"

"Touch me and I'll scream child abuse."

That stopped me dead in my tracks. "Well, I guess I'll just have to call the police."

"Go ahead. That crabby little cook of yours already did. And guess what the cop said? She said there ain't nothing illegal about what I'm doing, just as long as I keep my top on." She sighed. "So I put the damn thing back on, even though it's gonna give me a farmer's tan."

"What?"

"A farmer's tan. You know, when you can see the strap marks."

"Farmers don't wear straps—" I slapped myself for getting sidetracked. "You had your top off?"

She sat up, slowly opened her peepers, and then blinked like a bat when you shine a light in its face. (I don't do a lot of that, mind you; just enough to know.)

"It wasn't even off all the way. I just had the strings untied. I don't see what the big deal is. God made us naked, didn't He?"

"Yes, but then just about the very next thing He did was make us clothes. And I mean *clothes*, dear. Not bikinis."

"How do you know He didn't make bikinis too? It doesn't say He didn't, does it?"

"Never mind, I'm not going to argue with you. Just go on into the house."

"Like I said, *make me*."

"Okay, toots, if that's the way you want it."

I'm not as stupid as I look. I wouldn't lay a hand in anger on a thirteen-year-old child. I had no compunctions, however, about picking up the garden hose and giving the girl a good hard squirt. I'd aim for the mouth first, of course. Heaven knows it needed a good washing out.

I picked up the hose and turned on the faucet, but before I could squeeze the nozzle, a car barreled up the driveway and came to a screeching halt just inches from mine. I stared in dread as out jumped Lodema Schrock, my pastor's wife.

To say that I've never gotten along with the woman is like saying some politicians have been known to stretch the truth. She, I might add, has little or no grounds for her dislike of me. The reverse is definitely not the case. *Au contraire*. The woman is all ten plagues rolled into one.

"Shame on you, Magdalena," she cried, waving her arms like a symphony director. "I heard what was going on here, but I couldn't believe it. I had to see it with my own eyes." She gasped, whether from lack of oxygen or shock, I don't know. "A den of iniquity, that's what you're running here, Magdalena."

"I didn't give this child permission to dress like this," I cried.

Lodema Schrock continued to conduct her imaginary orchestra. "Just because you're a wanton woman, Magdalena, is no reason for you to corrupt this child."

Alison, who'd been sitting there with a smirk on her face, jumped to her feet. "Hey lady, watch your mouth! I ain't no child."

Lodema turned to me. "You see?" The fact that I could

still hear her was a wonder. Lodema's voice is capable of rising to inaudible registers when she gets truly excited, causing dogs all over the county to howl in agony.

"Do I see what?"

"Not even a day in your custody, and this pathetic child has turned into a heathen. Sodom and Gomorrah, Magdalena, that's what you should rename this place."

Alison was livid. "Hey lady, I told you I ain't no child, and I ain't no heathen. Like, what are you? Some kind of fossil from the Middle Ages?"

"Why, I never!" Lodema gasped. "You should be spanked."

"Spanked?" Alison laughed derisively. "Like, who's gonna do it? You and that fat ass of yours?"

Of course I could not tolerate such language. Neither could I stomach Lodema Schrock, and I mean that literally. I felt like throwing up, and since it was my grass, that simply was not an option. So you see, I had no choice.

I turned the hose first on Lodema. She squawked like a hen that had just laid an egg, while she ran in circles like a chicken that had just had its head cut off. I have a pretty good aim, if I say so myself, and she had a hard time dodging the blast.

"You'll pay for this, Magdalena! I'll tell all the ladies in the Sewing Circle! The Prayer Chain too! You'll be persona non grata!"

"Tell away," I cried gleefully. "Call the newspapers. Call the networks. Maybe *People* magazine will put me on their cover." Having already crossed the line, I might as well get full credit for my sin.

My efforts were certainly being appreciated by young Alison. "You go, girl!" she shouted.

The fact that I couldn't stand Lodema Schrock was no reason for Alison to show disrespect. And there was that matter of her foul mouth. I swiveled and turned the hose on her.

"Hey!"

"Now, you can tell on me too, dear."

"That ain't funny!" But unlike the spastic Lodema, Alison snatched up her towel and boogied through the front door of my inn. The girl might prove to be trainable after all.

Poor Lodema, however, must have been a hopeless child. She didn't have the sense to get in her car and drive away. And since after a while it isn't fun to hit a sitting duck—or running chicken—I shut off the hose. Although well water is essentially free, it does take electricity to pump it.

"You're welcome to come in and dry off," I said charitably. "I have an extra bathrobe that is way too big for me, but it might fit you."

Lodema had finally stopped running, and she glowered at me through dripping, colorless lashes. "You haven't heard the last of this, Magdalena. If we were Catholic, I'd get the Pope to excommunicate you. You can be sure, though, that I'll get the Reverend to do *something.*"

"Oh?" I wasn't the least bit scared, merely curious. Her husband, coincidentally, is a saint.

"Well, I might not know what it is yet, but it will be something drastic."

"That sounds exciting, dear. And when you talk to him, please remind him that I'm Beechy Grove Mennonite Church's largest contributor." I put a finger to my chin. "Hmm, let's see. Is the sanctuary scheduled to get a new roof this summer, or did the building committee decide we could wait another year? Whatever. But I seem to remember hearing it's going to cost ten thousand dollars that's not in the budget."

"You can't buy your way out of this!" Lodema shrieked.

I smiled sweetly and followed Alison into the house.

While it may be true that money can't buy happiness, it can for sure buy a whole lot of convenience. And privilege. I had no doubt that my pastor's wife was going to report me to the Sewing Circle, and the Prayer Chain too—maybe even get the latter to pray for me—but I was far from through at Beechy Grove Mennonite Church.

Thank heavens Alison is not the type to hold a grudge. In fact, she seemed quite taken with me. She chatted on a mile a minute about how I was so much more fun than her mom and dad.

"You're, like, totally awesome," she said to me right in front of Freni.

"Ach, du leiber!" Although a pious woman, my cook has a jealous streak a mile wide.

"No, really, I mean it. Like, my mom would have gotten totally pissed at that old lady, but she wouldn't have had the nerve to squirt her." Alison turned to me. "You do that often?"

"Not as often as I'd like."

"Man, I'm gonna like living here. So when do I get to see my room?"

"When will you remove those studs from your tongue?"

Alison stuck said tongue out defiantly. "Hey, you can forget that. These babies stay."

"Not if you want to."

"You're shooting me, ain't ya?" Actually she said a far cruder word, one I would never repeat.

"Like, I'm totally serious, dear." I had no intention of backing out of my agreement to take in Alison, but the art of bluffing is a skill I've been honing for years. After all, so much in life is dependent on the attitude we bring to it.

"That reeks!"

"Take it or leave it, dear."

"What if I get rid of one stud? Will that make you happy?"

"It's all or nothing. Since it's going to be nothing, it's a good thing you haven't unpacked yet, isn't it?"

"Hey, you ain't getting rid of me that quick!"

Then much to my eternal disgust, Alison twisted her tongue like a good Amish pretzel, and removed from it what seemed like pounds of shiny metal. She held out her hand.

"There! That better?"

"Gott in Himmel!" Freni, about to faint, was staggering for the nearest chair.

"That's wonderful, dear. Now throw them in the garbage."

Much to my surprise, Alison obeyed. "Sheesh, I can't believe I just did that," she said, wonder in her voice. "My mom could have never made me throw them away. You really are cool."

"Absolutely, dear, and don't you forget it."

Then, to reinforce this image of myself as a super-cool mom-in-absentia, I let her pick which one of my six guest rooms she wanted as her own. Unfortunately, there were guests registered to that room, so I told Alison she could have my room until those guests left. Just for the record, Alison picked the most expensive room I have. This display of good taste made me like the girl even more.

So, you see, I was feeling rather benevolent as I prepared to leave the PennDutch to interview my next suspect. Generosity of spirit does not always translate into open purse strings, however. I was just opening the front door to leave when Mayor Rachel Blank's shiny new car rolled slowly up my drive.

I was of half a mind to slam the door shut and bolt it. This inclination had nothing to do with the woman's sexual orientation, mind you, but my suspicion that she was there to ask for money. Certainly she was there to solicit my vote. The truth is, I was tempted to give her both, and therein lay my problem.

How could I, in good conscience, not vote for the best candidate for congressperson? But a vote for Mayor Blank was a vote against getting Melvin out of his position as Chief of Police. That was a sobering thought. The man was dreadful at his job, after all, and everyone knew that Zelda Root would make a far better Chief. There were, however, the ramifications to consider.

Melvin was Melvin, and I had no illusions that he would magically become competent if elected to state office. The only thing sure to change would be that his sphere of influence would be wider, leaving me to ask myself the following question: Which was more important, the good of Hernia or the good of the congressional district? And what *if*, Heaven forfend, Melvin not only won the election, but bamboozled the public and continued to climb the political ladder? There have been bamboozling idiots in the White House before, but none so dense as to ship ice cream by UPS.

Complicating the situation was the fact that Melvin was my brother-in-law. Susannah wanted desperately to be somebody, and being a congressman's wife was certainly a start. Frankly, I wouldn't mind being a congressman's sister-in-law, just as long as Melvin wasn't involved.

So you see, I would much rather have ignored the entire election. Alas, that is virtually impossible to do in this country, given the fact that our electoral processes generally outlast most marriages. I had no choice, therefore, but to fling open the door and paste a wide, fake smile across my mug.

As usual, Rachel Blank was impeccably dressed, in a cream linen suit, buttery tan pumps, and a gleaming single strand of pearls that matched the solitaire drops at her ears. Every dark hair on her head was in place and she was wearing a moderate, and not too unattractive, amount of makeup. I could certainly imagine Rachel as our next congressperson.

"Mayor Blank, what a nice surprise!"

"Hello, Magdalena. I hope I'm not disturbing your lunch."

"Lunch, munch, who has time for that? Unless, of course, you'd like some lunch. I'm sure Freni wouldn't mind throwing another potato in the pot." I laughed agreeably.

"No, thank you, I've just eaten. Do you mind if I come in for a minute?"

"I don't mind at all. But it will literally have to be a minute, because I was just about to head out the door on police business."

She seemed surprised. "Melvin stick you with one of his difficult cases again?"

Like I said, Melvin Stoltzfus may be a loser, but he's my loser now—I mean he's my *relative* now. Besides, Rachel was Melvin's boss. If Melvin lost both his job and the election, I might be forced to take him and Susannah in to live with me. I'd sooner have Mama back from the dead.

"It's no big deal," I hastened to assure her.

"It's the Clarence Webber case, isn't it?"

I motioned to one of the many rocking chairs I keep on the front porch for my guests' enjoyment. She nodded her agreement and we sat. There was no point in wasting a beautiful day inside.

"How did you know?"

"This is Hernia, Magdalena. What other difficult cases does he have?"

"Well, Anna Leichty has complained that someone's been throwing eggs at her outhouse."

"With or without her in it?"

We both laughed.

The mayor stopped suddenly. "It's okay, Magdalena. Melvin told me about the latest development."

"You mean all those little scars? Wasn't that sick?"

She shuddered. "People never cease to amaze me. To disgust me either. So, what is it Melvin has you doing?"

"Oh, he just has me checking on a few suspects. Like I said, it's really no big deal."

"Who does he suspect?" She pressed manicured but unpolished nails briefly against her lips. "Shame on me for asking. Sometimes I forget that, just because I head up the city council that hired Chief Stoltzfus, I'm not entitled to know everything."

I breathed a quiet sigh of relief. It may, or may not, be the mayor's business to know everything that goes on in a town. Speaking from experience, however, the fewer people involved in a murder case, the better.

"So, what brings you out here? My vote or my checkbook?"

She looked startled, and then laughed louder than before. I must explain, however, that in keeping with her polished appearance, Rachel had a cultivated laugh. Even at high decibels.

"You're too much," she finally said. "Zelda warned me about you."

"She warned me about you too."

A neatly plucked brow rose in a questioning manner.

"It's not that I don't find you attractive," I hastened to explain. "Which is not to say that I do, either. I mean, if I was, I would. But I'm not, so I don't. But it's nothing personal, I assure you."

"I'm afraid I don't follow you, Magdalena."

"I'm not gay!" I wailed.

The second brow shot skyward. "I'm afraid I don't follow."

"Zelda said that you were—well—what you do behind closed doors is really no one else's business."

If laughter is indeed the best medicine, Rachel Blank was going to leave my front porch in tip-top condition. Finally she remembered I was there.

"Sorry," she said, pressing fingers to mouth again in that coy, if somewhat affected, manner. "It's just that Zelda has such an active imagination."

"That she does." Zelda once told me that her parents were missionaries to the Belgian Congo and that she knew the famous mystery writer Ramat Sreym, whose parents were also missionaries. This is, of course, utter nonsense. I've known Zelda since she was knee-high to a grasshopper—make that a mantis—and to my knowledge she's never even been out of this state.

"Anyway," Rachel said, her demeanor restored, "you asked what I wanted from you. Well, here's the thing."

14

I hopped to my feet. "My checkbook's in the house. I'll be back in a jiffy." I started for the door, then stopped and turned. "But I have to warn you, dear. Since I'm undecided, and Melvin is my brother-in-law, I think I'll donate to both campaigns. Equal amounts, of course."

"Please, Magdalena, sit down. It isn't money I'm asking for—although I never turn down a donation. I'm here to inquire about renting your inn."

I plopped back onto my rocker. Take it from me. If your bottom is as bony as mine, plan your plopping carefully.

"Ouch," I said. "What do you mean you want to rent the inn? All six guest rooms? Because now that I'm a mother, I'm down to five."

If I ever get around to plucking my eyebrows—which has got to be some sort of a sin—I want perfectly arched ones like Rachel's. Just by lifting one, she can ask a question. Yes, I know, I can lift my brows too, but when they're this shaggy, the questions are unintelligible.

"I became a mother this morning," I explained. "No, I didn't have a baby, if that's what you're wondering. It's more like foster care. And she's definitely not a baby. But back to the matter at hand. Why do you want to rent my inn, when you have a perfectly good house right here in town?"

Rachel smiled. "Yes, it is a perfectly good house, but as you know, it's rather small. No, I want to rent the inn for a special occasion. For my election-night victory party."

"My, we're feeling confident, aren't we?"

Although there was a twinkle in her eyes, she glanced around melodramatically and leaned forward. "I've taken a poll. According to my figures, I'm in the lead by seventeen percent."

"Never count your chickens, dear. And you know, of course, this is a very popular inn. I'll check my calendar, but I'm sure I'm booked solid through the end of the year."

Rachel gasped softly. "All the way to New Year's?"

"A *year* from New Year's. Like I said, this is a successful establishment. Sometimes, however, there are cancellations. And sometimes—and I'm not making any promises—it's possible to shuffle things around a bit. I could at least put you on the waiting list."

"Oh, my. I've already invited the governor and his wife." She sounded curiously relieved.

"You've invited the *governor*?"

"Yes. Lorie and I were college roommates. In fact, we were double-dating the night she met Dinky."

"You call the governor Dinky?"

Rachel blushed. "That's a private joke. You mustn't mention it to anyone."

"Wow! The governor!"

I am ashamed to admit this, but I may have sounded fairly excited. You see, although I have hosted a number of celebrities at my establishment—from both the hills of Hollywood and the hills of greater Washington,

D.C.—I have never hosted a Pennsylvania governor. I've never even met one. And since it is my dream to not only meet a governor of my fair state, but be awarded a medal for all the contributions I've made to the Commonwealth of Pennsylvania, how I could not say yes to Rachel Blank?

"Look, Magdalena, if it's too much trouble—"

"Trouble, shmubble, I'll take care of everything."

"Great! And you do have a liquor license, don't you?"

My heart sank even as my hair stood on end. The very thought of serving spirits in my ancestral home was enough to cause five generations of spirits (mostly Yoders) to turn over in their graves.

"I'm sorry," I said, "but I don't have a license."

"Well." The perfectly plucked brows sagged a little as she gave that bit of information her serious consideration. "I'm afraid then I'm going to have to move my victory celebration to Bedford. You understand, don't you?"

I nodded mutely. I'd have to find another way to bring myself to Dinky's attention and win statewide recognition. I don't know what honors are within the governor's power to bestow. But this is the Keystone State, and I am a quasi-cop. Perhaps the Order of the Keystone Cops would be appropriate.

"Of course a contribution would still be nice," Rachel said smoothly. She is, after all, the consummate politician.

I wrote her a check, but it had two fewer zeroes than the one I had originally intended to write.

While my guests and Alison lunched on Freni's incomparable chicken and dumplings, I snacked on a bag of Fritos washed down with a pint of chocolate milk. This might not sound nutritious to you, but it is, in my opinion, a remarkably balanced meal. The corn in the chips is both a vegetable and a starch, depending on how you look at it; the milk is an outstanding source of protein and calcium, and the chocolate, besides being delicious, must surely count as a fruit. After all, cocoa beans come from cocoa pods, which are, essentially, the fruit of the cacao tree. It's as simple as that.

I am an excellent driver, if I must say so myself, and I lunched with one hand while I steered with the other. My route took me back into town on Hertzler Road, up Route 96, past Baughman Lane, where Emma Kauffman lives, and almost to the Pennsylvania Turnpike. I was swigging the last of the chocolate milk when I pulled into the tiny gravel parking lot of the church with thirty-two words in its name.

The First and Only True Church of the One and Only Living God of the Tabernacle of Supreme Holiness and Healing and Keeper of the Consecrated Righteousness of the Eternal Flame of Jehovah is nothing more than a whitewashed cinder-block building that could fit into the parlor of my inn. The parsonage—a mobile home set on plain cinder blocks—is almost as large. But from what I've heard, the members of this little congregation share among themselves enough verve and religious zeal to fuel a Southern Baptist Convention. A more fancy wooden church with stained-glass windows wouldn't stand a prayer, what with all the foot-stomping and hand-clapping that goes on during their three-hour-long services. This is not a judgment, mind you, merely an observation. This is a free country, and each of us is free to worship in our own peculiar way, even if it is indecorous.

I parked my car in the sparse shade of an ailanthus tree and crunched my way to the door. Mercifully, it was ajar a few inches. That meant Reverend Nixon was in and I didn't need to try the trailer.

"Knock, knock," I called cheerfully.

"Come in," came the doleful reply.

I stepped from the warm sunshine into a dimly lit oven. I've baked muffins in cooler, brighter places than that.

"Whoa!" I said. "No offense, Reverend, but you really should get an air conditioner."

Reverend Richard Nixon rose from the pews like a marionette on hidden strings. A tall, gangly man, he's the spitting image of Abraham Lincoln, sans facial hair. Reverend Nixon has the most protruding Adam's apple I've ever seen, and sometimes, particularly when viewed in silhouette, he gives the impression of having two heads. At any rate, he was wearing a brown polyester suit worn so thin in spots he could use it to sift flour.

"As a matter of fact, Magdalena, I was just working on that."

"You have a unit down there on the floor?"

"No. I was asking the Lord to provide."

"How much do folks charge the Lord these days? For a good air conditioner, I mean."

He smiled nervously. Perhaps he thought I was taking the Lord's name in vain—which of course I wasn't. Ask and you will receive, the Bible says. I merely intended to help the Good Lord keep His word. And although the Bible doesn't specifically mention tax write-offs, neither does it condemn them.

"Well, I saw a window unit for five hundred dollars, but—"

"You don't have any windows."

"Right."

"So how much would it cost to get a proper air conditioner installed? You know, cooling ducts, the whole works."

"I think it could be done for twenty-five hundred dollars. Three thousand at the most. But we could never raise that kind of money, Magdalena."

"You couldn't. But the Lord could." I fumbled in my purse—I didn't see how the congregation could read their Bibles and hymnals in that poor light—and withdrew my checkbook. "Four thousand. If there's any left over, buy yourself a new suit."

He gaped at me.

"Go on, dear. Never look a gift horse in the mouth— especially if she hasn't brushed her teeth recently."

He finally took the slip of paper, his hand shaking like a dog fresh out of water. "Praise God! Hallelujah!"

"I'll second that, dear. Now, if you don't mind, I'd like to get down to business."

He crammed the check into the inside pocket of his shabby coat. Clearly, what the Lord gave, Magdalena Yoder was not going to take away.

"Business?" he asked cagily.

"Don't worry, dear. There aren't any strings attached to that. It's a gift, pure and simple. However, I would like to talk to you about Clarence Webber."

His sigh of relief created a welcome breeze. "Ah, that. Sure, we can talk about Brother Clarence if you like."

Alas, the breeze was short-lived. "Mind if we talk outside, dear?"

He had no objection to following me to my car, where we sat in air-conditioned comfort. There is a good deal of traffic on Route 91, since it is the only way to Bedford, but I couldn't care less. There is absolutely nothing wrong about sitting with a man of the cloth—even threadbare cloth—in a parked car in broad daylight. Not as long as both parties keep their hands to themselves.

"So," I said, when we were settled in, "I understand you visited Clarence in jail."

"That's right. He asked me to pray with him. Read to him from the Bible. That sort of thing."

"Was he a member of your congregation?"

"We of the First and Only True Church—"

"I get the picture! Just tell me if he belonged."

"That's what I was trying to do."

"Then spit it out, dear."

"Well, like I was about to say, we of the First—"

"*Please,* Reverend Nixon, just get to the point."

He bit his lip. "The answer is no. You see, we don't have members in our church. Not official members on paper, at any rate. That's a human concept. Our membership is only in the Lord."

"How interesting. But did Clarence Webber attend services? You do have those, don't you?"

"Of course we have services." The enormous Adam's apple bobbed as he struggled to swallow his irritation. "And yes, Brother Clarence did attend from time to time. But he wasn't a regular by any means."

"I see. Do you visit all your—uh, attendees—when they end up in the hoosegow?"

The giant apple took on a life of its own. Quite frankly, given the confines of the car, I feared for my safety.

"Magdalena, we may be small, and what you probably consider to be a fringe denomination, but that doesn't make us all criminals. I've been pastor here for six years, and besides Brother Clarence, Sister Joan is the only worshipper to end up in the hoosegow, as you so quaintly put it."

"Oh? What was Sister Joan's crime?"

"I'm not at liberty to say."

"Well, if she was convicted as an adult, it's a matter of public record." I cranked up the AC and patted my pocketbook to remind him of my generous contribution to his creature comforts. "You could save me valuable time, dear."

His sigh raised the temperature of my car a full degree. "Sister Joan was a prostitute."

"*Really?*" I am ashamed to admit this, but the idea of

a real live prostitute in Bedford County was somehow exhilarating. Who would her clients be? Baptists and Methodists? Presbyterians and Catholics were a given. But surely not Mennonites or Amish.

"They only kept her one night at the county lockup. I bailed her out. Trust me, Magdalena, she'll never do it again."

"That brush with the law scared her straight, eh?"

"No. She wasn't very good. One of her clients turned her in. Said she couldn't hold a candle to the prostitutes in Pittsburgh or Philadelphia. Claimed he'd been swindled and wanted his money back."

"Figures." Even professional sinners in Bedford County were second rate.

He put his hand on the door handle. "So, did that answer all your questions?"

"I guess so. And it was nice of you to visit Clarence in jail, especially since you didn't know him all that well."

He shrugged. "I thought I knew him pretty well. Otherwise I wouldn't have married him."

15

Pumpkin Grits

Though this dish is hardly ever seen today, it is found in the old cookbooks of the South. The combination of pumpkin and corn is also seen in old-time stews and soups and surely comes from Native American cooking. You may use any of the dense winter squashes in place of the pumpkin, and canned pumpkin is a lot easier to handle than fresh. Just be sure it's plain pumpkin, not pumpkin pie filling. Pumpkin grits are especially good with ham, bacon, or sausages at breakfast.

1 cup puréed cooked
pumpkin
1 recipe Basic Boiled
Grits (hot)

Pinch of cayenne
pepper (optional)
Salt to taste
Unsalted butter

Beat the pumpkin into the grits. Season to taste with cayenne and salt. Serve with butter.

SERVES 4 TO 6

16

"Get out of town!" I cried. Now there was a sin to get excited about.

Reverend Nixon's long torso pivoted. "I interviewed him thoroughly of course. Marriage is not something to be undertaken lightly."

"Indeed not." I rubbed my hands together in anticipatory glee. "Has your denomination always allowed same-sex marriages?"

There is not a whole lot of room in my car in which to recoil, especially for a man six-foot-six. Fortunately both roof and windows in this model are fairly sturdy. The ceiling was going to require a good stiff brushing, but at least the glass held.

"We do not allow such things," he hissed.

"But you said—"

"I said I married him. I didn't say I got married *to* him."

"Oh."

"Brother Clarence married—" He paused.

"Spit it out, dear! You've got me on pins and needles."

"I would, Magdalena, but they asked me to keep this quiet."

"Marriages are also a matter of public record." I glared at his breast pocket containing the check. I could almost see through the flimsy fabric.

"Okay, you win. But this is only because you're here to investigate a murder."

"Murder? Who said the M word, dear?"

"Come on, Magdalena. I'm a clergyman, not a cretin. Clarence Webber dies suddenly in jail, and you're here giving me the third degree. I bet you gave it to everyone who visited him. Am I right?"

"Right as rain," I cried. It was time to steer the conversation back on track. "So who was Clarence Webber's mystery bride?"

"Zelda Root."

I jiggled a pinkie in my right ear. It was obviously not working right.

"The weirdest thing just happened," I said. "For a second I thought you said Zelda Root."

"I did. You know her, of course. She's the police officer down in Hernia. Has a bit of that Tammy Faye look about her, only taken to the extreme. Anyway, for some strange reason they had me drive down to Cumberland and perform the marriage there. At a justice of the peace's house, no less. Still, they put me up in a nice motel, and made arrangements for me to eat at a Cracker Barrel. I just love their potato soup, don't you?"

I can recoil without banging into the window or grazing the ceiling. I can't, however, do it without twisting my neck.

"Not my Zelda Root," I moaned.

Reverend Nixon had a surprisingly nice smile. "Your Zelda?"

"I've known Zelda since she was born. She grew up hanging around Melvin Stoltzfus, who grew up hanging around my sister, Susannah. I can't believe Zelda married Clarence Webber. She's still in love with Melvin, for crying out loud."

"What can I say? She and Clarence seemed to be very much in love." He pursed his thin lips. "Of course love is a very overrated emotion."

I thought of Aaron Miller and started to nod. Fortunately the pain in my neck put a stop to that. *True* love is not overrated, and I was pretty sure that my feelings for Gabe the Babe fell into that category.

"I don't suppose you knew that Clarence Webber was already married."

Reverend Nixon and I were going to have to sue each other for whiplash. *"What?"*

"In fact, near as I can tell, he died having four wives. Maybe even a whole lot more. Perhaps I should put an ad in the paper." I was serious about that.

Reverend Nixon was no longer listening. "Bigamy! I helped that man commit the sin of bigamy. Therefore I am just as guilty as he is."

"More than two would make that polygamy, dear. And really, you mustn't blame yourself. These things are hard to know in advance. Why, anyone could marry a polygamist."

Alas, that got his attention. He fixed his preacher's gaze on me.

"You of all people should know, Magdalena."

"What's that supposed to mean?" But I knew exactly what he meant. There isn't a literate, or hearing, person in the county who hasn't learned of my inadvertent sin. But it should be old news by now. This horse has been dead so long its hooves have been made into gelatin, the rest of it into glue.

I told the Reverend adios, gave him a gentle shove, and locked the car door behind him. Then I made a bee-line back to Hernia. The woman who keeps her face in a jar was about to be grilled like a weenie.

*   *   *

Zelda's car was in her driveway, but she didn't answer the door. Being a faithful reader of Ann Landers, I knew enough to give her at least a minute before jumping to conclusions. Then, because jumping to conclusions is virtually my only form of exercise, I concluded that Zelda Root was lying in a pool of blood, gasping her next to last breath, and that if I didn't immediately barge in to rescue her, said blood would be on my hands.

I tried the doorknob, and since it turned easily, I guessed that I'd made the right call. Just to be on the safe side, I announced myself loudly. There was, I suppose, a slim chance the woman might be in the shower, or otherwise indisposed.

Getting no response to my loud calls of "Zelda! Zelda!," I felt it my duty to search the house carefully. Perhaps she'd been bound, gagged, and stuffed in a closet. Or, and this is not beyond the realm of possibility, she'd been kidnapped and the ransom note had been stuffed in the bottom of one of her drawers. Not every kidnapper leaves the note in plain sight, you know.

I made a quick reconnaissance of all the rooms just to make sure Zelda wasn't lying out in the open, still taking that last breath. Then I got down to the real work. Less charitable folks might call it snooping, but they aren't pseudo-assistant policewomen like myself. If they were, they'd realize that there is no such thing as too much information in this business. Clues are only useful when they're found. Finding a guitar, for instance, would be very interesting indeed.

Zelda's front coat closet was a major disappointment; just coats, umbrellas, and three boots. The closet of her master bedroom (and I use that term lightly in this case) was equally divided between uniforms and civilian clothes. Stretching the entire length, from wall to wall, was a line of shoes; far too many, in my opinion, for a good Christian woman with a clear conscience. I clucked disapprovingly at this extravagance. When there are still barefoot children in parts of Africa and Asia, what does a woman in Hernia need with footwear in every imaginable style and color?

The contents of her drawers were even more disturbing. Clearly her mother had not taught the woman the virtues of ironing and folding underwear. Talk about getting one's knickers in a knot! The tangle of bras and panties was like a Rubik's cube.

Still reeling from that shocking discovery, I opened the closet doors of Zelda's guest room. What I saw there brought me, literally, to my knees. It was both an appropriate and an inappropriate gesture.

"Gott in Himmel!" I cried, reverting to my ancestral tongue.

I was kneeling before a shrine. On the wall before me hung an oil painting of Melvin in an enormous gilt frame. I'm not good at guessing size—or I never would have married Aaron—but the canvas alone was probably sixteen inches by twenty. The artist had managed to capture the essence, if not an exact likeness, of the exasperating little man. Bulging eyes staring in separate directions, crustaceous mandibles—the overall effect made me want to dash out for a can of Raid. My legs, however, were not capable of supporting me.

Below the painting stood a long narrow table draped in white. It was apparently an altar of sorts, and on either end was an electric candlestick, the kind some folks use for Christmas decorations. Between the lights—as if the vermin's visage weren't enough—Zelda had assembled a collection of some of the weirdest stuff imaginable. The things I could identify included a lock of hair, a tooth, a tooth*brush*, a golf ball, a man's handkerchief, and a ticket stub from one of the movie theaters over in Bedford. The unidentifiable stuff was just that—although some of the items were so gross that even had I known their identity, I wouldn't have been able to describe them.

I don't know how long I knelt there before I heard the music. Some sort of audio device—perhaps a CD player—had apparently been activated when I opened the closet doors. At first I thought it was a hymn, but then I recognized the theme song to the movie *Chariots of Fire*. Let me hasten to explain that I do not watch movies, but I do listen to the radio from time to time, and I know this catchy tune. What on earth it had to do with Melvin was anybody's guess.

I realized with horror that I was still on my knees. We Mennonites don't do a whole lot of popping up and down in our worship like Roman Catholics and Episcopalians, but we do kneel from time to time in earnest prayer. We definitely don't kneel in front of statues or pictures, especially ones of Melvin Stoltzfus!

"Forgive me!" I cried and staggered to my feet.

"The hell you say!" the Good Lord roared.

I don't know which was more shocking, the fact that God spoke to me, or that He'd sworn. Not that it mattered. Either revelation was enough to make me hit the floor again, and that's exactly what I did.

"I wasn't praying to Melvin," I whimpered. "You've got to believe me, I'd never do such a thing!"

"I don't exactly pray to him either—oh hell, why am I trying to explain this to you? You're an intruder, after all. I could have you arrested for breaking and entering."

I spun on my knees. "Zelda! Zelda Root!"

"Who did you think it was?"

"Uh—you, of course. It's just that you startled me. What are you doing here?"

"*Me?* I live here, in case you've forgotten. The question is, what are *you* doing here?"

"I thought you'd been kidnapped," I said. Exercising

an active imagination is not the same as lying. "I was looking for clues."

Zelda propped balled fists on nonexistent hips. "You should be looking for a loony bin that caters to rich Mennonite innkeepers."

I hopped to my feet. "Why, I never!" I paused to consider her suggestion. "Are there such places? And do you think they'd give back rubs? I'm prepared to pay a premium for a good masseuse."

"Magdalena! I'm not letting you get away with this. Either you tell me what you're doing in my house, or I'm running you in."

"You can't do that! I'm working for Melvin. *Saint* Melvin."

Zelda ignored my snide remark. "But I can. No police officer—even a real one like myself—is above the law." She snapped her fingers. "Rats! I haven't gotten around to cleaning the ladies' cell since our last female prisoner. And I certainly won't have time to wash those sheets today. Oh well, you'll just have to make do."

"At least the food is good," I wailed.

"Yeah, if it doesn't kill you first." She shook her head slowly. "You sure do a lot of wailing, you know that?"

"I can't help the way I speak. And that comment about the food was unfair. You know good and well that neither Freni nor I poisoned Clarence Webber." I tapped the toe of a brown brogan on Zelda's cheap carpet. "If you must know, dear, I'm here to investigate you."

The normally nimble Zelda teetered on her black platform shoes. "Why me?"

"You sure you wouldn't like to sit first? We could go into your living room. There's all those beanbag chairs and—"

In an effort to steady herself, she grabbed my left shoulder—and the black talons dug into my collarbone. I felt like I'd fallen on a rake.

"Magdalena, just tell me what this is all about."

I extricated the dark claws and prayed I wouldn't get tetanus. "You lied, it's as simple as that. You were married to the deceased, for Pete's sake."

Zelda swallowed so hard, I saw traces of an Adam's apple. Perhaps it really *was* Jimmy Hoffa hiding under all that makeup.

"I didn't lie, Magdalena. I just neglected to tell you something. How did you find out?"

"I can't squeal on my sources, dear. But you were married to Clarence, weren't you?"

She nodded.

"Yet you worship Melvin. What gives?"

"I don't *worship* Melvin. I merely venerate him. There is a difference, you know."

"That is so wrong." I know we are not supposed to judge, but surely the Good Lord intends for us to make exceptions, otherwise He would not have chosen to include the book of Judges in the Bible. "Besides, Melvin is—uh—how should I put this?"

"Melvin is the dearest, kindest man who ever lived. Just ask your sister, why don't you?" Zelda then launched into a litany of Melvin's supposed good qualities.

I clapped my bony hands over my ears. Unfortunately they acted more like hearing aids than plugs.

"Stop it!" I finally screamed. "You don't know the whole story. Melvin Stoltzfus and Saddam Hussein are identical twins, separated at birth. Their mother—Elvina Stoltzfus—was touring the Middle East and had a layover in Baghdad. I mean that literally, if you get my drift. Elvina returned to Hernia and gave birth, but the father followed her here, and kidnapped the son he thought looked most like him. If you don't believe me, look it up in the encyclopedia."

Zelda's eye muscles struggled to lift lids weighed down by heavy loads of mascara. "Is that really true?"

"No. But we shouldn't even be discussing Melvin. We should be discussing you. Why did you marry Clarence Webber?"

Zelda's sigh sent a cloud of face powder into the ozone. If El Niño returns, I am not responsible.

"All right," she said, "I'll tell you everything. But first let's go into the living room and make ourselves comfortable."

17

"Comfortable" meant the beanbag chairs. There is nothing comfortable about having my thighs and neck aligned at forty degrees, both at right angles to my back. The only thing comfortable one can do with beans is add ham hocks and make a good soup. Zelda's furniture could go a long way toward alleviating hunger in some small Third World country.

I made myself as comfortable as I could on what should have been somebody's supper. "Spill it," I said.

Zelda settled into her chair. "I married Clarence to make Melvin jealous."

"Say what?"

"Well, he married your sister, didn't he? So I married Clarence to get even."

"Melvin knows about this?"

"Of course."

"I wonder why he didn't tell me? Or at least Susannah—who would have told me for sure."

"Because I made him swear not to. Magdalena, it's not like I loved Clarence. It was—well, frankly, it was embarrassing."

"Did it at least work?"

Tears welled up in Zelda's eyes. "All he said was congratulations. And that I could have the day off."

"That cad!" I wasn't being sarcastic, mind you.

The floodgates opened, threatening to reveal the real Zelda. I was both fascinated and repelled by the transformation. Once-smooth cheeks were now fissured by gullies and, in some spots, deep ravines. Even an all-terrain vehicle would find it almost impossible to drive across that face.

"It was a horrible mistake," she sobbed. "I know I should never have done it. But just so you know, Magdalena, we never actually—well, you know what."

"Thank heavens for that!" I must confess, however, that having actually engaged in you-know-what with my pseudo-husband, Aaron, I am of two minds on the subject. On one hand I deeply regret losing my maidenhood to a lying, two-timing scoundrel. On the other hand, now I know what all the fuss is about—in my case, about three minutes.

Zelda quit sobbing and gingerly fingered her new crevasses. "I know what you're thinking, Magdalena. You're thinking that I killed Clarence so I'd be free again for Melvin. But in case you haven't thought of it, that would be just plain stupid. I mean, why not just get a divorce?"

"Why not indeed?"

She frowned, and the gullies on her forehead grew so deep I thought I heard the distant shout of coal miners. "I was going to get a divorce until he got arrested. But then after that, it was just too embarrassing. They publish divorce proceedings in the paper, you know."

"Indeed I do."

"Indeed this, indeed that. Magdalena, you're starting to sound pompous."

"Moi?"

"You see? Anyway, I certainly wouldn't have killed

him in jail. Not where I work. What kind of idiot do you take me for?"

I allowed Zelda the privilege of listening to the dulcet sounds of silence, during which I pondered the situation. The woman had a point; she was anything but stupid, and it would have been the epitome of stupidity to kill Clarence in the Hernia jail. Especially considering the fact that I'm prone to sticking my probing proboscis in there with some regularity. In the end, I decided to cross her off my mental list. After a minute or two I cleared my throat.

"You were married in Cumberland, Maryland, weren't you?"

She sat ramrod straight, an amazing feat in a beanbag chair. "How did you know?"

"The justice of the peace lived in this big white house, on top of a hill, and his wife, Bonita, made your bouquet from rhododendron blossoms. You honeymooned at a brand-new motel on I-70 right next to the Cracker Barrel. Am I right?"

"They were lilacs, not rhodies. Magdalena, were you spying on me?"

"Unfortunately not. Zelda, I'm afraid I have some bad news for you. Apparently Clarence Webber was a bit of a lothario. In fact—I don't know how else to say this—you were not the only woman he married in Cumberland."

"Why, that's utter nonsense, Magdalena. Who put you up to this joke? Susannah? It's not very funny, you know."

"It's not a joke, dear. It's the truth."

Zelda sank back into her bag of beans with a soft moan. "I can't believe this is happening. I'm a policewoman. I should have known."

"Woman's capacity to deceive herself is even greater than her capacity to deceive others. Words of wisdom from yours truly."

Zelda was· shaking her ravaged head slowly. "Who told you I was married?"

"Reverend Nixon, but I twisted his arm."

"Clarence was insisting we get married by this J.P., but I wanted a preacher there as well. He finally agreed if I paid all the expenses. I only picked Reverend Nixon because Clarence suggested him. Apparently he goes to that little church up by the turnpike. I can't ever remember its correct name."

"I don't think the Reverend can. It has thirty-two of them."

"Who?" she asked weakly. "Who was Clarence married to?"

"Sometimes it's better not to know the details. A little self-deception in this case might well be the antidote."

"Magdalena, quit talking riddles and cut to the chase. Who was that blankety-blank-blank [I wouldn't dream of quoting Zelda word for word] married to besides me?"

I took a deep breath. Don't for a second imagine I felt any pleasure in my task. Now, if it had been a case of Reverend Schrock cheating on Lodema, that might have been different story.

"Clarence was a busy man, dear. It seems he married Dorcas Yutzy, Emma Kauffman, and Agnes Schlabach. Possibly even more. But I'm pretty sure he never got around to marrying Richard Nixon."

My attempt to cheer Zelda went unnoticed. "Those were all women who visited him in jail. Under my nose! If Clarence were alive, I'd kill him." She clapped a black-tipped paw over the remains of her mouth. "I didn't mean that the way it sounded."

"Of course not, dear." I struggled to my feet. "Well, *tempus fugit.*"

"What is that supposed to mean?" She sounded testy.

"It's Latin for 'time flies.' I've got to skedaddle, dear."

Zelda walked me to my car, which proved, if nothing else, that she was a brave woman. "You do believe me, Magdalena, don't you? That I didn't kill Clarence."

Although Zelda was now off my list, it didn't hurt to keep her hanging. The Good Lord knows I've been wrong before.

"Mine not to reason why," I said. "Mine but to do and die."

"Riddles!" Zelda cried. "More riddles!" She sought to detain me with her lethal talons, but I dodged them deftly this time and made my getaway.

There is nothing like a nice drive to clear the cobwebs from the brain, but a car trip without food is like a bath without soap. Okay, so maybe that is a bad analogy, but in both cases something critical is missing. At any rate, rather than go all the way back to the PennDutch to stock up on provisions, I elected to visit Yoder's Corner Market, which was right on my way to Cumberland.

But first I stopped to use Hernia's *only* public phone. It hangs on the wall of a small wooden shed, a mere stone's throw away from the little grocery. This is where the Amish—who don't own phones, by the way, but are not averse to using them—make their calls. Usually there are several folks waiting in line, but today there must have been a dearth of news.

There must not have been too much happening back at the inn, either, because Alison picked up on the first ring.

"Hey, where are you?" she demanded.

"I'm out doing some errands, dear. Are you behaving yourself?"

"If you call doing nothing 'behaving'."

"Have you been out to see the cows yet?" Frankly, the reason I was calling is because I was worried the child might get too bored with life at the inn, and opt for reform school. While that decision wouldn't exactly break my heart, I was getting rather used to the idea of having her around.

"No, I ain't been to see the cows. Hey Mom, how come ya have this picture of my dad?"

"*What* picture?"

"The one ya got hidden under your undies and things."

"Alison Miller!" I shrieked. "Are you in my drawers?"

She giggled. "Don't get your panties in a bunch. I was only looking for a place to stash my stuff."

"Stay out of my drawers!" I roared. The truth be known, I was more embarrassed than angry. I'd buried that photo under my unmentionables the day Aaron revealed he was legally married to someone else. It was just too good a likeness to throw away. Although a part of me had always been aware that it was there, at the same time I'd also been—up until now—for the most part able to block it out.

"Okay, okay," Alison said, not without attitude. "I'll stay out of your stupid drawers. But you know what? I think it's kinda funny that my dad looks like that man who lives across the road."

"He most certainly does not!"

"Man, you sure get upset easily. You know that?"

"I do not!"

"Like now, see? You keep this up and you're gonna bust a gut."

I said good-bye to Alison before her prediction could come true.

Samuel Nevin Yoder, the owner of Yoder's Corner Market, is my first cousin. He recently revealed that he's been carrying a torch for me since childhood—"has the hots" was his cruder way of saying it—and has been trying to talk me into having an affair. Even if Sam were the third or fourth last man alive, I wouldn't consider his offer. For one thing, he's married. For another, the very thought of doing the horizontal hootchie-cootchie with a cousin, even were it legal, is repulsive to me.

Ever since Sam first told me about his feelings, I've tried my best to stay away from the store. But Yoder's Corner Market is the only place to buy food for humans in Hernia, and one should never venture to Maryland without provisions.

I steeled myself against Sam's advances and strode briskly into the store. Sam, thank heavens, was nowhere in sight, but I nearly ran over Susannah with my shopping buggy.

"Sis," she cried delightedly, "I've been trying to reach you. Where've you been?"

"Playing tiddlywinks, dear. What's up?"

"I've decided to throw a dinner party, and I want you to come."

"When?" With any luck, I already had something scheduled for that date.

"Tonight. Say, sevenish. Oh, and you can bring that little girl of yours if you like."

"She isn't so little, and I'm afraid I can't make it tonight anyway. I have to go to Maryland."

"Maryland?" The excitement in Susannah's voice was palpable. Maryland had been her stomping grounds as a rebellious teenager. No doubt it still held fond memories.

"It's business, dear, not debauchery."

She pursed her lips in disgust, but then smiled slyly. "I invited Gabe. He said he would come—provided you were there. Sorry, sis, but I told him you already said yes."

"Susannah!"

"Well, he is your babe, isn't he? Your boy toy?"

"He's the same age as me," I wailed.

"He is? Get out of town!"

"In fact, he's six weeks older."

She shook her head. "Really, Mags, you should do something about the way you look. Like cut your hair. Just because Mama wore her hair in a holy bun doesn't mean you have to. And I don't mean to be disrespectful, but lose that prayer cap as well. And your dresses—geez, they're from the dark ages. Hey, what's that word they use to describe Queen Elizabeth?"

"Dowdy," I said dolefully. "But she's really not. She's really a rather snappy dresser."

Susannah has selective hearing. "Yeah, that's what you are. Dowdy. That might work for a queen, sis, but not for you. Hey, if you want, I could give you lessons on how to dress. I wouldn't even charge you a dime."

That hiked my hackles. I pointed to the fifteen feet of filmy fuchsia fabric that flowed over and around her skinny frame. "You look like a half-unwrapped mummy, dear. There's no way I'm going to wear that."

"Of course not, sis. This style takes attitude to wear. No, I was thinking about a skirt—say, mid-thigh length, and a nice little twin set. Tangerine would be a good color on you."

"I'm a conservative Mennonite for crying out loud, not a go-go dancing Presbyterian."

Susannah laughed loudly. "Go-go? That is so retro, Mags. Hey, but let's not argue. You'll come, right?"

I nodded. Boy toy indeed. Still, if folks thought that was the case, it said less about my dowdy appearance than it did about my charming personality. Not every middle-aged Mennonite innkeeper can snag herself a boy toy.

Maryland might be only thirty-two miles away, but it is across the state line. The only time I'd been out of Pennsylvania was to go to Ohio. I hadn't needed a passport then, or shots for that matter, but that was Ohio, and I was there to visit Amish relatives. I was almost positive a passport wouldn't be needed for Maryland, but shots were probably a good idea. Alas, there would be no time for that if I wanted to make it back for Susannah's dinner party. I had no choice but to live dangerously on that account.

Just to be as safe as possible under the circumstances, I put the following items in my buggy: two one-gallon jugs of bottled water, a roll of double-ply toilet paper, three cans of Beanie Weenies, two cans of sardines, a six-pack of Three Musketeers candy bars, one large box of granola, one medium-size box of low-fat powdered milk, one small box of plastic spoons, a package of Styrofoam bowls, a single bag of trail mix, a jumbo bottle of that sanitizing hand gel that's been so popular lately, and a ball of string. One can never have too much twine, if you ask me. The last thing I plopped in the buggy was a roll of duct tape, an item that should be on the "must" list of every traveler contemplating a trip abroad.

Susannah had long since disappeared by the time I made my decisions, and Sam was at his usual place behind the register. He eyed my buggy with amusement.

"Going camping, Magdalena?"

"I'm going to Maryland."

"Then you'll need matches."

"You're right!"

He tossed a box on the counter. "On the house. So, how long you going to be gone?"

"Two hours minimum. Maybe three."

He nodded gravely. "Pays to play it safe."

"Say," I said casually, "you ever hear anything about a J.P. down there popular with the Hernia crowd?"

As proprietor of Hernia's only food store, Sam is privy to a lot of gossip, most of which he is happy to pass on. He threw a second pack of matches on the counter.

"So that's where you're headed, eh?"

"Yes. Do you know how to get there?"

"Doesn't that young man of yours know? Usually it's the groom who makes the arrangements when folks elope."

"I'm not eloping! And he's not a young man!" I slammed one of the water jugs on the counter, barely missing Sam's fingers. "I take it, then, you don't know."

Sam smirked. It is an expression I find particularly irritating on him, perhaps because we look so much alike. Same faded eyes, same thin lips, same nose worthy of its own zip code.

"Suppose I have heard of this guy? What's your interest in this, Magdalena? Melvin have you working on a case?"

"You must have had a slow day so far, Sam. You should know exactly what I'm up to."

"I don't gossip with my customers." He sounded genuinely hurt.

"Maybe not, dear. But you're the one who first told me that Elspeth Miller beats her husband, Roy. And it was you who broke the news that the Schwartzentrubers—the *Amish* Schwartzentrubers—on Rickenbach Road bought a transistor radio from the Wal-Mart up in Bedford. You even called me on the day the bishop finally decided to excommunicate them. And when Thelma Graybill's goiter—"

"Okay, I get the picture. But can I help it if folks like to talk to me?"

I waved a hand impatiently. "So, do you know about this J.P., or not?"

To get back at me he took his sweet time in answering. My favorite author, Ramat Sreym, could have written an entire book while waiting for Sam's response.

"Well," he finally said, "as it happens, I have heard of this guy. Dorothy's niece, Juanita, tied the knot there last year. Said the old geezer gave her the creeps."

"Dorothy's niece got married? Why wasn't I invited? Why didn't anyone even bother to tell me?"

"You've never even met Juanita, that's why. Like I said, she's on Dorothy's side of the family."

I sniffed. Sam had no business marrying Dorothy in the first place. The woman was a Methodist, for crying out loud.

"Anyway," Sam said, "the guy's name is Benedict something or other."

"Benedict Arnold?"

"That's it." Sam was serious. "Only it's the other way around. Arnold Benedict. Didn't we learn about a guy with that name in school?"

If my cousin had spent more time with his Yoder nose in his books and less time tying my pigtails into knots, he would have learned more.

"Benedict Arnold created some fancy egg dish," I informed my ignorant cousin. "Everyone knows that. I never heard of Arnold Benedict. But that's this guy's name, huh?"

"Yup. Shouldn't be too hard to find. Just look him up in the phone book. But like I said, be careful. Juanita didn't like him at all."

"I'll be as careful as a hen in a den of foxes." I tapped the bottle of sanitizing gel. "You charged me for this twice."

Sam feigned surprise. "I did?"

"You bet your bippy, buster. In fact, that's the third time this month you've overcharged me." I gave him a meaningful look. "I heard once that some store owners actually give their relatives discounts."

He deleted the charge. "You know, Magdalena, in some states it's not illegal for first cousins to marry."

I fished for my wallet. "Your point, dear?"

"Well, it's no secret that Dorothy and I haven't been getting along lately—"

"Sayonara!" I sang, as I grabbed my bags and scooted for the door. The wilds of western Maryland were awaiting me.

18

There wasn't even a guard shack at the border. Just a little blue and white sign that said MARYLAND.

I sniffed the air carefully. Mama had been wrong. There was no scent of sin, at least not as far as I could tell. Then again, I'm not all that familiar with the smell.

Cumberland is larger than Bedford, but not as large as Pittsburgh, and I found it surprisingly easy to get around. The people were friendly and spoke English. In fact, on my third try—at a Speedway gas station—I found someone who knew Arnold Benedict.

"I know *of* the man," Beth said. She was a big-busted woman in a green smock, about my age, and wore her hair in what Susannah mockingly calls a "holy-roller beehive." Her name badge, which was pinned to the apex of her bosom, bobbled with every word she spoke.

"Fantastic!" I cried. "Can you tell me where he lives?"

Beth had a golf-ball-size wad of gum in her mouth. Every three or four words she would stop to give the gum a quick chew.

"He lives in a big white house up 'top a hill on Beaver Pond Lane. To get there just keep going on this street 'til you get to the third stoplight. Go on through and get yourself going east on I-40. Take that 'til it meets up with I-68. Get off on the Willowbrook—I forget the number. Anyway, go through two lights and three stop signs. Turn left on Buttermilk, and then a sharp right on Beaver Pond. Should be the third house on your left." She rolled her eyes upward in thought. "Might be the fourth, though."

"What's the number?" I asked, only half joking.

"Six six six."

"You're kidding!"

"Yeah, I'm kidding. Don't know the number right off, but I can look it up for you. Wilma!" she barked. The gum unfortunately came sailing out and landed on the counter. Beth popped it back into her mouth. "Wilma! Where's the damn phone book?"

Wilma, who was standing just inches from Beth, shrugged, and went back to the business of handing a customer dirty change.

"Don't really need it," Beth said. "The number, I mean." She blew a bubble the size of an apple. "Just ask anybody out there. They'll tell you which house."

I nodded. "Is Mr. Benedict a friend of yours?"

Beth clucked, and for a second I thought she was going to spit. "Look, I'm a Christian woman, ma'am. I know we're supposed to love our neighbors, but that's taking it too far."

"I'm Christian too," I said.

She glanced at my prayer cap. "Yeah, I can see that you are. Mennonite, right?"

"Right."

"Only you ain't from around here."

"How could you tell?"

"Your accent. It's kind of funny." She clucked again. "But seeing's how you're a Christian and all, what do you want with old Benedict and his wife?"

"To convert him," I heard myself say. Oh, how my face burned with shame. It's one thing to lie about your age, or to tell your pastor you're too busy to teach Vacation Bible School when you're not, but to lie about doing the Lord's work—well, that's just plain wrong.

Beth clucked again. If she were one of my hens, there would be an egg by now.

"Good luck, is all I can say. I'll be praying for you."

"Thank you."

She let Wilma handle the customers and pulled me into one of the aisles. On the shelves I saw sardines, trail mix, and even powdered milk. My shopping spree at Sam's had been unnecessary.

"You ain't planning to go there alone, are you?" She punctuated each word with a snap of the gum.

"Yes."

Beth shook her head. "It's a brave woman that would risk her reputation like that."

"I'm not planning to use their services," I explained quickly. "I have a boyfriend—make that a man friend—back in Pennsylvania."

"Still, people will get the wrong idea. You sure you don't want to just mail them something? Like maybe a Bible?"

See where lying gets you? "I could do that too," I said. "But I really need to speak to them in person."

Beth shrugged. "Don't say I didn't try to stop you." She started back to the counter, where customers were beginning to pile up. Halfway there she stopped and turned. "Like I said, I'll pray for you."

"Please do," I said. I meant it.

Beth's directions were right on the money. It was indeed the third house. BENEDICT'S ESCORT SERVICE AND WEDDING CHAPEL the sign said. Even reading it with my funny Pennsylvania accent, there was no mistaking the words.

"Mama, I can smell the sin now," I wailed. Although, most probably, it was just plain garbage I smelled. There were bins lining the curb up and down the street.

Thank heavens Mama rarely answers me, and this was one of the days she chose to be mute. To keep it that way—and so as not to be a stumbling block to others— I removed my organza prayer cap and laid it gently on the seat. When Mama didn't throw a hissy fit, like roll over in her grave enough times to create an earthquake, I got out of the car and scurried up a cracked sidewalk.

The large house appeared to have once been a duplex. There were two doors, and about five yards from the building the sidewalk branched. For no particular reason I chose the left. Perhaps because that door had an eye-catching red bulb in its overhead light fixture. I said a brief prayer for courage and rang the bell.

A tiny woman with a face like a bleached prune opened the door on the first ring. She studied me closely before arranging the wrinkles into what was most probably meant as a grin.

"You here about the ad?"

"Yes," I said. I know, it was a stupid lie, but at least I wasn't bearing false witness against any of my neighbors.

"Come in."

I stepped into a dimly lit hall. "Oh, what pretty red flocked wallpaper," I said.

"Thank you. Some of the girls hate it. Mostly the ones who don't have any class."

"Looks very classy to me."

She led me into a large parlor that was sumptuously appointed, but a bit on the crowded side. It was virtually lined with chairs, all of them plush and covered in bright pink velvet that, frankly, clashed with the crimson wallpaper. Tiffany-style floor lamps dispensed a soft, mysterious light. At the far end of the room was a door hung with heavy crimson curtains tied back with tasseled gold braids. It was immediately apparent that the Benedicts loved to entertain.

"Have a seat," she ordered.

I chose a chair near the crimson-swagged door.

"Now pull up your dress a bit. I can't even see your knees."

"I beg your pardon!"

She shook her head. "Honey, you're not the first one to come here looking for a job dressed like an old-maid schoolteacher. Since some of the customers actually like that look, it's all right with me. But I'm going to have to see the goods—all of them—before you get the job."

"The goods?" Was it just my imagination, or was the thick faux-oriental carpet beneath my feet starting to vibrate?

"Don't be so bashful, honey. A woman your age has been around the block more than once."

"Excuse me?"

"Hey, this isn't your first job, is it?"

"Heavens, no! I've been working ever since I was a little girl. First I helped Mama and Papa around the farm, and then when they died—squished between a milk tanker and a truckload of shoes—I sold most of the livestock and turned the place into a thriving full-board inn. *Condor Nest Travel* called it 'the ultimate cross-cultural experience where the water is safe to drink.' They gave it four and a half feathers."

For some reason the prune appeared perplexed. "That farm stuff sounds kinda interesting, and I like the feathers, but that squishing is definitely over the top. And I don't know about that cross-cultural stuff. My customers are strictly heterosexual."

"Well," I said, choosing my words carefully so as not to sound morally superior. "I, for one, try not to judge others on what they may, or may not, be doing behind closed doors. After all, a person is more than his or her sexual orientation."

The prune pondered my words for a moment. "Oh, what the hell? Why not? It could potentially double our client base. You know, you just may be what the doctor ordered."

"So I got the job?"

"You sure do. But speaking of doctors, I want you checked out first. Then regular visits once a month—keeps the customers happy."

I nodded. Now that I'd made an entrée of sorts, I was eager to get started on my real job—that of interviewing Arnold Benedict.

The prune wasn't finished. "You're to charge the customers a flat fee of one hundred bucks an hour. You get to keep half. What you do for that half is your business." She chuckled. "If any customer looks at all suspicious—well, remember we're officially an escort service. You can spot an undercover cop, can't you?"

There comes a point when even the most naive amongst us—once supplied with enough clues—finally gets the picture. If it took me longer than most folks, that's thanks to my strict upbringing. Apparently even Mama was clueless for a while. But when that moment of realization finally came, the floor beneath my feet began to shake violently.

"Sister Joan!" I gasped. "She worked here, didn't she?"

The prune shook her head. "Nah, I don't think so. I'd remember somebody who looked like you."

"She's not my sister!" Susannah may be a slut, but she's not a harlot. *My* baby sister would never charge for what she could give away for free.

"Anyway," the prune said, "we don't use real names here. My girls go by nicknames like Candy, or Bambi."

"This isn't an escort service at all, is it?" I cried.

"Of course it is, honey." Laughter turned the prune's face into an accordion.

"No, it's not! It's a house of ill repute!"

The accordion froze. "You a cop?" she asked without moving her lips.

"No, but I work for one."

She'd been standing in front of me during my interview, and now she backed away as if I had some fatal communicable disease. I stood and tugged the hem of my dress down as far as it would go.

"Look, lady, I didn't come here to cause trouble. I just want to speak to Mr. Benedict."

"He's not here."

"Where is he?"

"Out of town."

"Where out of town?"

"Pittsburgh." She was back to being a prune again.

"Do you have a number where he can be reached?"

"Nope. Arnie does that, you know. Goes off for days by himself. Hell, last time he was gone for weeks. I'll tell him you stopped by."

I tried a smirk on for size. It seemed to fit.

"I was hoping to handle this myself," I said. "But—if that's the way you want it—I'll have to call my superior. You wouldn't happen to have a phone I could use, would you?"

The prune turned on a heel and disappeared behind the heavy curtains. She was gone a long time. Not one to waste resources—and time is our most precious resource—I sat and made out a list of menu suggestions for Freni, reviewed the math in my checkbook, and scraped the lint off a half-wrapped mint. I was steeling myself to sort through a jumble of receipts I'd been meaning to file, when I heard the sound of returning footsteps.

The prune was piqued. She was stomping like a vintner in a vat of grapes.

"It's about time, dear!" I called without looking up. After all, the prune did not have a monopoly on rude behavior.

The prune grunted.

"Yes, dear, I'll be with you in a minute. I'm trying to decide if I need to save the receipt for the new rice steamer I bought Freni at Wal-Mart. The warranty is only for parts, and even then, I have to send the whole thing back to someplace in Wisconsin for repairs. And guess who has to pay shipping? It hardly seems worth it, don't you think?"

The curtains parted with such force that the heavy metal rod crashed to the floor. That certainly got my full attention. Unfortunately, by then it was too late to run.

19

I read my Bible daily. I know for a fact that David killed Goliath. And even if he hadn't, the giant would be dead now. Biblical characters lived a long time, but not that long.

Still, the man standing before me seemed to have stepped right out of the pages of that Old Testament story. His head grazed the ceiling, and he had to stoop dramatically to clear the lintel. His chest had the girth of a steamer trunk, and with feet that wide the man would never have to wear snowshoes.

Despite his size, and unlike his Biblical predecessor, this giant was dressed in a rather snappy tailored suit. The charcoal gray was complemented nicely by a monochromatic slate blue shirt-and-tie set. He was also neatly groomed; his dark hair was parted on one side, his eyebrows kept under control. The only thing preventing him from being handsome—if you like gargantuan men—was skin the color of egg whites.

I'm a pacifist, and I'm supposed to turn the other cheek. However, I have an aversion to pain—my own, at any rate. But just so you know, it was not without guilt that I fumbled for my formidable set of keys. A good poke in the eyes, if I could reach either of them, would certainly buy me time. Barring that, a jab south of the equator, followed by a hard kick, should disable the giant long enough to get me out the door.

"My wife said you needed to speak to me," he said in a voice like a bass drum.

I stared incredulously. "Uh—that was your wife?"

"Bonita Benedict," he said. "We've been married thirty-two years. Not many people can say that these days."

I closed my purse, but held it tightly. I still had the option of whacking him below the equator.

"Mr. Benedict, I'm sure your wife—"

He held up a hand the size of a baseball mitt. Arnold Benedict's fingers were not sewn together, of course.

"I know what you're thinking, little lady. You're thinking that my Bonita robbed the cradle, aren't you?"

"If the snowshoe fits, dear."

His laugh could cause avalanches. "We're the same age, little lady. Born on the same day even. But Bonita likes to sunbathe. Does it all summer long, every summer. Me—I almost never go outside."

"Your wife wasn't sunbathing today."

"We both just got up," he said. "She's headed outside now."

I gasped, scandalized at the very thought of sleeping past noon. If I wasn't up with my chores completed by eight, Mama would throw ice water on my bed.

Tall, dark, and not quite so handsome seemed amused by my reaction. "You married, little lady?"

"No, and I don't see that it's any of your business."

"Marriage is one of the oldest institutions there is." He winked lewdly. "But not the oldest."

I gasped. "Mr. Benedict, I don't know what your wife told you, but I'm not here for a job, and I have no intention of saying anything to the authorities. *If* you cooperate by answering a few simple questions."

He pulled up two of the velvet-covered chairs, placed them side by side, and sat. One buttock on each chair. His knees were at eye level with me, and I struggled not to peek beyond these two watchtowers of decency.

"Shoot, little lady."

"Mr. Benedict, I understand you're a justice of the peace?"

He grinned broadly. "If you need me to be."

"Well, are you or aren't you?"

The grin began to fade. "Well, I used to be. Hell, I've got a minister's license. That's almost the same thing."

"*You?* A man of the cloth?"

"You betcha. In fact, you oughta be calling me Reverend."

"I don't think so. Where did you go to divinity school?"

The receding grin had stabilized and was now a sneer. "I didn't say anything about attending a school."

"I see. So you have one of those mail-order diplomas. What'd you do, send twenty-five dollars to an address in the back of a magazine?"

"There's nothing wrong with that. And the College of Universal Divinity charges two hundred bucks. 'Course you get a nice little service booklet for that. Real imitation leather binding too. Anyway, it's all perfectly legal."

"Maybe, but it's not legal to marry the same man over and over again."

He blinked. "I don't know what the hell you're talking about."

"Oh, but you do. You performed your little wedding service for Clarence Webber at least four times."

Who knew there was a shade paler than egg whites? "I still don't know what you're talking about."

"You most certainly do! I know for a fact you *married* Clarence to a woman named Dorcas Yutzy. Extremely tall—although not quite as tall as you—bottle-thick glasses, widely spaced teeth. Wears her hair pulled back in barrettes?"

"Little lady, I do a lot of marrying. I can't remember what they all look like. Least of all their names."

"How about Zelda Root? Take Tammy Faye, give her a boy's haircut, add five pounds of makeup, and voila. You remember her, don't you?"

"Like I said," he snarled, "I don't keep track of the ladies once they pass through here."

"That's too bad, because Zelda's kept track of you. And, as it just so happens, she's a policewoman."

Goliath struggled to his feet. "Time for you to go, little lady."

"In a minute, dear, I'm not done. I bet you married Emma Kauffman and Agnes Schlabach—"

I thought he was going to punch me, but instead he thrust a paw under each of my armpits and, holding me at arm's length, carried me the length of the parlor and to the front door. You can be sure I screamed like a banshee. I also tried to kick him along the way, but he held me off to the side. Although most of my kicks did nothing but stir up stale air, I did manage to get one good one to connect with his left kneecap. At least I think so, because my big toe hurt like the dickens for the next couple of minutes.

Still holding me, but just by one armpit, he opened the door, and with surprising gentleness deposited me on the top step. I scrambled down the flight backwards.

"I could sue you, you know!"

His response was to slam the door.

I decided to report to Beth, the Speedway cashier. She saw me coming and hustled me down an aisle, stopping between the cookies and the feminine hygiene products.

"So whaddya think?"

"That place is a den of iniquity, pure and simple."

Beth appeared to be working on the same wad of gum. "I told ya. So what happened?"

"Mrs. Benedict tried to give me a job."

"What kinda job? Like a maid or something?"

I chose my words carefully, so as not to sound proud. "An entertainer."

Beth clapped her hands to her breast, knocking her name tag askew. "You're kidding!"

"Oh, I'm sure she'd be happy to offer you one too."

"Really?" I could practically see Beth give herself a mental slap. "Of course I would never be interested in such a thing!" She fixed her eyes on mine. "You didn't take her up on it, did you?"

"I played along at first so I could get an interview with her husband. That was, of course, until I realized it wasn't an escort service."

"Escort service, my eye!" Beth blew a bubble that threatened to engulf her face. "And you should see some of those poor girls the Benedicts sucker into working for them. When they start out they look so wholesome, but boy, does that change fast."

"I don't get it," I said. "I thought that kind of thing was against the law."

The bubble popped, sounding for all the world like a backfiring engine. Either that, or a gun. A woman buying cigarettes from Wilma actually ducked.

"It is, honey," Beth said. "But those Benedicts are clever. As long as they maintain the façade of an escort service, and as long as the women that work there don't actually solicit, there's nothing the police can do. Believe me, we've tried to shut them down."

"Who is 'we,' if you don't mind me asking?"

She adjusted her badge. "My church. Folks in the neighborhood. Why, half the town."

I shook my head. "What about Arnold Benedict?

How can he get away with conducting bogus marriages?"

She shook her head in sync with mine. "That's a crying shame, isn't it? The fact is, according to the law, he qualifies as a minister. This freedom of religion thing has gone too far if you ask me."

"Amen to that! But even a kosher minister—pardon my mixing of ecclesiastical terms—can't marry the same man to more than one woman."

"He does that?"

"You bet your bippy. He married at least four women, that I know of, to the same man. Maybe lots more. He acts like it's all a joke. Like he can get away with it forever."

Beth squared her broad shoulders, her enormous bosoms straining the green smock. The badge trembled but remained straight.

"Well, we'll just have to see about that. The CCC will get to the bottom of this, I promise you. Arnold Benedict will spend time behind bars."

"CCC?" I'd noticed that she turned the gum with each letter, and I got a good view of her tonsils.

"Cumberland Christian Citizens. There wasn't a whole lot they could do about that escort business, but this marrying stuff is another thing. Marriage is a sacrilege, you know."

"I think you mean sacrament, dear."

She scowled, yet another reminder that sometimes I should leave well enough alone. "The Bible commands us to be monotonous."

"It does? Didn't Solomon have seven hundred wives?"

"That was in the Old Testament," she humphed. "You don't see the disciples getting married."

I bobbled my head to appease her. I'd already broken one of my cardinal rules: Never discuss religion with someone more devout than you.

We exchanged phone numbers, and she promised to keep me abreast of her efforts to land Arnold Benedict in the slammer. Then, almost as an afterthought, she snatched a package of sanitary napkins off the shelf. The kind with wings.

"Here," she said, "a little something for the road."

I took the package. Perhaps Beth had meant to give me cookies, but it didn't matter. A gift is a gift, and that was one horse's mouth I didn't want to look into again.

I'm not perfect. If I think hard enough, I can come up with at least half a dozen faults. One thing I am not, however, is paranoid.

A white car pulled into traffic behind me shortly after I left the Speedway. I noticed it at the first stoplight, because I—well, okay, I was checking myself out in the rearview mirror. I just wanted to see if I could see what Mrs. Benedict saw. Was it possible I was actually pretty enough to work as a you-know-what?

There was no indication that the driver of the white car saw me notice that vehicle. There was absolutely no reason for him or her to do so. In fact, I most probably wouldn't have even remembered the incident, except for the fact that the windshield of the car behind was tinted dark. Almost black. That irritated me no end.

Sighted folks who wear sunglasses during face-to-face conversations irritate me as well. It just isn't fair. The Good Lord intended for us to look each other square in the eye when we talk. If He meant for us to look at our reflections, then we would have all been born with the same head.

At any rate, when I was done appraising myself in the rearview mirror, I stuck my tongue out at the car behind me. Actually I stuck my tongue out at the image of that car in the mirror. I've read enough recently about road rage to know that minding one's business is the safest course of action. Surely the mirror wouldn't tattle on me.

Still, I remember feeling a bit uneasy after my lingual display. Just to be safe, I rolled the power window up on my side, leaving about a three-inch crack. The remaining three windows I closed tightly. I also began keeping track of the white car.

Sure enough, it followed me through the next light, and the one after that. My pulse began to race when at the fourth light it was still behind me. By the time I turned off Route 36 and onto Route 35, which eventually becomes Route 96 and the way home, I was in a state of panic. The gleaming white car with the menacing black windshield was practically riding on my bumper.

I know, a clear-thinking Magdalena would have pulled into the nearest sign of human habitation and begged for help. A technologically advanced Magdalena would have had a cell phone in the car. The Magdalena I've grown to know and love over the years responded by stomping on the accelerator.

The Buick had a fair amount of oomph, but then so did the white car. My one advantage, if any, was that I exhibited more confidence on the curves, and believe you me, Route 96 has more curves than a beach full of bathing beauties. Incidentally, I attribute my skill as a driver to the fact that Papa took me to the state fair when I was eight and let me drive the bumper cars. At any rate, I was able to keep a good deal of distance between myself and my pursuer, as long as I didn't let up on the gas.

Unfortunately—perhaps it was the stress brought on by the bizarre job interview—I forgot that one of the turns is not a curve, but a right angle. I might even have been able to correct that oversight, had not the car behind me smashed into my rear bumper.

The next thing I knew I was airborne, soaring over some cottonwoods that bordered a creek, then over the creek itself, finally coming to rest in the V formed by two primary trunks of a massive sycamore.

It was not a comfortable landing.

20

Grits Polenta

Polenta is Italian cornmeal mush. It's a great favorite these days for its affinity for full-flavored cheeses. This dish is made with grits, which gives a slightly coarser texture to the cornmeal polenta and also a more substantial body. Since almost any word sounds better than grits, tell your picky-eating friends it's polenta first.

1 recipe Basic Boiled
  Grits (hot)
½ cup freshly grated
  Parmesan cheese
1 cup crumbled mild
  goat cheese, such
  as Bucheron

Salt to taste
2 cups Tomato Sauce
  (recipe follows)
¼ cup thinly sliced
  scallions (green
  onions)

Combine the grits, Parmesan, and ½ cup of the goat cheese in a mixing bowl. Season with the salt. Pour the mixture into a well-buttered medium-size baking dish. Let cool completely, then invert and cut into 1½-inch squares.

Preheat the oven to 425° F. Generously butter a medium-size baking dish.

Arrange the polenta squares slightly overlapping in the prepared baking dish. Spoon the tomato sauce over the polenta, but don't try to cover it evenly. Leave some areas sauceless so the polenta can toast up a little. Bake in the oven until very hot and bubbling, about 12 minutes.

Sprinkle the remaining ½ cup goat cheese and the scallions over the polenta. Return to the oven to just heat the cheese and scallions, about 1 minute.

SERVES 4 TO 6

Tomato Sauce

2½ tablespoons peanut oil
1 cup chopped onions
⅓ cup chopped carrot
½ cup chopped celery
2 cloves garlic, chopped
2 cans (28 ounces each) tomatoes

½ teaspoon dried thyme
½ teaspoon dried basil
½ teaspoon dried oregano
Pinch of red-pepper flakes, or to taste
Salt to taste

Heat the oil in a large saucepan over medium-high heat. Add the onions, carrot, celery, and garlic, and cook until the vegetables are tender, about 15 minutes.

Add the tomatoes with their juice, and stir with a

wooden spoon, breaking up the tomatoes. Add the seasonings and cook, uncovered, until the desired thickness is reached, about 1 hour. You may purée the sauce if desired.

MAKES 6 TO 7 CUPS

21

———◆———

I passed out. The 1986 Buick I'd bought as a cure for
pride did not contain an airbag. My bony chest hit the
steering wheel a split second before my forehead hit
the windshield. My nose hit something as well, because when I came to, both it and forehead were
bleeding profusely. I took one look at myself in the
rearview mirror—the skin on my forehead was split
open, like a weenie held too long over a campfire—
and fainted.

The second time I regained consciousness I knew better than to get a gander at the goo. From what I could
detect by feel, the bleeding had stopped. Of more concern to me than my head—which was now throbbing—
was the fact that my chest felt like it'd been hit by a
baseball bat. My left side ached as well, and just the act
of moving my right hand up to touch my nose produced
excruciating pain in one of my ribs.

"Oh Lord," I moaned in all earnestness, "take me
now."

The Good Lord appeared to have other plans. He
left me sitting there, throbbing and moaning, as late af-

ternoon turned into dusk, and then into a night as black and dismal as any I'd ever experienced.

Of course I tried to lower the window some more and call for help—even a long, narrow face like mine can't fit through a three-inch crack—but the Buick's power windows were not about to budge with the motor off. I had not shut the motor off, by the way. When I gained consciousness the first time, the car was as silent as a married man alone with his wife in a restaurant. Turning the ignition key did absolutely no good.

To my great delight, the horn worked fine. At least it did at first. Eventually, though, it began to sound like an anemic lamb two pastures over, and I decided to save what little juice there was left in the battery for emergency use of the lights.

Sleeping that first night was impossible. Pain and fear contrived to revive me every time I nodded off. For the most part I just sat there, willing the hours away. I prayed a lot too, but to be honest, they weren't the most respectful prayers I've ever composed.

I blamed the Good Lord for having allowed the accident in the first place. At the very least, I informed Him, He could have sent a rescue squad to my aid the moment I landed in the damn tree (I'm afraid I did use the D word, which may have contributed to the delay). Finally, driven to it by desperation, I made all kinds of promises I know now I can't possibly keep.

They say God answers prayers in mysterious ways, and I wholeheartedly agree. By dawn's early light, what so proudly did I hail, but the roll of duct tape I'd bought at Sam's Corner Market. It was sitting on the passenger seat right beside me, although the rest of my provisions had scattered hither, thither, and yon.

I prayed some more—this time without as much blame—and got the distinct impression that I was supposed to do something with the tape. But what? I could barely move. Then suddenly, like a bolt out of the blue, I had a vision of a blue bolt. Wrapped in the blue bolt of chiffon was my sister Susannah.

Of course! The Good Lord meant me to wrap that duct tape around my chest like I was a mummy. No doubt I had a cracked rib or two, which was causing the severe pain. Those ribs needed to be held in place, and the duct tape just might do the job. But a fat lot of good that knowledge did me. To wrap myself would be to cause even more intense pain. Unbearable pain, even.

"Why are you torturing me?" I cried.

The Good Lord, as usual, said nothing. Not aloud, at any rate.

There is, however, inside each of us, a still, small voice that can only be heard if we silence the din in our minds. After moaning and complaining a good deal—it was my right, after all—I finally calmed down enough to hear the voice.

"African women give birth in the fields," it said.

"What?"

"They do it all the time. Look, Magdalena, you can either sit there helplessly, or you can do something to make things better. If African women can deliver their own babies in the fields, and then walk back to the village on their own two legs, then you can wrap a piece of silly tape around your bony chest."

"But it will hurt!"

"Are you a woman or a wuss, Magdalena?"

"A wuss," I wailed.

"Have it your way then, Magdalena. Just remember, I offered My help. Oh, and by the way, you sure wail a lot."

The short hairs on my head stood. The long hairs, fortunately, remained coiled in the semblance of a bun.

"Lord, was that You?"

Again there was no answer.

*   *   *

I thought about what had just happened. Perhaps the still, small voice had indeed been the Lord. More likely it had just been me. I'm in the habit of not only talking to myself, but answering myself as well. This is not, as some people think, a sign of mental instability, but rather of intelligence.

Whomever the voice belonged to, it had made a lot of sense. I could sit there—and sitting was virtually all I could manage under the circumstances—and do nothing, or I could bite the bullet, so to speak, and take the suggested course of action. I bit.

Wrapping one's own broken ribs with duct tape may not be quite as painful as giving birth in a field, but it is surely a close second. During the process I learned that my vocabulary was far more extensive than anyone, least of all myself, had previously thought. I also learned that wetting oneself is not the end of the world.

But when it was all said and done, the tape worked miracles. I could move the upper part of my body without feeling like someone was taking a crowbar to my chest. This meant I could finally assess my situation.

Alas, what I learned on that score wasn't good. Neither door would open. The two-door vehicle had become quite firmly lodged in the crotch of a massive sycamore. What's more, the crotch that cradled me was a good twenty feet off the ground. Had I been able to open the window the night before, and somehow managed to crawl out, I most probably would have fallen to the ground and broken my scrawny neck. All the duct tape in the world, and all the king's men, wouldn't have been able to put together this horsy again.

I was trapped, but at least I was safe. I said a prayer of thanksgiving and set about trying to improve my situation. Two things that very much needed attention were my lacerated forehead and broken nose. A fly had found its way through the cracked window and was determined to settle on the open wound just below my hairline. As for my nose—every time I turned my head, it felt like it was going to spin off into space. Somehow I needed to cover the gash and splint the proboscis. But with what?

"Think, *dumkopf*," I said aloud. "This isn't brain surgery we're talking about. There's got to be something you can use."

It was then that I heard my mother's voice. It was as loud and clear, and grating, as it had ever been when she was alive.

"Use what you have," Mama said. It was what she always said when I asked for a new outfit. Mama was the ultimate mixer and matcher.

"All I've got is what I bought at Sam's," I wailed. I retrieved the spilled items from the floor and stacked them on the seat. "And this!" I held the package of feminine goods Beth had so generously given me.

"You've got more than enough," Mama said. That was the last I heard from her for a while.

For once, Mama was right. If necessity is the mother of invention, then surely dire need is the daddy. First I cleansed the open wound on my forehead as best I could with a wad of toilet tissue and antibacterial cleansing gel. It hurt like the dickens of course, providing me with an opportunity to repeat a few of the words that had escaped my lips earlier. Taping the sanitary pad on my forehead was easy and relatively painless.

Taping a sanitary pad along the length of my considerable nose was a bit trickier. It was also a whole lot more painful. My poor schnozz kept shifting about like a gear in the hands of a city driver. By the time I finally got the wings secured with tape, my nose was bleeding again. To stanch the flow, I plugged both nostrils with wads of toilet paper.

After attending to my wounds I was able to settle

down a bit. I wouldn't say I was comfortable exactly,
but the situation was bearable. I ate two sardines for
breakfast, sipped a little water, and napped. When I
awoke I was ravenous, so I devoured the rest of the
sardines for lunch. Not knowing how long I had to
make my provisions stretch, I even drained the oil
from their can, taking great care not to cut my tongue
on the sharp edges. After all, a Magdalena without a
tongue is like a flashlight without batteries.

For the remainder of the day I ate sparingly, drank
even more sparingly, and tried to amuse myself—when
I wasn't praying—by telling myself stories. Alas, I am totally without imagination, and my stories kept putting
me to sleep. In a desperate attempt to stave off bore-
dom, and on the off chance that it might lead to my discovery, I fashioned a kite of sorts by taping the
paper-light Styrofoam bowls to a length of string. A long
strand of toilet paper served as a tail. I anchored the
kite to my steering wheel before slipping it through the
crack above the window. Unfortunately there wasn't a
breath of wind, and the strung bowls hung limply down
the trunk of the massive tree, the toilet-paper tail cas-
cading almost to the ground.

Eventually I became so bored, I resorted to cleaning
out my purse. That's when I found the small notebook
that I use as a memory prodder. It was like finding gold,
and I immediately started a journal of my ordeal. In it I
recorded the date—based on the assumption that I had
not been unconscious for more than a few hours—how
I felt at the time of writing, and a few details I thought
might be of interest to any loved ones who survived me
(in the event I croaked in the crotch of that sycamore).

Perhaps you have always wondered how folks who
find themselves in circumstances such as mine attend to
their personal needs. I know I've always been curious.
Well, you'll have to keep wondering. At least about the

details. Suffice it to say, one of the Styrofoam bowls was put to good use, and the giant sycamore which held me prisoner, nourished as it was, would continue to grow healthily for years to come.

At any rate, although my first full day in the tree passed tolerably well, my second evening was—uh, Hades on earth. I was just finishing my Beanie Weenie supper when the first of the mosquitoes found me. She must have had her cell phone with her, because within minutes she was joined by a swarm. There was virtually nothing I could do to stop the invasion. Because I'd been physically unable to remove my dress and slip before wrapping my chest, I had nothing to stuff in the space, and I was now out of duct tape. My dirty bloomers, if you must know, had gotten the heave-ho hours earlier. There was nothing to do but suffer.

Perhaps it was because of all the mosquitoes in the area, but I've never heard so many bullfrogs in my life. They bellowed like raging bulls, from dusk until dawn. Even my sister, Susannah, who once slept through an earthquake while visiting San Francisco, would not have gotten more than a wink. I made a mental note to send the people of France a thank-you note for all the amphibious legs they'd eaten.

But the next day was even worse. While the frogs slept and the mosquitoes took a much-needed break from their feeding frenzy, forty-five million fat, fearless flies found me. I can only conclude that I'm sweet, because they were all over me like white on rice. Eventually I gave up trying to slap them. Like those folks I've seen in pictures of Australia's outback, I let them crawl where they would.

I had more important things to think of than just insects. There seemed to be a pattern developing. First blood, then frogs, vermin, and flies. It had yet to hail—although no doubt it would—and I was too high up to be reached by wild beasts of any size. I couldn't re-member all the plagues off the top of my wounded head, but I was pretty sure that the final one was the death of the firstborn. And I, Magdalena Portulacca Yoder, was the oldest child!

"Oh Lord, please make it quick!" I implored.

I suspect the Lord had His own daily reminder in front of Him, opened to the M's. I did everything but die quickly. My mosquito bites festered, I ran out of food and water, and just when I thought things couldn't get worse, a cold front blew down from Canada. It wasn't cold enough to kill the flies and mosquitoes, mind you— it was June, after all—just cold enough to make me shimmy and shake like a pagan Presbyterian on a disco dance floor.

"Oh, Lord," I begged through chattering teeth. "Take me now!"

The Lord finally listened.

22

I saw the light. It was every bit as beautiful as I'd imagined it would be. I was in a tunnel of some sort, and floating toward it, feeling absolutely weightless. At the end of the tunnel, silhouetted by the luminance, were two figures, one male, the other female. The male figure I took to be the Lord. The female figure had to be Mama.

Before I could get close enough to make positive identification, the female figure spoke. "She looks awful, even for Magdalena. Isn't there anything else we can do?"

"Mama? Is that you?"

"She's delirious," Mama said, and turned to the Lord.

I must have been nearer the two than I thought, because the Lord took my face in both His hands and cradled it gently. Then He lifted my eyelids with His fingertips.

"She's conscious," He said. "We just need to give her a minute."

"I made it, didn't I?" I cried. I don't mind confiding what an immense relief it was to learn that I had indeed made it to the right side. I know, as a Christian I am supposed to feel assured that I am saved, and I do for the most part. But I still have a few doubts; I am human after all. Well, at least I was.

"You made it, all right," the Lord said. "Just hang in there. The ambulance will be here soon."

"They have ambulances in Heaven?" I thought no one ever got sick there. Then again, Heaven had streets, didn't it? Gold streets, to be sure, but they had to be used for something.

"She's definitely coming around," the Lord said. "She heard me say ambulance."

I smiled up at my Maker. "To take me to Your mansion in the sky, right?"

"Delta Dawn," Mama began to sing, "what's that flower you have on?"

Mama's voice sounded no better than it had when she was alive. In fact, it sounded very much like Susannah's. Mama even looked a bit like Susannah.

I blinked and tried to focus.

"You see?" the Lord said. "If I know Magdalena, she'll try to sit up any second now. We have to stop her. She needs to be X-rayed before she's allowed to move a muscle."

The Lord was beginning to sound very much like my neighbor and uh—dare I say man friend—Dr. Gabriel Rosen. Gabe the Babe, I've been known to call him in private.

I closed my eyes tightly, and opened them once more. Sure enough, that wasn't Mama's mug I was staring at. The Lord's either. And I certainly wasn't in Heaven.

"Where am I?" I demanded.

"You're in some stupid woods," Susannah said. "You were in a terrible car wreck of some kind and have maxi-pads taped to your face. It's lucky you didn't die."

"The car!" I was lying on my back, looking up. I turned my head one hundred and eighty degrees, but couldn't see a car of any description. Only the stupid woods. "Where's my car?" I demanded.

"Mags, honey," Gabe said, "we'll fill you in on everything later. What you need to do now is just rest."

"What I need now is water," I croaked.

Gabe shook his head. "Sorry, hon. There's a stream nearby, but I don't know if it's potable. But the ambulance will have an IV and—"

I tuned him out for a while. An ambulance meant strangers. A hospital meant even more strangers. There were people I couldn't trust at the moment, one of whom drove a white car with tinted windows and wanted me dead.

"No ambulance," I said emphatically.

"Don't be silly, Mags." Susannah grinned happily. "Gabe said I could ride in the back with you. We'll have fun."

"No ambulance!" I shouted.

"Hey, hey," Gabe said. "Take it easy, Mags. You'll only do yourself harm."

I tried to prop myself up on my elbows, but the pain was too intense. "It's a matter of life and death," I groaned.

Gabe glanced at Susannah as if to reassure her. "Our Mags is exaggerating."

"I am not! For your information"—I paused to gasp—"I'm not talking about my injuries. I'm talking about a murderer on the loose. The one who pushed my car over the edge of the embankment."

That got their attention. They shut their mouths while I opened mine. First I swore them to secrecy—an un-Mennonite but necessary thing to do—and then I filled them in as quickly as I could. I had to leave out many details, but with the ambulance on its way, there was no time to waste. Whenever either tried to interrupt, I waggled a finger weakly at them.

"So you see," I said in summary, "this person thinks I'm dead. I've got to keep it that way."

Gabe shook his handsome head. "Just how are we supposed to do that? Whisk you away right now and stash you someplace where no one will find you?"

"Exactly."

"Mags, honey, I know you take this detecting thing seriously, but this is carrying it too far. You need medical help."

"Which you can give me, dear."

"But I'm a cardiologist and—"

I found the strength to wave my hand at him. "Please stop arguing, and just do as I say. I've got it all figured out. You can take me to the hospital over in Somerset County if you really want X rays and all that. Nobody knows me there. Then I can stay with you until I'm well enough to get around." I pointed at Susannah. "And you, dear, will help me with a disguise. Fifteen feet of filmy fabric will take a little getting used to, but I'm sure I can manage."

"What about your car?" Gabe asked. "We have to report the accident. If we don't, the ER in Somerset will."

"We'll tell them I fell from a tree. And anyway, I'll register under an alias."

"Oh sis, you're so crafty," Susannah cooed. "I'm so proud of you. But what are you going to tell Melvin?"

I did my best to arrange my dry, cracked lips into a maternal smile. "Need we tell him anything, dear?"

She clapped her hands in glee. "A secret! I just love secrets."

"I was hoping you'd say that. But Freni's another story. Not only is she as stubborn as a bulldog, but besides you two, she's the only one who will really care if I don't show up."

"What about Alison?"

"We only just barely know each other," I said. "Besides, I think she's too young to keep such an important secret."

Gabe gave me an incredulous look. "You're wrong about nobody caring. The entire community is stunned by your disappearance. You're all anyone talks about."

"Yeah, sis, you even made the front page of *The Broad Top Bulletin.*"

"That's good," I said, trying not to dwell on my fame, "because that confirms my death in the eyes of my would-be assassin. Still, we tell Freni."

Gabe sighed. "Okay, suppose we go along with this. Somerset County is too close for the tests I want run. I know someone up in Pittsburgh I can trust. Runs a private clinic. That meet your approval, Sherlock?"

"That's fine, Watson."

A second later we heard the distant sound of a siren.

Gabe and Susannah did an admirable job of hustling my busted bustle to Gabe's car before the paramedics—who had had to travel all the way down from Bedford, seeing as how we were in Pennsylvania—arrived. Of course Gabe complained the entire time that what he was doing was not only stupid medicine, but ethically wrong. Susannah, of course, thought it was just plain fun.

On the long drive to Pittsburgh I filled them in some more—although I didn't tell them *everything*. Susannah means well, but, her delight in keeping secrets aside, she sometimes can't tell her lips from the next person's ear.

They in turn related how, the day before, Susannah had been driving by herself down Route 96, searching for me, when she'd spotted "the funniest-looking kite I'd ever seen." She mentioned the sighting to Melvin, who dismissed the strange object as being nothing more than trash. She then called Gabe, who thought investigating the object was worth a shot. By then it was dark, however, and they decided to wait until the next day.

That night the mother of all thunderstorms rolled through, and the next day the funny kite was nowhere to be seen. Still, Susannah remembered its approximate location and the two of them, Gabe and my sister, set out on foot to find its source, hopefully me.

"You were lying about twenty yards from your car," Gabe said.

I slurped the last of the chocolate shake they'd bought me at the first McDonald's we came to. I'd wanted more than just a shake, mind you, but Gabe had insisted I break my fast with liquids. No matter, that simple shake did far more to restore my health than an IV would have.

"Yes, but how did I get down?"

Gabe, who was driving, stroked my arm with his right hand. "Get down from what, hon?"

"The tree!"

"What tree?"

"The giant sycamore my car landed in when it went sailing off the road."

Susannah, who was in the backseat filing her nails, patted my other arm. "She's delusional again," she said, presumably to Gabe.

"I most certainly am not! My car was wedged in the crotch of a tree. I couldn't get the doors open."

"Hon," Gabe said softly, "your car wasn't in a tree. And both doors were wide open."

"Are you calling me a liar?"

"Of course not. It's just that you've been under a great deal of stress. You might have a concussion and well—uh—"

"What he's trying to say, sis, is that you've been seeing things."

Gabe nodded, but kept his eyes on the road.

"Well, I haven't! Okay, so maybe I thought Gabe was God and you were Mama, but that was only for a few seconds. My car was wedged in that tree, and that's a fact."

"Whatever you say," Susannah said.

Those were fighting words, and I could tell by her tone that she'd rolled her eyes. Wisely, I let it go. I knew the truth, and that's all that mattered—well, until I got my strength back, and could prove what I'd said was true. In the meantime, it was best to cooperate as much as possible.

My maturity paid off. Gabe's friend at the clinic confirmed that, although I'd suffered a slight concussion, there had been no permanent damage to my noggin and I was well on my way to recovery. Being a reasonable man, he stopped short of certifying me as sane. Then again, who really is? As for my ribs—two of them had hairline fractures, but they too had already begun to heal. The doc said I'd done a bang-up job with the duct tape. Even the gash on my forehead was coming along nicely. Only my nose was problematic. Apparently maxi-pads, even the type with wings, don't make good splints. The prognosis for my proboscis was that I was going to either have the thing reset at some point or risk sinus problems. I chose surgery—but opted for a later date. In the meantime I had an important fish to catch and fry.

I spent just three days at the clinic, and then Gabe settled me into an upstairs bedroom at his house. In my absence the inn had been closed and Freni, bless her heart, had taken the munchkin Alison home with her. True to their word, Gabe and Susannah had shared news of my discovery, and subsequent recovery, with my elderly cousin. I was just putting my new toothbrush away when Freni and her husband came galloping up the drive in their open summer buggy.

By the time I got downstairs the couple were inside, panting from exertion. "Ach!" Freni squawked when she saw me. Then, defying five hundred years of inbred inhibition, she threw herself at me, clasping me tightly in her stubby arms.

"Ach!" I squawked back at her. Freni may be short, but she's every bit as heavy as a millstone. Even Arnold Schwarzenegger would have staggered under her weight.

Meanwhile Mose, whose genes do a better job of keeping him under control, fidgeted nervously. "Good to see you," he said.

I extricated myself from Freni and shook Mose's hand. Then I hugged him. I hugged Freni again too.

"Rumors of my death have been greatly exaggerated," I said.

Despite the bottle-thick lenses she wore, I could see the tears welling up in Freni's eyes. "Yah, dead, that's what we thought."

"Freni made me drive all over the county to look for you," Mose said, his accent heavier than usual. "I am sorry I could not find you."

I smiled through tears of my own. The thought of a septuagenarian Amish man roaming the byways of Bedford County in his buggy looking for me was touching beyond words.

"So what do you eat when you are dead?" Freni asked, in a rare attempt at a joke.

"Not your chicken and dumplings, dear. Mostly sardines and granola. But as you can see, I'm fit as a fiddle now—a couple of scratches and bruises notwithstanding."

Freni studied me closely for the first time. "Ach, the nose. It goes this way, and then that way."

"Just think, dear, now it will be harder to stick into someone else's business."

She nodded. "So, how long will you be dead?"

"Just as long as it takes. How's Alison?"

"A good child, Magdalena."

"Really? You think so?"

They both nodded.

"She helps me with the milking," Mose said. "And the horses! She loves the horses."

"Still, it must be a little crowded, what with Jonathan and Barbara and the three babies."

"Yah," Freni said, a naughty gleam in her eye. "Barbara complains that now we are too many. She wants always to know why I take this Alison home with me."

"What did you tell her?"

"I ask her if she thinks the child would be better off with that no-good papa of hers in the land of a thousand ponds."

"That's lakes, dear. And I think there's supposed to be ten thousand of them. Does she know I'm still alive?"

Freni frowned. "Susannah said not to tell anyone."

"Susannah was right. Too many people know already. Say, Freni, how well did you know Emma Kauffman?"

Both Freni and Mose seemed to shrink. Mose looked as if he were looking for a hole into which to crawl.

"Which Emma Kauffman?" Freni asked, as if she didn't know. "That is a very popular name."

"*The* Emma Kauffman, dear. The one who turned her back on your faith to paint."

"Ach, that Emma Kauffman." Freni turned her head so I couldn't see her eyes. "So why do you want to know?"

"It's part of my investigation, dear—and incidentally, this is also top-secret information. Anyway, I just want the name of someone—maybe an old friend, or family member of Emma's—she keeps in touch with. Someone who might be able to shed some light on her character."

Freni clucked dismissively. "And this I should know?"

"Hannah Zug," Mose said, his voice a harsh whisper.

I smiled at him.

He shuffled from foot to foot, but not having found that hole, it got him nowhere. "They are sisters. It is known that Hannah finds it difficult to obey the Ordnung. She does not agree with this ban that has been placed on Emma. It is said she sometimes goes to see her. There is talk even—"

"Ach!" Freni waved her arms at Mose in a vain attempt to silence him.

"There is talk," Mose said defiantly, "that Hannah will herself be banned. This is a very sad situation, yah?"

"Yah," I said. "I mean, yes. Do you know where Hannah Zug lives?"

"She lives with her husband," Freni snapped. "Mr. Zug. Magdalena, is it necessary for you to speak with Hannah?"

"Absolutely."

"Why? What will you learn?"

I shrugged. "I don't know. In an investigation like this, things sometimes turn up that you can't anticipate."

Freni grabbed one of my arms. Her short fingers are capable of extracting juice from a walnut.

"You will not be so hard on her, yah?"

"I promise."

She gave me what was meant to be a meaningful stare, but the thickness of her lenses made her come across as comical, rather than threatening. At last she sighed.

"Hannah Zug lives on Gindlesperger Road. The third white farmhouse after you cross Kanagy Creek. You will see by the flowers."

"The flowers?"

Freni took a deep breath. She apparently had a great deal to say about the flowers, but before she could get one word out, Gabe's front door flew open and in waltzed Susannah.

"Here I come to save the day!" she sang.

I stared at her in disbelief.

23

My baby sister was dressed in a navy blue skirt-suit, cream silk blouse, pantyhose, and black patent-leather pumps. Her shoulder-length hair, which normally resembles a wheat field after a windstorm, was styled into loose but orderly curls. Near the tip of her nose rested a dainty pair of what we used to call granny glasses. Her makeup had been applied so sparsely that it almost looked natural. I say "almost," because even though this application fell well within the range of what passes for normal, any idiot knows it takes a day well below freezing to produce apples on the cheeks.

In short, however, Susannah could have passed herself off as a bank president, a flight attendant, or a Methodist church lady. Perhaps I should have been overjoyed by this transformation, but I found it unsettling.

"Where's that hideous little beast?" I asked suspiciously. The suit jacket was fitted and there didn't seem to be room for even the most minuscule of mangy mutts.

Susannah patted the left half of her bosom. "My Shnookums is right here."

As if on cue, my sister's left breast began to bulge. Within seconds it was writhing and pulsating, like a small volcano about to blow. Then, just when I thought it would erupt, the bulge moved across Susannah's sternum and her right breast more than doubled its size.

"Ach!" Freni had covered her face with her hands, but her fingers were spread wide enough to allow a good peek. Mose had discreetly turned his back.

"He likes to change cups every now and then," Susannah said matter-of-factly. "I think it gets hot under this jacket."

"Then lose it, dear," I suggested.

"The jacket?"

"The canine in a cup. What do you think that does for his self-esteem?"

Susannah frowned. "I never thought of that. Are you saying I might be giving him some kind of complex?"

"It could be, but not to worry. I heard there's a good pooch psychiatrist in Philly. Dinky demented dogs are his specialty. He has a tiny leather couch in his office, just over a foot long." I sighed dramatically. "The thing is, dear, he charges a hundred dollars an hour."

"Really?"

I was just kidding, but Susannah apparently wasn't. And I know for a fact that Mose and Freni had taken me seriously, because they fled before any more of my inane English prattle could penetrate their already beleaguered brains.

"So where's the hunk?" Susannah asked, looking around Gabe's living room. Doggy doctors were already just a dim memory.

"He's in his study working on his book. You know, that mystery with the Yiddish-speaking, kick-boxing grandmother as the sleuth? Anyway, sometimes he doesn't show his face for hours."

Susannah clapped her hands. "Goody. Then we can get right to work and surprise him."

"Excuse me?"

"Wait right there!" Susannah popped outside and reentered a moment later pulling an enormous suitcase on wheels.

"What's that?"

"Your disguise."

"Think again, dear. I'm not going anywhere dressed as a suitcase."

"Don't be silly. There's costumes and makeup in here." Susannah dragged the case into the middle of the room and hoisted it onto Gabe's coffee table. She opened it, displaying a bewildering jumble of wigs, clothes, and cosmetic implements. The inside of that valise was every bit as messy as her room had been when she was a teenager.

I backed off after a cursory glance. "I thought we agreed I was going to dress like you. I don't see any mummy clothes in there."

"Very funny, sis. I thought about that, and decided it wouldn't work. There can only be one *me*, especially here in Hernia. So, I've decided to make you over into somebody so different nobody would ever suspect it was you."

"And who would that be?"

"Somebody glamorous."

Susannah was true to her word. I've met a lot of the Hollywood crowd over the years (my inn is a popular getaway for the shallow but wealthy) and have learned that a lot of the image those folks project is just smoke and mirrors. What I mean is, few of them are perfect physical specimens when viewed up close, without the benefit of hair stylists and makeup men. Some of the men are shockingly short, and most of the women have long since forgotten their natural hair color. Why, even the Good Lord probably doesn't have teeth as straight and white as your average starlet's.

My baby sister knew all that, and had taken it into account. She plucked, puttied, and pulled on yours truly. She even used a bit of duct tape. When she was done, about an hour and a half after she began, I was a curvaceous blonde in a short—by my standards—hot pink dress, with a somewhat wayward nose. My errant schnozz aside, I was downright beautiful.

"There!" Susannah said with satisfaction. She stood behind me while I gazed into Gabe's bathroom mirror. "What do you think?"

I caught my breath. "I'm just too good to be true."

"Look, you even have cleavage."

I did indeed. "Can't take my eyes off of me."

"You like that dress, huh?"

I stroked the silky fabric. "I feel like Heaven to touch."

"And I want you so very much."

I whirled. Gabe was standing in the doorway, his blue eyes twinkling.

"Gabe!" My hands flew to cover my cleavage.

"Wow," he said, "you look really hot, you know that?"

"I look like a trollop."

He chuckled. "Boy, I could get really used to this."

"Well, don't. As soon as I wrap up this investigation I'll be getting back into some good Christian clothes."

Gabe frowned. "You mean you're actually planning to go out dressed like that?"

"Why not?" The truth is, I had no intention of leaving Gabe's farmhouse dressed like the Whore of Babylon. Surely there was something else in Susannah's bag of tricks I could wear. If the Good Lord approved of cleavage, he would have given Eve a push-up bra instead of an animal skin when she shed her fig leaves.

Gabe's frown turned into furrows. A skilled farmer

could have planted corn kernels in those disapproving creases.

"Because like you said, Magdalena, you look like a hooker."

I fixed my faded blue orbs on his sparkling sapphires. "Is this observation based on personal experience?"

"Hey, give me a break, Mags. I was just being honest."

I tugged at the plunging neckline. My gifts may be modest, but the duct tape Susannah had used, plus a product called Bosom Buddies, had all but made my cups overflow. They were teacups to be sure, not mugs, but a gal can't be choosy.

"And if I did go out like this?" I asked.

He had the audacity to laugh. "Well, you won't, of course, because I forbid it."

"You *what*?"

"You heard me. No girlfriend of mine is going to strut her stuff looking like that."

I'd shed my faithful brown brogans for a pair of pink pumps. I stamped one so hard the bathroom mirror rattled. "No one, but no one tells me what to wear. If I want to strut my stuff—as you so crudely put it—I will."

Susannah clapped her hands with glee. "You go, girl!"

Gabe's face was grim. "And just how do you plan to get where you're going?"

"You said this morning at breakfast that you'd loan me your car. In fact, you said that thanks to the revisions you had to make on your novel, you might not be sticking your head out that door for days. Possibly even weeks."

Gabe grunted and tossed the keys in my general direction. "Go ahead and make a fool of yourself. See if I care. But you'll have the whole town talking, you know that."

Gabe's keys had fallen on the floor, but I snatched them up before he changed his mind. "That's *if* they figure out who I am. But let's say they do—what business is this of yours?"

At a loss for words, Gabe glared and then strode back down the hallway. No doubt somebody was going to pay for my contrariness, if only in the pages of his mystery.

"Wow," Susannah said, as the last echo of Gabe's footsteps faded, "you're something else, sis. I always thought you were kind of—well, you know—a stick-in-the-mud. But you know something? You're pretty cool after all."

"Not in hot pink, I'm not." I whipped the fractional frock off over my head, taking with it Goldilocks' tresses. "Now give me something decent," I ordered.

"Oh man," Susannah whined, but did as she was told.

When I pulled into Hannah Zug's gravel drive I was blond again, but I'd shed the tight pink dress in favor of a royal blue one with princess seams and a skirt that came well below my knees. I was still quite shapely, mind you; I just didn't look like I was out to welcome home the fleet. I was still wearing pumps as well, but now they were black (Susannah didn't have *everything* in that suitcase).

Freni had been absolutely right. Someone in the Zug family had a green thumb. Maybe yellow, red, and purple fingers too. I had never seen such a profusion of flowers, certainly not on an Amish farm.

While Amish do cultivate flowers—they are a gift from God, after all—their beds tend to be simple in design, the different varieties arranged neatly in rows. The Zug flower garden seemed to have been lifted from an English country estate. The plants bordering the drive were low and compact, giving way to successively taller flanks; the colors swirled as on a painter's pallet. The perfume nearly knocked me off my pumps.

I stooped to sniff a particularly redolent rose in the

middle of a bed. "Aaah," I said aloud, "now that's what Eden must have smelled like."

"Thank you," the rose said.

"You're welcome—". I recoiled in shock. I would have fallen off my shoes for sure, had I not finally noticed the young woman on her hands and knees behind the rose bush.

"Good heavens!" I gasped for breath. "You scared the living daylights out of me."

The woman stood and smiled. She was holding a mason jar containing dozens of scrabbling Japanese beetles, and multitudes of other flying, buzzing, and wiggling insects.

"In Eden, they do not have these bugs, I think."

"Have you tried Sevrin? It will work on the beetles for sure."

"Ach, these chemicals I do not like to use."

I nodded. "It was just a thought. Personally, I like to let my chickens do most of the work in my garden. But then again my garden isn't nearly as nice as yours. Say, you wouldn't happen to be Hannah Zug, would you?"

Admittedly, it was a stupid thing to say. The bug lady was petite, and herself a blonde. She looked about as much like Emma as I did. She was, however, quite clearly an Amish woman, belonging to one of the more conservative sects in Bedford County.

My question startled the bug lady. Her eyes widened, and the knuckles on the hand holding the jar turned white.

"You are from the newspaper, yah?"

"Excuse me?"

The National Intruder." She looked as if she would have happily flown away on the back of a giant beetle, given the opportunity. I could see her eyeing the farmhouse, calculating the time it would take her to run to safety.

"I'm not from that gossip rag," I said.

"Then you have come to sell me something, yah?"

"Absolutely not, dear. I'm a friend of your sister's."

The jar in Hannah's slim little hand shook. "I must go," she said softly, and began to thread her way delicately, but rapidly, through the flowers.

"But I am," I wailed. "Well, at least I know her."

Hannah reached the drive and broke into a trot. I have longer legs, so keeping up with her was no trouble.

"I'm a Mennonite!" I cried. "I'm Magdalena Yoder, owner of the PennDutch Inn!"

"Magdalena Yoder is dead," she called over her shoulder. "You should not play such games."

"Everybody *thinks* she's dead. But I was in a car accident, you see, and two people very dear to me whisked me away before the police arrived. Because they, the police, can't find my body, they think I drowned in some creek. Anyway, I can prove who I am."

Hannah froze, and I nearly plowed into her. Fortunately I'd been adept at hopscotch as a girl, and I applied some of those moves now. Two hops and a skip and I was in front of her. I whipped off the silly wig.

"You see? It really is me!"

I might as well have been Calista Flockhart claiming to be Mrs. Santa Claus. Hannah tried to step around me. One move, though, and I had her blocked.

She shook her head. "Magdalena Yoder was a famous woman. I have seen her picture many times in the real newspaper. She did not look like you."

"That's because I'm wearing makeup. Tons of it. You have to believe it's me."

She sighed. "I did not want to be rude, but Miss Yoder does not have the same nose."

"That's because I broke it!"

She peered at my probing proboscis. "Maybe. But the rest of you—it is not the same."

"Well, normally I don't wear royal blue, and of course I never ever wear pumps. Why, a body could break a leg on these. That little hop and a skip I did was pretty remarkable, don't you think?"

"It is not the clothes. They are English, I can see. It is—ach, how should I say this? Magdalena Yoder is like a pancake. You are like two muffins. Two very big muffins."

"That's just duct tape! Susannah squished them together—well, never mind. Just trust me. Normally I'm a carpenter's dream."

She considered that for a moment. "So who are your enemies? If you are really Magdalena Yoder, you will know the answer to this question."

"I don't have any enemies, dear," I said at last. "Well, none that I'm aware of."

Hannah was a quick little thing. She feinted to the left, stopped on a dime, and made a mad dash around me on the right. She took the front steps like a gazelle on steroids. A couple more seconds and she would be in the house.

Suddenly it hit me, and I knew what she was after. Alas, it was too late to intercept her physically.

"Melvin Stoltzfus!" I yelled at the top of my lungs. "That menacing mantis is my nemesis. And Lodema Schrock is the bane of my existence!"

Hannah turned and smiled.

24

"Come in," she said. "I will make us some tea, yah?"

I scurried up the walk, but when I got to the steps, I prudently removed the pumps. Hannah held the door open for me.

"Thank you."

She followed me into a large but sparsely furnished room. A plain wooden bench flanked one wall, two chairs the opposing wall. In between there was enough space to hold a dance—not that I would know from personal experience, mind you.

Hannah seemed to read my mind. "The church will be held here on Sunday. The benches are now in the barn, yah? They will be brought in Saturday, but today I must clean the floors. Then tomorrow and Saturday I will cook."

I nodded. Most Amish sects, unlike we Mennonites, meet for worship in private homes on a rotation basis. This requires each family to have a fairly open floor plan, with space to accommodate as many as a hundred worshippers. The wooden benches upon which the worshippers sit, and which are communally owned, are shuttled from home to home by horse-drawn wagon a few days prior to the service. After the service, which lasts more than three hours, a communal meal is served. Because of the effort and expense involved, families seldom have to host more than once in a calendar year.

We entered Hannah's kitchen, which was spotless, but harkened back to the turn of the century—the nineteenth century. The sink was supplied with water from an artesian well by a hand pump. The icebox was just that—a squat insulated box in which a chunk of ice sat, melting slowly, surrounded by soggy perishables. The stove was made of solid cast iron and used wood for fuel. The firebox looked large enough—please forgive a mind that has seen death once too often—to accommodate a human body.

Hannah bade me sit at a sturdy oak table while she stoked the fire and added several pieces of wood. Then she filled a cast-iron kettle at the pump and placed it on the burner nearest the firebox.

"You like molasses cookies?" she asked.

"Love them."

"Milk with the tea, yah?"

"Lots."

"Sugar, yah?" It was more of a statement than a question.

"Oodles of sugar, if you don't mind."

"Ach, you are the same as me."

"Isn't that the truth," I said. It never hurts to affirm one's affinities with the subject of a forthcoming interview. Lucky for me, I really did love molasses cookies and sweet milky tea. But I would have pretended to prefer gingersnaps and lemon if that's what I thought she wanted to hear.

The technology may have been a hundred or more years old, but the water heated quickly, and soon we were sipping our tea and munching what truly were some of the best cookies I've ever eaten.

"So, tell me," Hannah said, looking away almost shyly, "why you do not like this Melvin Stoltzfus."

"Because he's a nincompoop."

"Yah?" Hannah, whose English vocabulary was unquestionably more limited than mine, was clearly alarmed.

"The man's an idiot," I explained. "A *dumkopf*!"

She nodded somberly. "Yah, it is a sin to say this, but I feel the same."

"Really? What did he do to you?"

"He gives my husband a ticket, because the horse does not wear a diaper and—uh—"

"I get the picture, dear. Would you pass the cookies, please."

She handed me the plate. "So, Miss Yoder—"

"Please, call me Magdalena." I learned long ago that being on a first-name basis fosters intimacy, which is a prerequisite for confession.

"Magdalena," she said, obviously relishing the privilege, "you did not come here to talk about the police chief. Or Lodema Schrock with the serpent's tongue. It is about my sister, yah? Because she is a famous artist, yah?"

"Yah—I mean, yes. Well, to be totally honest, it's not so much her I wanted to ask about, but her husband."

Hannah's eyes grew to the size of molasses cookies. Her face paled to the color of milk.

"You knew about him? This Clarence Webber?"

"Of course, dear. I make it my business to know everything. What I want to know now is, how well did you know the man?"

"Ach, not so much! And Emma, she does not know the man either. I ask her, how can you marry this man?"

"What did she say?"

"She says it is love at first sight. Do you believe in this love at first sight, Magdalena?"

"Well—uh, let's not talk about me, dear. How did your sister meet Mr. Webber? And where?" The truth

is, I did believe in love at first sight. I fell in love with
my Pooky Bear—a.k.a. the scoundrel Aaron Miller—
instantly, in a cow pasture, and look how that ended. I
fell in love with Gabe over the course of an evening,
but that was still going strong.

Hannah sighed, the color returning slowly to her face.
"She met him at one of her painting shows. Over in
Bedford."

"How long before they were married was that?"

She shrugged. And then, leaning across our cups, whispered, "Magdalena, these questions are very difficult for
me. You see, I am not supposed to see my sister."

I nodded. "Because of the ban."

"Yah. But sometimes I cannot help it. I must see her,
even if it is a sin."

"I understand. I have a sister too. Susannah may get
on my nerves more than a bad case of poison ivy, but
she's still a huge part of my life." I smiled encouragingly.
"Believe me, dear, I won't tell a soul about your visits to
your sister."

She looked at me, her eyes filled with gratitude. "I try
to follow this ban, Magdalena, but I cannot." She
paused. "You ask how long between when they meet
and when they marry—I think maybe just two weeks.
Emma does not like to talk about it, yah?"

"But you did meet Clarence, right?"

"Yah, but I was not invited to the wedding." She
stared sadly at her tepid tea. "I did meet this man—after
they were married. I saw him only once, but I did not
like him. There was something—ach, how do I say this?"

"He seemed evil?"

She frowned. "Perhaps that is too strong of a word.
But swami, yah?"

"Swami?"

"Ach, that is the wrong word. But he was smug, yah?
And I did not trust him."

"Smarmy!" I ejaculated. "That fits him to a tee."

Hannah beamed. "Smarmy. I want to tell Emma this, but of course it is too late."

"You're close to your sister, aren't you?"

"Yah, we used to be very close. Not so much now, of course."

"Why do you think Emma was attracted to Clarence? Face it, dear, he wasn't all that good-looking."

She smiled. "Yah, there were better-looking men— but nobody for my Emma."

"You mean she's picky?"

Hannah excused herself to put the kettle back on. She waited until she was sitting again before answering.

"Magdalena, you are a woman of the world. In the world it is very important to be pretty, yah?"

"Unfortunately it helps. Not that I would know from personal experience, mind you. I have, however, read a few articles." Frankly, it's a wonder my toilet tank hasn't collapsed under the weight of all the *McCall's*, *Ladies' Home Journal*, and *Reader's Digest* magazines I keep stacked on the lid.

She nodded. "Well, my Emma is not so pretty, and of course she cannot marry an Amish man."

"Are you saying she was desperate?"

"Ach!"

"But you are saying that, aren't you?"

Hannah grabbed my wrist. Her fingers, which had milked countless cows, might as well have been made of steel. There was no breaking away.

"It is the clock," she said. "Always it strikes. You feel it too, yah?"

I sat motionless, trying to hear the clock, or maybe, if it was a grandfather clock, feel its vibrations. Except for a low rumbling emanating from the firebox, the distant drone of the windmill, and the closer drone of a fly, the Zug world was silent.

"Sorry, dear, but I don't hear a clock."

She pointed at my stomach. "The baby clock! Do you not hear it?"

"Oh that!" Alas, the batteries in my baby clock had all but run out. Even if I found a man to ring my chimes, it probably wouldn't do me any good.

"So you see," Hannah said, "Emma had to get married. Even now that she is no longer Amish, she feels that she must be married to have a baby."

I gasped. "Is she pregnant?"

"Ach, no! I mean for the future."

"I see. So it was really a marriage of convenience."

The kettle was steaming like a miniature volcano. When Hannah rose to turn it off, I got up as well.

"You've been very helpful," I said. "But I have to ask you a huge favor."

She turned from the stove, suddenly wary. "What is this favor?"

"You must forget you saw me."

"How is this possible?"

"Well, not literally, of course, but you mustn't mention our little chat to anyone. And above all, you can't, under any circumstances, tell anyone that we talked about Clarence Webber. Do you give me your word?"

I knew that, as an Amish woman, she would not swear to silence. As a Mennonite, I would not ask her to. A simple "yes" would have sufficed, but I could see in Hannah's eyes that she couldn't wait to tell her sister about my visit.

I didn't like to threaten her, even by implication, but it was too important to let go.

"Remember, I am promising you that I will not go to the bishop and tell him about your visits with your sister. Surely you can promise me not to tell anyone, especially your sister, about my visit here today."

Hannah gave me her word.

*   *   *

If you can't trust your town's policewoman, then who can you trust? Maybe her hairdresser. At least it was worth a try.

I knew from previous conversations with her that Zelda Root got her bizarre haircuts at Paul Rue's House of Hair up in Bedford. I'd driven by there once or twice and seen the large collection of wigs in the window, so I knew Paul Rue did more than cut. I also knew that Paul was from Paris—or at least he pretended to be from the City of Lights. That was the most common rumor. Others, however, have variously reported he was from Hungary, Russia, and even Andorra. Not that it really mattered, though, because this was Bedford County. Paul could have been from Parsippany, and we would have thought him exotic.

They say that Tuesday is the best day to go shopping, get your car fixed, or visit a government office, because for some strange reason Tuesday is the day most Americans prefer to stay at home. It appeared that Americans preferred not to patronize the House of Hair on Thursdays either. There was no one in the shop except Mr. Rue when I entered, so I got waited on by the head honcho himself.

"What a hideous wig!" he cried, in his charming accent. He clapped his hands to his cheeks. "It looks like a dead muskrat, no?"

I smiled ruefully. "The wig is blond. Muskrats are brown. And just for the record, they're incapable of love."

He grinned and extended a well-manicured hand. The proffered paw was the size of a child's hand, in keeping with the man's diminutive stature. He was, after all, no larger than a twelve-year-old boy.

"I like you already," he said. "Zee name is Paul. And you are?"

"Portulacca." It was, after all, the truth.

"Is zat your family name?"

"Does it really matter, dear? Think of me as Cher. Or Madonna. One name is all I need."

He had me sit in a genuine imitation leather chair. Then with a snap of his wrist he spun the chair so that I faced the mirror.

"Vell, den, Portulacca, vhat can I do for you today? Besides get rid of zat ting for you."

"That's basically it. I'm hoping you can help me select a better model, or"—I snatched the faux locks off my sweating head—"come up with a more flattering hair-style."

Paul gasped, his hands finding comfort on his cheeks again. *Mon Dieu!* It *eez* zee muskrat."

I gave him an abbreviated version of my evil eye. "Not hardly, dear. This is all home-grown protein."

He shuddered. "Vee must cut it off! It is disgraceful for a beautiful woman like you to have hair like that, no?"

"No—I mean, yes! I mean, what's wrong with it?"

"You are just joking, yes?" He'd picked up a scissors and was gazing at my head with all the longing of a quarantined child looking out the window at freshly fallen snow.

"I most certainly—" I caught myself just in time. "You know, dear, I was thinking of a hairdo like the one you gave Zelda."

"Thelda?"

"Zelda Root. The policewoman from Hernia."

Paul Rue recoiled in horror. I spun around to face him.

"What's the matter now?" I demanded.

"Zat—woman," he said between gasps, "her name must never be spoken in here."

"Oh, really? What did she do? Forget to tip?"

He waved the scissors like a conductor's baton, punctuating each word. "She lie to me, yes? She make promise to marry me so zat I can get my green card, and then, voila, she is marry somebody else."

"Oo-la-la," I said. "That had to hurt."

"Like zees!" He pantomimed stabbing his own breast. "Now vhat vill I do?"

"Go back to Paris?"

He scowled. "Paris? Never!"

It occurred to me that the stories I'd heard about Mr. Rue might be wrong. Maybe he wasn't French after all. I decided to fish for the truth.

"Then maybe Moscow, dear. You'd look good in a fur coat."

"Bah! Moscow, eet eez too cold."

"Berlin then. It's supposed to be a happening city."

"No vay, Berlin. Zee language eez too difficult. It makes me pit."

"I think you mean 'spit,' dear. How about Rome? It's nice and sunny there, and Italian is such a romantic language."

"Maybe yes, but zee people drive always too fast. Eez crazy, no?"

"Spain?"

"Vhere zay keel zee balls?"

"I beg your pardon?"

He gave me a pitying look. "Een zee ballfight."

"Andorra?" I asked desperately.

"Vhere?"

"Never mind, dear. Wherever home is, I bet it's lovely."

"Yes, of course, but eet is not as beautiful as zees. I love zees country. Zay vill have to drag me avay." He laid the scissors across his heart and began to hum "The Star-Spangled Banner." About two bars into it he stopped abruptly. "Are you married, Portulacca?"

"Moi?"

"Yes, you!"

I shook my head reluctantly. "I was once, but I doubt if I'd ever do it again." That contained a kernel of truth, because I'd never marry anyone other than Gabe the Babe, and at this point that seemed highly unlikely. The Babester and I were of different faiths, and neither of us had any intention of converting. While the good doctor didn't have any problem with marrying someone outside of his faith—or at least I assume that was the case—I could never marry a non-Christian. For one thing, Mama would spin so fast in her grave, the heat generated would melt both polar ice caps, flooding much of the eastern U.S. When that happened, Hernia might well become a beach town, home to a bevy of buxom bathing beauties, and I would surely lose Gabe. So what would be the point?

Unless—my pulse started to race—Reverend Schrock gave us his blessing. That would make it a whole different ball game. Mama wouldn't dare object to a proper Mennonite minister officiating at the wedding, even if there were a rabbi present. But would Reverend Schrock agree? Quite possibly! After all, his was a mixed marriage, wasn't it? Good and evil!

Paul must have sensed the shift in my reasoning. He eyed me shrewdly through peepers that were mere slits.

"But you vill change your mind if zee price is right, yes?"

Never dismiss a business offer until you've heard all the details. "My prices tend to be rather high, dear. What did you have in mind?"

25

Jalapeno Grits Casserole

Some folks who won't eat grits in any other form will line up for this spicy version. It's sort of a party dish, definitely special enough for company.

*1 recipe Basic
    Boiled Grits*
*2 cups shredded
    sharp Cheddar
    cheese*
*½ cup (1 stick)
    unsalted butter,
    cold, cut into
    pieces*

*3 large eggs, lightly
    beaten*
*3 tablespoons
    minced seeded
    fresh jalapeno or
    cayenne peppers*
*Salt and freshly
    ground black
    pepper to taste*

Preheat the oven to 350° F. Generously butter a deep 2-quart baking dish.

Prepare the grits, add the cheese and butter, and beat until smooth. Stir in the beaten eggs and peppers and season with salt and pepper.

Pour the grits into the prepared baking dish. Bake until the grits are set and the top is lightly browned, about 35 minutes.

SERVES 6

26

"Half ownership in zees shop."

More details were needed. "Would this be a marriage in name only, or would I have to—uh—submit to—uh, live up to certain obligations?"

Paul's eyes widened with horror. "In name only, of course!"

"Well! You don't have to be so vehement about it."

"So, you vill do it?"

"I didn't say that. And I didn't say I wouldn't. But I will say this: Any man I marry has to be capable of holding up his end of a conversation. There's nothing worse than sitting in a restaurant across from two hundred pounds of mute meat."

"Talk? Eez zees vhat you vant?" He spun one of the adjacent faux leather chairs in my direction and plonked his pretend-Parisian patootie on the pink pleather. "So, let us talk."

"Well, dear, why don't we chat about Zelda's marriage to the recently deceased Clarence Webber?"

He made the same face I made once when served escargot. "Zee man vas a Philistine!"

"Oh no, dear, I don't think he's from the Middle East."

He shook his head. "I mean he vaz a barbarian. He drove a red BMW, yes? But I have dem over to dinner at my house, and I serve dem filet mignon. Zees man—zees Philistine—he ask for A-1 steak sauce!"

"I prefer a good ketchup, myself."

Paul dropped the scissors so he could clap his cheeks. Unfortunately the scissors landed point down. There followed a string of invectives in a dozen different languages, none of which I recognized as French. Finally, perhaps after concluding he still had the potential to produce a parade of petit Pauls, he returned to the subject at hand.

"Thelda vas a lovesick voman, *n'est-ce pas*? She vanted always to marry this Vermin Stoltzfus—"

"Actually, that's Melvin—never mind. I like your way better. Please continue."

"So, like I vas saying, Thelda marry zees Clarence Vebber to make Vermin jealous. But it not vork, yes? Eet only break Thelda's leettle heart. I say to her before she marry, zees man is no good. Vhy you peek him and not me?" He paused.

"And vhat did she say?" I begged.

"She say eet eez because he make her to feel like very much voman."

"Is that so?"

He nodded vigorously. "So I say to Thelda, 'Vhat am I? Chopped leeber?' Vell, she no can answer."

"Perhaps she didn't understand your question, dear. At any rate, it's a crying shame Zelda thought she had to marry Clarence. I would have thought just flaunting him in Melvin's face would have done the trick—well, except for the fact that Melvin is, and has always been, in love with my sister, Susannah. Still, what good did actually marrying him do?"

Paul poked the air with the scissors. "Dis eez what I ask, no?"

"Yes?"

"Thelda, she not happy veeth zees question." He sighed. "But, I vill tell you my opinion. You vant to hear it?"

"Absolutely. Spill it, dear."

"Zees Vebber man vas pressuring her, yes? Das vhat I tink. But vhy, I ask myself."

"Vhy, indeed?"

Paul scowled. "Are you making fun of me?"

"Oh, no, dear. At least not intentionally. Please, go on."

He punished by making me wait. I ignored his childish behavior by making faces at myself in the mirror.

"Vell," he finally said, "I tink maybe zees man had money problems, yes?"

"No!"

"Yes, I tink so. I tink maybe he vas in trouble veeth zee mub."

"Zee mub? I mean, the *mub*?"

"Yes. And I tink maybe zee mub vanted to make for him heavy shoes."

I chewed on that for a while. It was almost as tough as overcooked leeber. Eventually, however, even the dimmest of us can see the light if we try hard enough.

"Mob!" I cried, jumping from my faux leather seat. "Organized crime! Is that what you mean?"

"Yes, but of course. Vhat else do you tink?"

"I think we may need to find an interpreter. Correct me if I'm wrong, but it's your belief that Clarence Webber married Zelda to get at her money?"

"Yes, now you are cooking with oil."

I sighed. "That's because your theory has run out of gas. Zelda Root is a lowly policewoman. She's so poor she has to borrow from the church mice."

Paul grinned. "Zat is vhat she vants you to tink. Thelda is a very reech voman."

"Don't be ridiculous, dear. I've known her since she was knee-high to a grasshopper. No, make that knee-high to a gnat. She's an orphan like me, but when her parents died they left bupkis. You see, Robert Root was a dreamer and a gambler. He was always investing in companies that went nowhere, like the Mars Mining Corporation or the Trans-Syria-Israel Railway. He even played around in the stock market. I remember, because everyone in Hernia laughed when he bought oodles of shares in this silly new company called Microsoft—oh, my stars! Why, that sneaky Zelda! She even made me pay when she took me out for my birthday."

"You see?" Paul crowed triumphantly. "Zat is vhat zees Clarence Vebber vas after."

I plopped the blond tresses back over the remnants of my brown bun. Then I arranged my features in a passable smile.

"What about you, dear? How do I know you weren't after more than just a green card?"

"Oot!" Paul leaped to his feet, punching the air wildly with the scissors. "Get oot of my shop zees minute!"

If the man had been on top of Everest, the ozone would have been in serious trouble. As it was, my poor schnozz came dangerously close to undergoing yet another alteration. I did what the little man asked, and skedaddled.

It was only a hop, skip, and a jump from the House of Hair over to the home of Agnes Schlabach, the woman with thirty-two cats, but I knew better than to visit her in my new persona, even given her so-called senior moments. Let's face it, although my nose had been reshaped, it was hardly smaller. And wearing a wig and a bright blue dress did not disguise the fact that I'm five feet ten inches tall. As for my voice, there's only so much one can do with a cross between Julia Child and nails on a chalkboard. Perhaps if I adopted an accent, like Rue Paul. But which accent?

No, it was much easier, and no doubt much wiser, to beat around the bush. To approach the problem sideways. The bush I decided to circumvent belonged to Virginia Chalk, one of Agnes's next-door neighbors. I'd seen Virginia's name on the mailbox when I'd been to see Agnes the first time, and I was filled with both admiration and horror. I, for one, would not advertise my marital status at the curbside if I lived in a city, even one the size of Bedford. The world is filled with kooks, some of them very dangerous, and some of them looking specifically for single women. Still, it was nice to see that Miss Chalk did not mind if the world knew she was unattached.

She didn't seem to mind unexpected visitors either. "Come in," she said without any sort of preamble. "You're a welcome interruption."

"I am?"

"Certainly. Writer's block," she said, tapping her head. "It's time I came down out of my creative clouds. When I get back, the scene will either fall into place, or it won't. If it doesn't, it wasn't meant to be."

I stared at my elegant surroundings. "You're a writer?"

Virginia Chalk had a cheery, infectious laugh. "I take it you've never heard of me. That's funny, because most visitors—at least in recent years—tend to be fans."

"Well, I saw your name on the mailbox a couple of days ago. Does that count?"

She laughed again. "Please, have a seat." She pointed to a shellback chair upholstered in pale yellow silk. Without waiting for me, she sat on a similar chair across the room.

I sat. "You know, dear, it's awfully brave of you to

have your name out there on the box. Doesn't that make you just a wee bit nervous?"

"Not with Tinkerbell around."

"Who?"

"Just a minute." She got up, went to the back door, and whistled. A second later it sounded like the Hernia High football team was headed my way. I threw my arms over my head and cowered.

Virginia laughed yet again. "This is Tink. She won't bother you, unless she perceives you as a threat to me. She would have broken down the door if she needed to."

I stole a peek at the largest dog I'd ever seen. With the right traces, you could hitch it to an Amish buggy, and finding a saddle for it would be no problem.

"You sure she doesn't bite?" The beast was panting like a satiated husband, yet slobbering like a teething baby. Perhaps she saw the word "snack" written across my forehead.

"Not unless I give the order."

"You're kidding, right?"

"Not in the least. Tinkerbell is half Doberman, half Great Dane. She's very protective of me—does exactly what I tell her."

"Would you please tell her to go back outside?"

"Sure thing." Virginia herded the monster to the back door and returned to her seat. "Now, where were we?" she asked brightly. "Ah yes. About my name on the mailbox. I have to, you know? There are two other 'V' Chalks living on this street; a Virgil and a Vance. Neither of them are related, by the way."

"So I guess we have to chalk that up to coincidence," I said wryly.

Virginia Chalk chortled. "So what can I do for you, Miss—uh, I don't believe I ever got your name."

I fished in my purse for a notepad and pen. "My name

is Portulacca Miller. I'm a stringer for the *Somerset Daily*."

"Oh, really? I've never heard of your paper, and I used to live in Somerset."

In for a penny, in for a pound—of guilt, that is. "Well, that's because we're a brand-new paper. This is my first assignment, you know." I sniffed the air conspiratorially. "Anyway, I heard that next door there might be a human-interest story about cats."

"Cats?" She sighed. "I was hoping you weren't one of those petition ladies. Usually you come in pairs."

"I beg your pardon?"

She stood. "We really have nothing further to talk about, Ms. Miller. I've told your group that what Agnes does in the privacy of her own home—or even in the privacy of her yard for that matter—is her own business. I know that some of you think you have the animals' welfare in mind, but like I've told them all a million times"—she paused dramatically—"read my lips. Agnes does *not* mistreat her cats. They have food and fresh water at all times, and she cleans their litter boxes daily."

I remained seated. That way if lightning struck me, I wouldn't have so far to fall. And while it's true, I do have the gift of gab, it was going to take some fancy and creative tongue-work to salvage this conversation.

"I'm not talking about *real* cats," I purred. "I'm talking about *Cats*, the Andrew Lloyd Webber musical. I know it left Broadway a year or two ago, but I'm taking a survey. Do you think there should be a revival?"

Virginia appeared startled by my question. "You're serious?"

I smiled pleasantly. "Well, Mr. Webber has to base these decisions on something."

"In that case, the answer is no."

I pretended to jot down her answer. What I really did was write Virginia's age—not that I knew, mind you, but she looked to be about fifty-five. She was a very attractive woman with large hazel eyes and an abundance of shoulder-length auburn hair, accentuated by a single streak of gray.

"I see," I said. I flashed her another warm smile. "Any idea how your neighbor—uh, Agnes, isn't it—might feel about a revival of the musical?"

Virginia slipped back into the shell chair. "Agnes will be thrilled to know it's even being considered. She saw it over one hundred times."

"Get out!"

"Well, they weren't all on Broadway. She saw it in Philly at least six times. And Pittsburgh—well, I thought she was going to wear out the highway between here and there."

"Of course she took her husband with her, right? I mean, I can't imagine she'd drive all the way to Philly by herself."

The large hazel eyes regarded me with surprise. "You knew she was married?"

I nodded. "I like to do a background check on my subjects first."

"Is that so? I thought you said this was your first assignment."

"Well, it is, for *this* paper." I pretended to consult some doodles on my pad. "I believe she was married to a Clarence Webber. Am I right?"

"Yes, and it's a shame, if you ask me."

"His death must have been quite a shock for her."

She pushed a lock of hair away from her left eye. "I'm not talking about his death. I meant it was a shame she fell for his brand of malarkey."

"Do tell!"

"Hey," she said, suddenly warming to me, "care for some lunch? I was just about to make myself a bite anyway. How about salami sandwiches and beer? We can dish over that."

I was ravenous, not having eaten a proper breakfast. Gabe's not into bacon and eggs. In fact, he doesn't even keep cereal on hand. While I am fond of bagels and cream cheese (I pass on the lox), I'd grown tired of them lately. Breakfast this morning had been pumpernickel toast and strawberry preserves.

"A salami sandwich would hit the spot." I screwed up the courage to say the four words forbidden in the Rosen house. "White bread and mayo?"

"If you like."

"And you wouldn't happen to have a nice slice of ripe tomato to throw on that, would you?"

"As a matter of fact, I have. You want that beer in a glass?"

I sighed. "I'm afraid I don't drink."

"No problem," she said cheerfully. "Will diet cola do?"

"Sounds wonderful."

She excused herself to prepare our repast, and I set about snooping. This bit of nosiness had nothing to do with Clarence Webber's death, but everything to do with my personality. I just adore learning the details of how other people lead their lives.

For instance, without leaving the yellow shell chair—thanks to an extraordinarily pliable neck—I was able to learn the following about Virginia Chalk. She loved horses as well as dogs (which might explain the horse-size dog), her favorite colors were yellow and rose, she subscribed to *Romantic Times*, *The Ladies' Home Journal*, and *The Anglican Digest*, and in addition to beer and salami sandwiches, she was fond of Hershey's Nuggets. The little gold wrappers were everywhere.

When Virginia returned bearing two wicker trays with our food, it was as if she'd never left the room. In fact, she began talking while still in the kitchen, so I missed the first half of her statement. The second half sounded like "he was a crook."

"I beg your pardon, dear?" I said.

She handed me my tray. "I said, I knew from the moment I met him that he was a crook. I mean, why else would a young, good-looking man like that try and charm his way into—well, let's just say Agnes Schlabach is a bit eccentric."

"The thirty-two cats?"

She settled back in her own shell before answering. "There *were* thirty-two, but one got out, and was never found."

I gasped. "You don't think it was Tink, do you?"

"No, but Agnes does. We were friends before that. I mean, really good friends."

I took a bite of my sandwich. The mayo was exquisite.

"But you seem so different."

Virginia shrugged. "Like I said, I'm a writer. I work alone all day, but I like to come up for air every now and then, and Agnes was always there for me to talk to. I really miss her."

"How long has it been? I mean, since the—uh, missing cat incident?"

She took a swig of her beer. "That just happened last Tuesday."

I took a swig of my diet cola to celebrate that good news. "So that means you were still friends with Agnes when she married this crook."

Virginia slammed the beer bottle down on her lap tray, nearly upsetting it. "I tried to stop that marriage, but Agnes wouldn't listen. Even after I told her what I knew."

"And what was that?" I asked breathlessly.

27

"Clarence Webber came on to me first."

"Get out of town!"

The hazel eyes seemed to have crystallized. The woman was definitely serious.

"He appeared one day at the front door—just like you—only he pretended to be a fan. You might think it strange, Portulacca—may I call you Port?"

"By all means, dear. Please, continue."

"Like I said, you might think it strange that a writer—especially one of my renown—would tolerate fans just dropping in, but the truth is most of us have humongous egos. Why else would we expect people to pay us for our thoughts and words? At any rate, I invited him in for a brief chat—Tink was right in the room, by the way—and he immediately started putting the moves on me."

I jiggled pinkies in both ears to make sure they were in proper working order. I wasn't about to miss a word.

"What kind of moves, dear?"

"Well, not physical—not at first. But he was blatantly flirtatious. I had the most beautiful eyes, he said. My hair was like burnished copper—yeech. I wanted to retch. I tried to hustle him out the door, but he was relentless with the come-ons. Finally, just to shut him up, I agreed to go on a date."

I shuddered. "And then what? Where did you go?"

"Oh, just out to eat, and then to a movie. Some silly date movie—nothing you'd expect a man to suggest, unless he wanted to worm his way into your heart."

"And?"

"Of course he hadn't! But apparently he thought he had. We went out for coffee afterward and he started asking personal questions. The most personal questions you can imagine." She lowered her voice to a whisper. "Financial questions."

I clapped my hands to my cheeks, a la Paul Rue. Asking financial questions was unconscionable. Prude that I am, I would rather give my body away than my bank balance. I'm sure most Americans would agree.

"You didn't tell him anything, did you?"

"No, but that didn't stop the questions. How much did I get as an advance? How much could I expect in royalties? Then, when he couldn't get any answers out of me, he started asking questions about Agnes."

"What kind of questions?" I took a large bite of my sandwich. Both it and the conversation were getting juicy.

"Basically the same kind of questions. Financial ones. Said he'd heard rumors that Agnes was an heiress of some sort. Wanted to know if it was true."

"Which of course, it isn't," I said, taking care not to display the masticated mayo mix.

"Oh, but she is."

My mouth fell open. I swallowed hastily when I saw the look on Virginia's face.

"What kind of heiress?"

"Steel."

"The metal?"

Virginia nodded. "The Schlabachs were farmers locally. Not especially well off, but not hurting either. Agnes's mother, however, was from Pittsburgh. *Her* father was one of the original steel barons. As strange as it might seem, Agnes Schlabach is probably the richest woman in Bedford County."

And here I thought that distinction belonged to me. "Are you sure?" I wailed. "She doesn't look rich to me."

"Exactly. That's the way the old money likes it."

I chewed on that, and my sandwich, for a good long while. "I suppose," I finally said, "that Clarence Webber's sole interest in Agnes was her money."

"Bingo. I told Agnes that, but of course she wouldn't listen. This might surprise you, Port, but some women grow blinders when they think they're falling in love."

"How silly of them," I said, and moistened a finger that I then used to pick crumbs off my lap.

"Well, it happens. Believe me, I know. That's how I make my living."

"Falling in love?"

She laughed. "I wish. No, I write historical romances."

"You don't say! You mean those bodice-rippers I see on the rack at Wal-Mart?"

"*Please*, Portulacca, we don't like to call them that. That's a pejorative term. Most of them are very well written. Just because they appeal to a wide audience doesn't mean we aim for the lowest common denominator. In fact, my latest, *The Pict's Pecs*—set in medieval Scotland—won three literary awards. Yet, unlike most literary novels, it was a *New York Times* bestseller." She beamed. "I don't mind telling you it sold over a million copies."

I could feel my eyes bulge. I've never been very good at math, but it was beginning to sound like I was the *third* richest woman in Bedford County.

"Just what is your royalty rate?"

"Eight percent," she said guardedly.

They say write what you know. I tried to imagine a romance novel set amongst the conservative Mennonites I knew, even the Amish. It wouldn't be a bodice-ripper, that was for sure. More like a cape-grabber. And when I got down to writing that essential nitty-gritty scene, I'd have to draw on a well of experience so shallow you couldn't dip a braid into it. After all, Aaron Miller was not exactly Casanova. Still, isn't that what the imagination is for? To create fantasy? And for the right sum, I can be mighty creative.

"What was your advance?" I asked innocently.

Virginia was kind enough to allow me to finish my sandwich before escorting me to the door.

On my way back to Hernia I stopped off at the church with thirty-two names. I was just pulling into the gravel parking lot when the significance of the number thirty-two struck me. That was the same number of cats Agnes Schlabach owned. Surely it was just a coincidence. After all, the average human has thirty-two permanent teeth, and there couldn't possibly be a connection between chompers, cats, and church.

I knew there would be no fooling Reverend Nixon with Susannah's disguise, so I whipped off the wig at the last moment. As usual, I found the good preacher inside the tiny church. This time he was on his hands and knees scrubbing the floor. As he worked he was whistling a tune familiar to me as a Mennonite: "Shall We Gather at the River." As a way of gently breaking the news that I was still alive, I whistled along with him.

For the first couple of bars of our duet he didn't seem to notice. It wasn't until we got to the refrain, and my whistle ran dry (causing me to come in late) that he looked up. The poor man's face turned to chalk as he gave a strangled cry. Then, before I could reach him, he slumped to the floor, knocking over the bucket of Murphy's Oil Soap and water.

I read somewhere that folks who have fainted should have their heads elevated. Or perhaps it was their feet. Since the Reverend was lying facedown in a pool of soapy water, I didn't think it would hurt to start with his head. I dragged him to a dry spot about ten feet away and propped his narrow head on a pile of hymnals. I briefly considered pinching his nostrils together and breathing into his mouth.

Fortunately, before I could commit to such an intimate gesture, the good Reverend came to. However, upon seeing my comely mug so close to his, he fainted again. I gently slapped his gaunt cheeks, and managed to revive him. Alas, a slightly longer glance at me, and he was out once more.

I waited patiently until he came around the third time. "It really is me," I blurted. "Magdalena Yoder. Big as life and twice as ugly."

His eyes flickered but finally remained open. "Where am I? Heaven?"

"I don't think so, dear. Not that I wouldn't be there to greet you, mind you—assuming, of course, my arrival date preceded yours."

"Hell?" He was in danger of fainting again.

"You're not listening, dear. I said my name was *Magdalena Yoder.* I'm certainly not in Hell. I'm not dead, and neither are you."

He struggled to a sitting position. "But it was in the papers. It was even on television."

"They said I was dead?"

"Not exactly. But they said you were missing. I knew you were working on the Webber case, as of course did Chief Stoltzfus, and, well—it just kind of got around that you had—uh—"

"Kicked the proverbial bucket?"

He nodded. "There were reporters here from all over the county. Law-enforcement personnel too. Someone even brought in a psychic, which, frankly, I think is a sin."

"It wasn't that Diana Lefcourt, was it?" I cried, although I was relishing every word that spilled from Richard Nixon's wafer-thin lips.

"Yes, that was her name. She dressed even stranger than your sister, if you don't mind my saying so. And half the time she didn't speak in English."

"That's because she thinks she's the queen of Egypt."

"But Egypt doesn't have a queen."

"You're quite right, dear, but Diana thinks she's the wife of Pharaoh Tutankhamen. She calls herself Ankhesenamen."

"She really believes that?"

"I think so. The woman is as nutty as a pecan pie. Anyway, what did she say about me?"

He frowned. "She claimed to have talked to you 'on the other side.' Said you told her that you had drowned in Miller's Pond. That nice Jewish doctor who lives there now brought someone in to drag the pond. Of course, they didn't find you. However, they did find a four-foot channel catfish. Who knew they could get so big? I don't suppose you could talk that doctor into letting me fish—" He caught himself. "Magdalena, as a Christian, I hope you don't believe in that stuff. The Bible quite clearly warns us about consulting with witches and the like."

I waved a hand dismissively. I hold no truck with psychics, if only because the concept of a working psychic is an oxymoron. Anybody who could really see into the future—or the past, for that matter—wouldn't have to work for twenty-five dollars a reading. Now, fortune cookies are another matter. Who's to say that the Good

Lord doesn't speak to us through those little slips of paper?

"I want to hear more about my supposed death. How did folks react?"

"Well, that doctor friend of yours was pretty broken up. Your sister too. In fact, it was her that asked me to lead the Lord's Prayer at the community memorial service."

"There was a *memorial* service?"

"Well, it didn't start out that way. It started out as a community prayer service to pray for your safe return. Somehow it ended up as a series of tributes to your life and contributions to the community. We all gathered at the picnic shelter up on Stucky Ridge."

"Move over," I said.

I made him scoot so I had plenty of room to spread out as I laid my horsy head on the heap of hymnals. Neither Gabe nor Susannah had said anything about a memorial service. No doubt they thought my head was far too big already.

"Was it well attended?" I asked.

He nodded. "Virtually everyone in Hernia, and it seemed like half the people in Bedford. That's why they held it outdoors."

"Details!" I cried.

He rubbed his eyes, as if still not quite believing I was a flesh-and-blood woman. "Well, your Reverend Schrock preached the sermon. His wife sang."

"Thank heavens I missed that! Was she off-key?"

"Every note. Oh, and the Hernia High band played 'Amazing Grace.' "

"On key?"

"A few of them. Anyway, then members of the community stood up and delivered short eulogies—well, most of them were short. Melvin Stoltzfus—may the Lord forgive me for what I am about to say—droned on interminably."

"That figures. He didn't launch into one of his political speeches, did he?"

"Oh, no. It was all about what a wonderful woman you were—I mean, *are*—and how much he was going to miss you. Toward the end he was even crying."

"He *was*?"

"Magdalena, practically everyone there shed a tear at one time or another. I, myself, confess to having been misty-eyed. Especially during the mayor's speech."

I bobbed to a sitting position. "Her Honor spoke at my memorial?"

"Hers was the final eulogy. She praised you for being such a solid citizen, for always keeping the folks of Hernia foremost in your mind, heart, and deeds. You would not be just another highway statistic, she said. You would never be forgotten. She even hinted that someday there might be a statue of you erected in Founder's Park."

"Get out of town!" I am ashamed to say it, but those past few minutes with Reverend Nixon in the church with thirty-two names had been the happiest of my life. The real Heaven, with its slippery gold streets and mollusk-secreted gates, couldn't possibly have been any better—except, of course, for the presence of the dear Lord. But He is, after all, everywhere, isn't He? I mean, a statue of moi in Founder's Park? How much better could it possibly be?

"A life-size bronze statue," Reverend Nixon said.

I thought my heart would burst with joy. "I don't even care if pigeons poop on me!" I cried. "Do you know what pose they'd like? When do they want to get started?"

Reverend Nixon reached for my nearest hand. His fingers felt like unbuttered toast.

"Magdalena, look at me," he said gently.

"I am looking at you."

"Now look around you. Where are we?"

"In your tiny little church. So, what's your point?"

"We're not dead, are we?"

"That's right. That's what I kept telling you over and over—" My heart sank. If I hadn't been sitting, it would have ended up somewhere near my skinny ankles. "There isn't going to be any statue, is there?"

"I'm afraid not. There will, however, be a great deal of rejoicing."

"You really think so?"

"I'm positive."

I hauled my bony carcass off the floor. "Wow! You know, Reverend, I really enjoyed talking to you."

He unfolded his even bonier frame and, in a series of jerky moves, managed to hoist himself to a standing position. He pointed to the nearest bench. I sat as bid, and after another series of awkward maneuvers he joined me. It was like watching a life-size marionette.

"What brought you back to see me?" he asked without further ado.

"It's about Clarence Webber, of course."

"What about him?"

"Well, I've begun to see a pattern in the women he was involved with."

"What sort of pattern?"

"For one thing, two of the women were surprisingly wealthy. I mean, I never knew Zelda Root had money. And I wouldn't have guessed that about Agnes Schlabach. Emma Kauffman is, of course, another story. For what she charges for those paintings—well, I was thinking of going to art school. Now the fourth, Dorcas Yutzy, appears to be just an underpaid teacher, but I wouldn't be surprised to discover that she too was sitting on some sort of golden egg."

"Is that the only similarity you've noticed between those four?"

"Funny you should ask, Reverend, because it's not. I don't mean to sound judgmental, but all four of them are what my sister, Susannah, would call DOMs."

"DOMs?

"Desperate old maids. Only thing is, now none of them are old maids. Not since they married that scoundrel Clarence."

"I see. Magdalena, you've obviously been giving this a great deal of thought. How honest have you been with yourself?"

"What do you mean?"

Reverend Nixon looked away from me to a plain wooden cross that hung on the wall behind the pulpit. The interior of the little cinder-block church was as dark and gloomy as any dungeon, but a thin strip of light had somehow managed to penetrate and was illuminating the left edge of the cross.

"Magdalena," he said softly, "you're a very wealthy woman, are you not? Please be honest with me."

"Well, I couldn't buy and sell Donald Trump, but I can afford brand names at the grocery store."

"I asked you to be honest."

"Okay, so I could afford English brand names flown in special from London if I wanted. But what has that to do with Clarence Webber?"

"Are you married, Magdalena?"

"Of course not. You know the answer to—hey! Just what is that supposed to mean? Do you think I'm desperate?"

"I don't," he said quickly. "But do you think Clarence might have thought that?"

"Well, if he did, then he was a fool." We Mennonites, incidentally, do not use the word "fool" lightly. "I have a boyfriend, you know."

"I know that now. But did Clarence? Magdalena, tell me how you met him."

I huffed with irritation. "Well, if you must know, it was when I sold my BMW through an ad in the paper."

"What were your first impressions?"

I tried to re-create the dead man's face in my mind. His living face, mind you.

"He was okay-looking, I guess. *If* you like the blond Adonis type, which I assure you I don't."

"How did Clarence seem?"

"Well," I said grudgingly, "he was charming in that oozing sort of playboy way. Not that I hang around a lot of playboys, you understand. But I've had a few stay at my inn."

"Were you attracted to him?"

"Absolutely not! I already have a boyfriend, like I told you."

"I'm not suggesting you acted on your desires, Magdalena. I merely wanted to know if you were tempted. And," he added quickly, "being tempted is a very normal thing. It is not a sin. Even Jesus was tempted."

"Stop it!" I shouted, placing both hands over my ears. "I don't want to hear any more of this nonsense."

"Very well," Reverend Nixon said. "I think you have your answers."

28

I left the church with thirty-two names in a snit. What a silly notion that I, a respected businesswoman, leader in my community, and pillar in my church, could possibly fall for a con man like Clarence. That was just absurd. Preposterous.

Yes, the man had charisma, but so did our recent President, and you didn't see me throwing myself at him when he stayed at my inn. And anyway, I certainly wasn't desperate. I'd been married, for Pete's sake, if not in name, then in deed. Besides, like I said, there was Gabriel Rosen. Do you think the other ladies had a handsome Jewish doctor waiting in the wings? Of course not.

Okay, so Clarence Webber had asked me out to dinner the night I sold him the car. Big deal! It was just dinner at the Coach Room Restaurant on South Richard Street. It didn't mean anything. The only reason I didn't tell Gabe was because I knew he would be jealous, and I didn't want to hurt him.

Neither can I help it that Clarence asked me out to dinner the following evening. I had to accept. It was either that or hurt his feelings, because, you see, I'd learned the night before that Clarence Webber was an extraordinarily sensitive person. And when that second evening, in the main dining room of the famous Jean Bonnet Tavern, he leaned across the table and kissed me, how was I *supposed* to react? Was I supposed to scream and slap him? I think not. Although it's really none of your business, I will share with you that when he drove me home afterward, and tried to kiss me again, I turned and made him kiss my cheek.

Now that I've come clean, it's imperative that you believe me when I say I was *not* jealous when I saw him the next afternoon, riding around Bedford in my red BMW with a bleached-blond floozy at his side. For all I knew, the bimbo could have been his sister. The fact that I followed them for several blocks is not germane to this issue either. I was merely waxing nostalgic over the car, savoring that one last glimpse.

I am a sensible, God-fearing woman with both enormous feet planted squarely on the ground. I simply do not fall for the Clarence Webber type. However, Reverend Nixon was another story. Don't get me wrong. I wasn't at all attracted to the latter's lanky frame, not in the least. But, just to show you how honest I am, I will confess to being attracted to his title. Reverend and Mrs. Richard Nixon, now *that* had a nice ring to it.

Here in Bedford County, being a preacher's wife counts for something. As a preacher's wife I could give that snooty Lodema Schrock a run for her hymnals. Maybe Beechy Grove Mennonite Church was ten times larger than Reverend Nixon's cinder-block structure, and had a proper congregation, but the Mennonite church didn't have thirty-two words in its name. Sure, a church with an unwieldy moniker might be seen as a turn-off by some, but with the right woman at the good Reverend's side, it could be turned into an asset.

I had no doubt that with my tutelage, Richard Nixon could be turned into the next Robert Schuller. Like the Crystal Cathedral, the church with thirty-two names could become nationally famous. Of course it would have to be expanded a good deal, maybe even turned into a complex containing an Amish theme park. Amishworld, we'd call it. We could offer buggy rides, taffy pulls, barn raisings, quilting parties—

"You stupid idiot!"

My reverie was ended by the owner of the car next to me. My thoughts had managed to see me all the way into downtown Bedford. It was rush hour (and believe me, they have one) and I had inadvertently drifted halfway into the neighboring lane.

"Sorry!" I shouted, and pulled into the nearest available parking space.

It was an eight-minute walk from my car to the Bedford County Courthouse. Completed in 1829, it is the oldest courthouse in Pennsylvania still in use for judicial purposes. At any rate, it was five on the button when I arrived, and apparently not a good time to do business.

"We're closed," the clerk said crisply over her shoulder. Her voice was oddly familiar. "We've all gone home for the day."

"No, you haven't; you're right there."

"We're still closed," she said, without even looking at me. "Come back tomorrow morning at nine."

"All I want is to look up somebody's death certificate on your computer. It will only take a minute."

"You're not going to make me call security, are you?"

"Go ahead and call them, dear." I whipped off the blond wig, which I'd worn into town. "Call the newspapers too. Because they're going to have a field day when they learn you refused service to a dead woman."

The stubborn clerk turned, and when she did, her mouth opened like the unsecured tailgate of a truck. My mouth, which was a good deal smaller, opened wide as well.

"Magdalena!" she gasped. "It can't be!"

"Thelma? Thelma Rensberger?"

The clerk—and it was indeed Thelma—closed her mouth. Fortunately she closed her eyes as well, because she'd started to faint. It would be awful to have to see the floor rise up to meet one's face, wouldn't it?

I still had a sore rib, but somehow I managed to vault over the counter and catch Thelma Rensberger by the armpits before she beaned herself on historic marble. I laid her gently down the rest of the way.

She came to almost immediately. "It is you!"

"As big as life, and twice as ugly. Especially now that my nose seems to be headed off in two directions."

Thelma struggled to her feet, gave me the once-over, and threw herself into my arms. "I can't believe it's really you!"

"Seeing is believing, dear. It's not necessary to squeeze me like a lemon over a pitcher of iced tea."

"Same old Magdalena," Thelma said happily. She was grinning like the Cheshire cat.

"Same old Thelma," I said.

Indeed, Thelma was a childhood friend, who didn't seem to have aged a day since I last saw her twenty-some years ago, waving to me through the window of a Trailways bus bound for the Big Apple. The woman was under the illusion that she was the next Beverly Sills. If the opera didn't pan out, at least she would wow them in Broadway musicals. I hadn't heard from her since.

"Everyone thinks you're dead," Thelma said. She tried to pinch my arm, but I slapped her hand away.

"And I was under the impression that you were living in New York. Why didn't you write to me?"

Thelma blushed. "It was all so overwhelming. Do you

know they charge thousands of dollars' rent for a one-bedroom apartment in Manhattan?"

I did some quick mental arithmetic. "That's really not too bad for a year's accommodations, dear."

"Not a year, Magdalena. A *month*."

"Get out of town!"

"That's exactly what I did. I moved to New Jersey and got a job teaching music in an elementary school. Then I got married and had three kids. The kids are grown and scattered now, and Carl died last year. A couple of months ago I decided I really missed Pennsylvania, so I put the house on the market. Do you know it sold the next day? Anyway, I moved back here last month and right away started looking for a job. I'm really lucky there was this opening. It has nothing to do with music, of course, but it keeps me occupied."

"You could have called me," I said accusingly.

She hung her mousy brown head. "I know. It's just that it's sort of embarrassing for me to have come back to Bedford County without having fulfilled my dreams. Especially since I made such a big deal of it when I left. You'd think I'd know better, though. Almost every day someone I know from the past comes in, and I have to explain all over again. Gee, I may as well just take an ad out in the paper."

"Well, welcome back."

"You too. All everyone's been talking about is your death. I kept hoping they had the wrong Magdalena. I was pretty sure of it, in fact, when I heard you'd been married."

"Thanks a lot!"

"Oh, don't get me wrong. I didn't mean that you couldn't find a husband. It's just that you were always—well, sort of picky."

"And plucky." The heavy front doors to the court-house clanged shut, and I could hear the security guard rattling her keys. "Look dear, why don't we do lunch soon? Then we can take our time yapping. In the meantime, there is something I really need to find out now."

She sighed. "Yes, I did smoke pot. But I didn't inhale. Magdalena, you have to believe me. Everyone in New Jersey was doing it back then."

"I don't care about that! I came here on a quest, and that's to look up Clarence Webber's death certificate."

She stared at me. "How odd you should say that."

"Why is that?"

"Because I had to process his will. It was my second day here on the job, and my first solo assignment. I guess it kinda stuck in my mind."

I had hoped to find a copy of his death certificate, and if luck was really on my side, a copy of his birth certificate as well. You see, I had a nagging suspicion that Clarence Webber was somehow connected to those sleazy Benedicts down in Cumberland. How else could he get away with all those illegal marriages? At any rate, I certainly had not anticipated the opportunity to scrutinize his will.

"You'll let me look at his will?"

"It's in probate," she said. "Anyone can look at it. Are you thinking of contesting?"

"Moi? Why would I do that?"

"Why else would you want to see it?"

I lowered my voice to a whisper, even though the constant clanging of doors and clinking of keys made eavesdropping next to impossible. Still, there's a lot of truth to that adage about the walls having ears. Around here they tend to have eyes as well. When they start speaking, I'm packing up my Samsonite and moving to New York City. I can afford three thousand bucks for a nice apartment.

"Look dear, I'm surprised it didn't come up in one of the dozens of conversations you must have had about me during my recent demise. But you see, I've been investigating Clarence Webber's death."

"Oh yeah, I remember now. Someone did say something about you playing second fiddle to that incompetent police chief down there in Hernia."

"Second fiddle, my eye! I'm first violin!" I took several deep breaths to calm myself. "So how about it, dear? When can I see the will?"

She glanced at the guard who was approaching us. "Not now. You have to wait until morning. Can you be here at nine?"

"Nine's fine, but now would be ever so much better." I gave her my best sad puppy-dog face, which is quite a feat considering I look a lot more like Trigger than Rover.

She squirmed. "I can't. I might lose my job. Is there anything specific you want to know? I remember a few of the details."

"Like what? Spill it all."

"Well, for starters, Mr. Webber left his entire estate to his parents."

"He did?" Who knew that snakes kept track of their families?

"Yeah. The funny thing is, though, their name isn't Webber."

"What is it?"

"Some kind of eggs. That's what it made me think of. But I forget the word right now."

"You mean like boiled or scrambled?"

"No, something fancier."

"Poached? His real name was Clarence Poached?"

"No—Benedict! That's what it is. Arnold and Bonita Benedict."

"Eureka!" I yelled as the last piece of the puzzle fell into place.

29

My yell brought the security guard running. Fortunately, or unfortunately, depending on one's point of view, the lady in uniform was someone I knew: Louise Tidweiller, who lives down the road from me in Hernia. When Louise saw my resurrected face she stooped to kiss the marble. But she wasn't hurt, I'm sure. While Thelma revived Louise, I slipped out the still unlocked east door.

Now, I'm a firm believer in following the rules of this great country. Breaking the law is a sin. On the other hand, we are all sinners, are we not? The Bible clearly says so. But since I don't dance, drink, smoke, or cheat on a spouse—and I've never committed murder—I find myself in need of some small transgression so as not to disprove the Good Book. Therefore, I have chosen speeding as my sin of choice.

I pressed the pedal to the metal, and while Gabe's car was no BMW, I made record time traversing the distance from Bedford to Hernia. And since this small sin was in the pursuit of justice, my guardian angels kept Smoky the Bear out of my way. I saw neither hide nor hair of the men with sirens, and when I reached Dorcas Yutzy's tiny house the predominant sound was the screech of my tires.

Despite my noisy arrival, I had to ring the bell five times before Dorcas answered. "Hi there," she said, when she finally opened the door. "I was hoping you'd come by."

It was my turn to register shock. "Aren't you going to faint?"

She giggled. "Should I?"

"I'm dead, dear. That deserves at least a semi-swoon."

"But you're not dead."

"Well, I'm supposed to be. Don't tell me you didn't know. Reverend Nixon said virtually everyone in Hernia was at my memorial service."

"Oh, I was there, of course. But you see, Magdalena, Mary Mast just called to tell me that Lodema Schrock had called and told her the news. That your death had been a mistake."

"Schrock!" I shrieked. "How did Lodema know about me?"

"Reverend Nixon, I think."

So much for the sanctity of the confessional—well, the wooden bench in this case. Richard Nixon was definitely off my list of marital prospects. Having the word Reverend on one's address labels would not be worth the lack of privacy. Without a doubt he'd look in my drawers.

Dorcas must have seen the furrows on my forehead. "We're all glad you're alive and well. At least Mary is."

"I'm sure Lodema is too," I growled. "Who better to pick on than moi, Hernia's resident bigamist?" I slapped my mouth when I realized my faux pas. "Strictly speaking, Aaron was the bigamist, not me, which means you're not really a polygamist." I slapped my mouth again. Sometimes it takes a little more to make it behave.

Dorcas started to shut the door. "Well," she said, "I'm really glad to see for myself that you're really all right. Thanks for coming by."

I slipped a size eleven in the ever-narrowing crack. "Aren't you even going to ask me in?"

"Well, Magdalena, I would, but you see, Mother's already in bed and—"

I sniffed the air. "Something smells delicious."

Dorcas beamed. "That's just supper."

"What are you having?"

"Pot roast with mashed potatoes and gravy. And green beans cooked with bacon. Oh, and for dessert there's strawberry shortcake with genuine whipped cream."

"I don't suppose you'd have enough for a guest?" Gabe's idea of fine cuisine was splashing Worcestershire sauce over Lean Cuisine.

Dorcas nodded. "Come in," she said, but she didn't sound at all happy.

"You're going to what?" Gabe was clearly an unhappy babe.

"She asked me. I can't very well hurt her feelings."

I could practically feel his pheromones through the phone. "But then you'll come straight home, right?"

"Not exactly."

"Magdalena, what the hell is going on?"

"I have a theory—about who killed Clarence Webber."

"Dorcas Yutzy?"

"Look dear, I'm not at liberty to talk now." I held my hand loosely over the transmitting end of the receiver. "Just water will be fine," I called.

"What was that?"

"Drink orders," I said. "Did you know Dorcas Yutzy drinks wine?"

"No, I didn't, but—"

"Her mother drinks beer, if you can believe that. Funny thing though, I never see her mother around. Maybe it's all that beer. She's in bed right now."

He sighed. "Magdalena, what time *can* I expect you home?"

Home! There was that H word again, and what a lovely word it was when emanating from Dr. Rosen's luscious lips. Alas and alack, to share a home with Gabe wasn't within the realm of possibility. I could never give up my belief that Jesus was the Messiah and Gabe— well, one can't very well browbeat another person into becoming a Christian, can one? Although it's been done before, forced conversions seem to me to be the antithesis of Christ's message. Besides, even if I came to accept his continued status as a Jew, what about my commitment to poor little Alison Miller? It had been a long day.

"I'll be there when I get there," I said patiently. "It won't be days this time, I promise."

Gabe hung up without another word.

"So what did he say?" Dorcas Yutzy asked. Despite her large size she'd managed to materialize out of nowhere wielding a large wooden spoon.

"He said to tell you hello."

Dorcas lit up like a jack-o'-lantern with two candles. "Oh really?"

I felt bad about my little fib. Perhaps speeding wasn't my only sin after all.

"Listen, dear," I said, in an effort to both change the subject and get down to business, "I came to ask you a favor."

The lights in Dorcas's pumpkin burned even brighter. "Anything. You know that. We're friends, Magdalena."

"Good, I was hoping you'd say that. Because after supper I need you to ride with me down to Cumberland."

Dorcas gulped. "Tonight?"

"Sure. It's a beautiful evening and—"

"Magdalena, it's supposed to rain."

I chuckled pleasantly. "Well, that's why they make cars with roofs. Come on," I coaxed, "it will be good for you to get out of the house."

"I can't leave Mother alone, Magdalena. Not at night. And there's no time to get a sitter."

"Then we'll take her with us. But I'm afraid she'll have to stay in the car when we get there."

"Uh—we can't take her."

"Why not?"

"Well, for one thing, it would be rude to wake Mother. She had a rough night last night, and she's just now gotten to sleep. Besides, she gets carsick. You don't want that to happen, do you?"

I considered the consequences briefly. It was Gabe's car, after all. And he was a doctor. Weren't they used to a bit of yuck?

"I don't get it," I finally said. "You leave your mother alone all day during the school year, don't you? Why can't you just let her sleep for a few hours?"

The big galoot took a step back. "What's so important about Cumberland?"

"There's something I need to check with the Benedicts. And I need you along for protection."

Dorcas blanched. "Why me?"

"Well, you're big and strong. You teach gym, don't you?"

"Yes, but why not just go to the police?"

"Because I only have a theory. I don't have proof. Besides, seeing you again might jog their memories. At the very least, it will put the fear of God in them." I smiled pleasantly. "I mean that in the nicest way."

Dorcas stared at me through the thick lenses. "I should think seeing you risen from the dead would be enough. Anyway, can't it at least wait until tomorrow?"

"Apparently not. I want to catch them off guard, and thanks to Lodema Schrock's dialing finger, it may already be too late."

Dorcas sighed. "Okay, we'll let Mother sleep while I come with you. But first let's eat."

"It's a deal."

I followed her into the tiny kitchen. The smell of Dorcas Yutzy's pot roast was as seductive as any man. Bottled, it would make an excellent cologne for the Babester.

I had just popped the last cream-slathered berry in my mouth when I felt the thump under my feet. I licked my lips so as not to spray when I spoke.

"That's odd," I said. "It feels like there's someone tapping under your floor." The Yutzy home had linoleum flooring, but the dinette table was centered on a brightly colored area rug. The vibrations were coming from beneath the rug.

Dorcas grinned. "You're a hoot, Magdalena, you know that?"

"Hoot! Hoot!" I flapped my arms, pretending they were wings.

Dorcas stood. "You have such an active imagination. It's only the water pipes." She stretched, literally touching the ceiling. "Come on, we better get going."

"Not without doing the dishes, dear."

"Oh, don't worry about them. They'll still be there when we get back."

I shook my head in wonder. And to think Dorcas's people had once been Mennonites. If I so much as left a coffee mug in the sink, Mama rolled over in her grave. Perhaps that's what I was feeling under my feet: Mama doing a preemptive roll.

"Let's at least rinse them, dear," I suggested. "Once roaches find you—oh my gracious! Did you feel that?"

"Feel what? I didn't feel anything." Dorcas Yutzy had me by the arm and was dragging me to the door.

"It felt like an earthquake under my feet. Well—not that I've felt a real earthquake, mind you—but I can imagine what one feels like, and that was it. Either that or Mama. It certainly wasn't water pipes."

Dorcas pulled harder. "You're so silly, Magdalena."

I dug my heels into the linoleum. Because they're so narrow, they make great crampons.

"Aren't you the least bit curious?" I demanded. "Okay, so maybe it wasn't Mama, or an earthquake, but there's something going on under your house. It wouldn't surprise me if it was termites. They're not capable of pounding, of course, but if there are enough of them, they can make an entire building shimmy and shake. Fall down even. Last summer the Neuhauser family over in Somerset had the floor drop out from underneath them. One minute they were lying in bed, the next thing they knew, they were in the cellar. Broke every one of Lizzie Neuhauser's jars of preserves." The truth is, the Neuhausers weren't just lying in their bed, if you get my drift, but I didn't know Dorcas well enough to tell her that.

Dorcas nearly tugged my arm out of its socket. It was, of course, wasted effort. For a gym teacher she was remarkably out of shape. She panted while I preached.

"Or it could be raccoons living under there. You certainly don't want that. Cheryl Bontrager had a family of raccoons living in her attic, and they stole all her silverware. Didn't even leave her a spoon. Of course Cheryl could stand to lose a little weight—"

"Magdalena," Dorcas begged. "Can't we just go?"

Whatever it was under the house was now tapping out a regular beat. Three long beats, then a short one. The pattern repeated itself. It had to mean something.

I wrenched free of Dorcas's grasp, and flipped back

one end of the rug. I squatted, not quite believing what I saw.

"This is a trapdoor, isn't it?"

Dorcas said nothing.

"I know about the tunnel," I said. "It's legendary. But I didn't think the entrance would be so obvious. However, it looks like you tried to cover it up."

She remained silent, but the tapping grew louder. I could hear the muffled sound of a human voice.

"There's someone down there," I cried. "Did you know you have company?"

"Leave it alone, Magdalena." Dorcas's voice surprised me with its sharpness. "Please, just go home."

"No can do, dear. Hold on," I called to whoever was on the other side of the door, and shouldered the table aside. The door popped open like a jack-in-the-box.

30

Spinach and Parmesan Soufflé

Soufflés made with grits do without the heavy white-sauce base of the more classical versions. The grits take the place of the sauce, giving both body and strength to the eggs, and the result is less rich and fatty and more nutritious. This spinach soufflé can be prepared two or three hours ahead of time, covered, and baked at the last minute.

¾ cup freshly grated
  Parmesan cheese
1 pound fresh
  spinach
3 large eggs,
  separated
1 tablespoon
  unsalted butter
1 recipe Basic

Boiled Grits,
  cooked until very
  creamy
Salt and ground
  white pepper to
  taste
Pinch of cayenne
  pepper
Pinch of freshly
  grated nutmeg

Preheat the oven to 350° F. Generously butter a deep 2-quart baking dish. Sprinkle the bottom and sides with 1 tablespoon of the Parmesan.

Rinse the spinach well. Discard all the stems and coarse leaves. Put the spinach in a pot with just the water that clings to the leaves and wilt over high heat for 3 to 4 minutes. Drain, rinse under cold water, and drain again. Press the water out of the spinach with your hands and coarsely chop.

Put the spinach, egg yolks, and butter in a food processor and run until mixed well but not puréed.

Combine the spinach mixture with the remaining Parmesan. Stir in the grits and season to taste with salt and white pepper, cayenne, and nutmeg. Whip the egg whites until soft peaks form and fold them into the mixture. Transfer the batter to the prepared baking dish and bake about 30 minutes. The soufflé should be nicely puffed with a gentle brown crust on top.

SERVES 6

Souffle Plus

For a memorable first course or a light luncheon entrée, add a bit of any of the following to the soufflé base. Then transfer to individual buttered ramekins for baking.

Back-fin crab
Diced cooked lobster
Finely shredded
 country ham
Chopped cooked
 asparagus

Crumbled Roquefort
Diced sautéed
 chicken livers

31

I fell back, hitting Dorcas's knees with my head. While I may be a numskull, mine is not a numb skull. Dorcas and I both moaned with pain.

Meanwhile the jack was struggling to get out of the box. "Help me," it said.

I jerked to a sitting position and stared at the jack. Rachel Blank stared back.

She'd obviously been having a bad day. Her normally impeccable do looked like an abandoned chicken's nest. Her mascara was running in black rivulets down her face. A strip of duct tape hung from one corner of her mouth.

"Help me," she croaked. "Dorcas Yutzy is a lunatic."

"I am not! Magdalena, don't believe a word this woman says."

"Yes, she is," Rachel rasped. "I was trying to find you—thought you might be here. The second she opened the door, Dorcas went nuts. Believe me, Magdalena, she's stark raving mad."

"I am not!" There was pain in the big galoot's voice. "And anyway, she attacked me. I think she wanted to kill me." She glared accusingly at Rachel. "You would have killed my baby, too, you know!"

Ms. Blank blinked. "Don't be ridiculous! Besides, I don't even believe you're pregnant."

Dorcas, bless her oversized heart, was not easily stifled. "Magdalena, she asked me all kind of questions about Clarence, like had he ever talked about her. I told her he hadn't, but she wouldn't believe me. Kept saying I was holding back. What would I be holding back?"

I swiveled to look at Dorcas, but all I could see were her bruised knees. "I've a hunch you're about to find out, dear."

I turned back to Rachel. She was standing on something hidden beneath the floor that wasn't very stable. The bulk of our esteemed mayor's weight was supported by her arms. She reminded me of some of the rock climbers I'd seen hauling themselves to the top of Stucky Ridge.

I smiled at her. "Why should I help you?" I asked. "You tried to kill me as well."

Rachel had the temerity to feign surprise. "I don't know what you mean."

"Oh, yes, you do. At my beautiful memorial service you stood up and vowed that I would be remembered, and not just as another highway statistic. Well tell me, dear, how did you know my disappearance had anything to do with a highway?"

Rachel blinked. "You're grasping at straws, Magdalena. It was only a guess on my part."

"Well, grasp this, dear. You rammed the back of my car just as I was making that tight curve coming back from Cumberland. You must have seen me sail over the treetops. Then, when I went missing, you made the stupid assumption I was dead. Well, surprise, I'm not!"

"Now *you're* sounding like a lunatic. May I remind you, Magdalena Yoder, to whom you are speaking? I'm the mayor of this crummy [she actually used a word that I can't repeat] little town, in case you've forgotten."

"Madam Mayor," I said, my voice dripping with sarcasm, "I haven't forgotten a thing. For instance, I remember that when you left Hernia, lo those many years ago, you were a shy little thing. Nobody thought you'd stand a chance in the big wide world outside of Bedford County. Then one day you showed up on TV doing the weather reports from Philadelphia. The next thing we knew you were running for mayor." I sucked back some of the sarcasm because it was making the floor around me slippery. "Everyone was stunned. Some were even thrilled. Local girl makes good, that kind of thing. What nobody stopped to ask was, what were you doing during those ten years between college and the days you prattled on about cold fronts? Were you raising children in New Jersey like Thelma Rensberger? I don't think so! No, I'll tell you what you were doing."

The smug mug by the rug challenged me. "Oh, yeah? What was I doing?"

"You were working as a prostitute for the Benedicts down in Cumberland."

Dorcas gasped. "Is that true?"

"That's what you and I were on our way to find out, dear, when this raven started tapping at the door."

Dorcas had the gall to giggle. Perhaps she really was a lunatic.

"It was a window, Magdalena," she said.

"What?" I snapped.

"Poe's raven tapped on a window, not a trapdoor."

"Would Watson dare contradict Holmes?" Before she could answer I plunged on. "I did a little digging at the courthouse this afternoon, and guess what I learned? Clarence Webber was once Clarence Benedict. He was Arnold and Bonita's son. I don't know why I didn't pick up on that right away. I mean, he kept bringing his pigeons home, didn't he?"

"Pigeons?" Dorcas asked.

"Okay, his wives. I only meant that you were easy marks."

"I wasn't a pigeon," Dorcas said adamantly.

"We were all three of us pigeons, dear. Even I found myself having to struggle to resist his considerable charms. You see, Clarence had a knack for finding a woman's weak spot—her Achilles' heel."

Dorcas gasped again, threatening to deplete the small room of its oxygen. "You married him too?"

"Oh, no, dear. But that was his plan. That, and extortion, not to mention credit card fraud."

"Well, I never married him!" Madam Mayor was still trying to hoist herself out of the hole, and was panting like a sheepdog in August.

"That's because he already had his hooks in you," I said with confidence. "He was blackmailing you, wasn't he?"

Rachel risked falling back down into the hole by using one hand to rip the tape the rest of the way off her smeared face. Her look of defiance was astonishing.

"That son of a bitch," she roared. "What I did—working for his parents—was *years* ago. I was barely more than a girl. I haven't been in touch with any members of that family since then, yet he remembered me!"

"Perhaps you should be flattered, dear. You are—and don't take this the wrong way—somewhat of an attractive woman."

She lacked the courtesy to acknowledge my compliment. "He right away threatened to cut a deal with Melvin, unless I coughed up a hundred thousand dollars." It was unintentional, to be sure, but she actually coughed. "Now, where would the mayor of a one-horse town like this come up with that much money?"

"So you killed him."

"You can't prove it. You certainly can't prove that I caused your accident. There were no witnesses!"

"I think I can. Body shops keep records of repairs, you know. Your front bumper must have been severely damaged. Maybe the whole front end of your car."

"You practically made me total it," she said accusingly.

"There, you see?"

"But that still doesn't mean anything. I could have hit a deer. A large buck can do a lot of damage."

"It wasn't a buck, but a Buick. And there's undoubtedly paint from your car still on mine. The impact sent me sailing, all the way over a creek and into the crotch of a giant sycamore." I turned around again to address Dorcas's knees. "Although when Gabriel and Susannah found me, the car was on the ground. I couldn't figure that out at first, but then I remembered the awful storm. It must have knocked the car plumb out of the tree. Did the winds hit hard here too?"

The knees bobbled, an indication that their owner was nodding. "It was awful. I thought the roof was going to blow off at one point."

I turned my attention back to the villain. "I hope you like stripes, Your Honorableness, because you're going to be wearing them for a long time."

Mayor Blank looked at me blankly. "But I was supposed to win this election."

"Don't feel bad, dear. You win a free ticket to jail. Do not pass Go."

"Bitch!"

My intent was to stick my foot out and bring it down ever so lightly on her extended fingers. I wasn't really going to hurt her. You have to trust me on that one.

Rachel Blank, however, had other plans. With lightning speed she grabbed my ankle and before I could dig myself in with my other crampon-like heel, she'd pulled me into the hole with her. Then, while I was still in shock, she used me as a stepping stool and scrabbled out of the tunnel. The next thing I knew the trapdoor slammed shut and I was engulfed in darkness.

It wasn't utter darkness. I've seen that before, and not just in the heart of Aaron Miller, that bigamist ex-husband of mine. Once, on one of my few vacations, I visited the Lost Sea Caverns in Tennessee. Deep in the bowels of the earth the guide turned off the lights so we could experience true darkness. It was terrifying.

At any rate, there was a definite, albeit dim, light source in Dorcas's tunnel. I would have supposed that a passageway between two houses—for indeed that was its purpose—would follow a straight line. Quite possibly its builders had encountered a rock too large to dispatch, because this corridor curved sharply to the right, just meters from where I stood. I would also have supposed an underground chamber of any kind to be damp and musty (the Lost Sea Caverns certainly were), but the air around me, although cool, was exceedingly dry.

The walls, roof, and ceiling of the tunnel appeared to be made of reinforced concrete, not brick or fieldstone as I had imagined. It occurred to me that during the atomic bomb scare of the fifties, the Yutzy family had converted their infamous tunnel into a shelter. If that was the case, they weren't the only family in Hernia to do it. The John Burkholders, on the south side of town, are said to have built a series of underground rooms with enough space to accommodate their ten children and twenty-three grands.

My parents, on the other hand, believed that building a bomb shelter was the desperate act of a faithless person. The launching of the first nuclear missile should be a time of rejoicing, because that meant the Good Lord was just seconds behind, on a cloud, with trumpets blaring all around. And what if, I asked Papa, Jesus chose not to time His return with the machinations of Nikita Khrushchev's thumb? Well, there was always the outhouse. It didn't have bunk beds like Laurie Burkholder's subterranean palace, but it had an exceptionally deep pit.

Thus, expecting to find a protective chamber of some sort, I walked toward the light in Dorcas's tunnel. I was not disappointed. The room I entered was perhaps twelve feet square. While that is not palatial, it must be remembered that there were only three people in the Yutzy family: Dorcas and her parents. What I did not expect to find were more people. A man and a woman—in bed together!

"Excuse me!"

I wheeled, and then turned again. There was something very familiar about the woman. She was lying perfectly still, which, incidentally, is the only way a true lady acts in bed. This woman's pose, however, didn't seem quite right. I couldn't see her left arm, but her right arm was suspended stiffly over the man's chest. Although I couldn't see the man very well, he too appeared unnaturally stiff. Either they were mannequins or—

"Mrs. Yutzy? Mrs. Yutzy, is that you?"

No answer.

I took a few baby steps forward and cranked up the volume a notch. "Mrs. Yutzy, I don't mean to be rude, but what were you doing down here in a bomb shelter with Mayor Blank?"

Elizabeth Yutzy stared vacantly up at the ceiling. The gentleman in bed with her did the same thing. There was an electric candle fastened to the wall just above the headboard, and its feeble light did nothing for their complexions. They both looked sort of—well, dead.

"Don't they look peaceful?" a voice behind me asked.

I literally jumped out of my shoes—well, at least my left shoe. At any rate, grinning goofily at me was the big galoot herself.

My heart was pounding like a madman on a xylophone and I was in no mood for games. "Dorcas! Don't you ever sneak up on me again!"

"I didn't mean to scare you, Magdalena. I thought you heard me coming."

"I did no such thing!" I peered around her. "Where's the murderess? Where's Rachel Blank?"

"Still in the kitchen, but out like a light." Dorcas giggled. "I conked her on the head with a dinette chair. Then I tied her to the table. This time I did a much better job. She won't be getting loose."

I breathed a sigh of relief, then remembered the dimly lit duo behind me. "Dorcas, please tell me those are papier-mâché figures on that bed over there."

Dorcas was probably staring at me behind the thick lenses. All I saw were two dark circles.

"Do you think that beige dress looks all right on Mother, or should I have put her in peach?"

I shuddered, my worst suspicions confirmed. Elizabeth Yutzy's hearing problem was worse than anyone in Hernia imagined.

"Who's the man with her?" I asked weakly.

"Why, Daddy, of course."

"Dorcas, dear," I said, choosing my words carefully while trying to edge around her, "your daddy ran off to Cleveland with a barmaid from Bedford."

"No, he didn't."

"Yes, he did. Ask anyone in town—well, anyone over thirty, because that happened a good number of years ago."

The grin on the big gal's face almost split it in two. "He died of a heart attack, Magdalena. He didn't run away. It was my idea to put him down here. He and Mother couldn't bear to be apart, you see. Then when Mother died last spring—"

"*Last* spring?"

She nodded. "Easter Sunday. I'm afraid I had to miss church."

"But what about—I mean—uh, I don't want to be indelicate, but—"

"Oh, that. Well, you see, this shelter was designed to keep out contaminated air. It has its own purification system, which means I can control the humidity level. Did you know, it's actually drier in here right now than it is in the Egyptian desert?"

I gasped as the awful truth sank in. "You mean your mommy's a mummy?"

"Yeah, I guess you could say that. You see, I teach biology as well as gym, and it's really not that hard to do if you have the right setup. Now the eyes—"

I ducked around her and raced back down the tunnel to the trapdoor. She made no effort to stop me.

32

"What's this glop?" Alison pointed to the serving bowl nearest her.

"It isn't glop, dear. It's Freni's special mystery salad."

"Well, it looks like glop to me."

"Ach!" Freni squawked.

We were having a family dinner at the PennDutch, which still remained unopened to guests. Seated around the massive oak dining table, made by my ancestor Jacob "The Strong" Yoder, were my sister and her husband, Melvin, Freni and her husband, Mose, the very handsome Gabriel Rosen, and of course the urchin Alison.

"Forget the glop," Susannah said irritably. She turned to me. "So Mags, go on with your story. What happened then?"

"Then," Melvin said, arranging his mandibles in a sneer, "Magdalena came running to me for help."

"Well, you are the police chief," I said. "I can't be expected to do everything for you."

"*Was* the police chief, Yoder. With Rachel Blank out of the picture, I'm a shoo-in for the congressional seat."

"Don't be too sure, dear." The election had been postponed, and in a weird twist of fate, the Reverend Richard Nixon intended to run against the cocky Melvin. The good pastor was assured of at least thirty-*three* votes—mine being one of them.

"No, no, no," Susannah cried, pounding the table with her knife handle, "I meant, what happened to the bodies in the basement?"

"It was a bomb shelter, dear. Anyway, the folks out at Evergreen Cemetery gave them a proper burial this morning. It was a private ceremony, of course. Besides Dorcas and my minister—hers wouldn't come—Melvin and I were the only ones there."

"And why did Dorcas put the mayor in her basement? Why didn't she just call the police?"

"Well, it turns out that Clarence found out about her parents' bodies in the basement, and must have told Rachel about them. When Dorcas didn't cooperate with her, Rachel threatened to expose Dorcas's secret. Dorcas panicked. Unlike the mayor, Dorcas is not a killer. So she just locked Rachel in the bomb shelter until she could think of what to do."

"What will happen to Dorcas?" Alison asked. "Will she go to jail?"

I tried not to smile at the girl. During her stay with Freni and Mose she'd taken to wearing Amish clothes. Even given the fact that half of Alison's genetic material is of Amish derivation, she looked remarkably authentic—except for the hot pink lip gloss and a silver stud in each ear.

"Well, dear," I said, "the laws of the Commonwealth of Pennsylvania require one to report a death, which, of course, she didn't. And while, practically speaking, the bomb shelter is as good as any burial vault, technically it doesn't qualify. Under the circumstances, I don't think Rachel Blank is in a position to press any additional charges, though."

"So, Dorcas is going to jail?"

"If I have anything to say about it," Melvin Stoltzfus growled.

I glared at him. "Which you don't." I turned my attention back to my young charge. "She's going to be hospitalized. It's clear she's suffered a complete nervous breakdown."

"I think she's psychotic," Susannah said. "I saw basically the same story in a movie once."

Freni nodded wisely. "Ach, these English. So many are not right in the head, yah?"

"Dorcas Yutzy had Amish ancestors," I reminded her. "Maybe way back, but still up there in the family tree. The same thing goes for the Honorable Rachel Blank. Little Miss Murder herself."

Mose cleared his throat. It was meant as a warning to Freni not to pursue that angle any further. Freni frowned, but wisely held her tongue. At least for a little while.

In the ensuing silence Susannah picked a choice morsel from her plate and dropped it into the loose folds of her bosom. I could hear the snap of Shnookums' sharp little teeth as he gobbled his mistress's goodies. One day he'd gobble the wrong goodies and Susannah would have room for an even larger dog.

Freni, however, could not be stifled indefinitely. "This Rachel Blank, she is a Presbyterian, yah?"

"No," I said before my Presbyterian sister could get her bloomers in a bunch, "Rachel was a Mennonite— that is, until she went off to that fancy-shmancy college and became an agnostic."

Freni smiled, finally satisfied. "Yah, too much education."

I let that one go, and for a few minutes we dined peacefully. Except for a series of loud belches from Alison, and the continued snapping of Shnookums' teeth, the casual observer might have guessed we were a fairly normal family.

Leave it to Susannah to upset the apple cart with a bad case of the giggles.

"Susannah," I said sternly, "if that dog's doing what I think he is, you take him outside right now."

"What?" She laughed. "Oh, Mags, you're so silly. It's nothing to do with my widdle-piddle puppy."

"Then what does it concern?"

"It's a secret."

"So keep it a secret," Melvin hissed.

"Too late, dear. Out with it now."

"Well"—she had herself a good little laugh—"if you insist."

"I do. It isn't fair to the rest of us unless you share your joke."

"Okay, but you asked for it. It's about those scars on Clarence Webber's back. Melvin said he wasn't tortured exactly, but that he liked to be whipped. If there was no one around to do it for him—well, he did it to himself."

"And that's funny?" It was anything but. It was actually very sad. Pathetic, even. Apparently Zelda had just this morning confessed that she'd seen Clarence perform his strange ritual with wire stripped from Agnes Schlabach's shepherd's flute. She had not told anyone earlier, for fear that she might somehow be implicated. After all, it was she who allowed the flute in the cell.

Susannah had no clue, or didn't care, that she had just opened a Pandora's box. "Why would he whip himself?" Alison asked, her eyes as wide as Freni's corn muffins.

"It's a sexual thing," Susannah said matter-of-factly.

"Ach!" Freni and Mose cried in unison as they each clapped a hand over one of Alison's ears.

"Hey, I'm not a baby!" Alison protested, and tried pushing away the protective hands. Fortunately she was no match for the Hostetlers, who milk cows on a daily basis.

Susannah was still clueless. "I can't imagine my Mel-kins doing that. He doesn't even like to be spanked."

Melvin groaned.

"Sick," Alison said. "Yuck! Man, you people sure live in a weird little town."

Aware that their censoring hands did no good, the elderly couple resumed eating. Alison shook her head, as if to clear it of their presence.

"This has been an exceptionally bizarre case," I admitted. "There's a lot about it I don't understand myself, and I thought I'd seen just about everything."

"What I don't understand," Gabe said, "is how the mayor was able to poison a prisoner at the city jail. Is access that free?"

We all turned and looked at Melvin. Even Susannah got in on the act.

Without moving his head, our Chief of Police was able to avoid our questioning eyes by training both of his on the ceiling. There is a footprint on the ceiling, just like at his office—don't ask me how it got there—and Melvin stared at this while mumbling his response.

"I'm sorry, dear, but I didn't hear you."

Melvin's right eye left the footprint and found my face. "All right, Yoder, so security may have been a little lax. But don't worry, I've already taken care of that. I let Zelda go this morning."

"Go? Go where?"

"I fired her."

I wagged a finger at him presidential style. "Then hire her right back. Make her go to counseling, if you want, but get her back on the team."

"You can't make me," he said, like a small child.

Fortunately for Melvin, the telephone rang. I answered it in the kitchen.

*   *   *

"PennDutch Inn," I said mustering my last ounce of false cheer. "We're not open for business now, but if you give me your name and a number—"

"Magdalena, this is Reverend Schrock."

"Hi Reverend!" How quickly false cheer can change to genuine dread.

"Magdalena, I've been thinking about our conversation this morning."

"Oh?"

"You know, what you asked me after I officiated at the interment of Dorcas Yutzy's parents. *After* you made sure Melvin was way out of earshot?"

"I know what I asked you, Reverend! What I don't know is your answer."

There was a pregnant pause; one long enough to allow half the women in Hernia to become with child.

"And?" I asked when three minutes were up.

"And the answer is yes."

"You're kidding!"

"I wouldn't joke about something this serious. And it is a serious decision on your part, Magdalena. You realize that, don't you?"

"Yes, but—"

"And a lot of people won't understand. Folks like my Lodema, for instance. There may be things said that shouldn't be. You might get hurt."

"Sticks and stones!" I said, barely able to contain my joy.

"Oh, and speaking of Lodema," he said, "I want to thank you for spraying her with your garden hose that day."

"You *do*?"

"She goes too far a lot of the time. It's good that you stand up to her."

"I do my best."

"It seems to me that if you go ahead as planned, you'll have a lot more opportunity."

We both laughed.

"Nu," Gabe said, "so who was that on the phone that's got you grinning from ear to ear?"

"Was it for me?" Alison asked with the hope of the young. "I sent Boyz II Men this phone number, by the way."

"It was probably for me," Susannah said. "I left a message with Studs R Us. They promised to call me as soon as the manager came in for the night shift. Sorry, sis, but I gave them your number."

Melvin was beside himself. "Studs R Us?"

Susannah smiled. "It's a dog-breeding service, poopsie."

"But that rat's a mutt!" I cried.

"Shhhhh!" Susannah pointed to her bulging bosom. "He doesn't know that. Besides, they have a special registry of"—she silently mouthed the word—"nonpedigreed dogs. You make a video and everything. It's like a dating service."

Alison rolled her eyes.

Feeling generous, I graced my sister with a smile. "Well, you're wrong, dear. That phone call was for me. It was from Reverend Schrock."

"Ach!"

"Don't worry, Freni. He actually thanked me for spraying his wife with water."

"Then why are you so happy?" she demanded. "It is not nice to keep us in suspenders."

"I think the word is 'suspense,' dear. And I'm smiling because the Reverend has agreed to co-officiate at a wedding."

"Whose?" Gabe asked, his curiosity piqued.

"Yours," I said. "Yours and mine. That is, if you'll agree to marry me."

"Is that a proposal?" Gabe asked, without missing a beat.

"Yes."

"Then my answer is yes," he said.

"Really?"

Gabe pushed back his chair and strode around to my end of the table. Before I had a chance to catch my breath, he planted one on me. Right on the kisser.

"Mazel tov!" Alison cried.

"Ach!" Freni gasped.

"Aooow!" Shnookums wailed.

You see? Just like I said, we were pretty much a normal family.

33

Grillades and Grits

Grillades are small, thin cutlets of beef, veal, or pork. Actually you could use chicken breasts for this recipe as well. In New Orleans, this is a robust way to start the day—it's a traditional breakfast for hard-working Creoles. It's also a great brunch dish, needing only a watercress salad and crusty French bread to make us think of those banana-tree-shaded patios in the Crescent City.

3 tablespoons bacon
  fat or lard
3 tablespoons all-
  purpose flour
¼ teaspoon salt
⅛ teaspoon freshly
  ground black
  pepper
1 pound thin pork
  loin cutlets

1 cup chopped
  onions
¼ cup chopped celery
½ cup chopped red or
  green bell pepper
1½ cups canned
  whole tomatoes,
  chopped, with juice
1 small fresh cayenne
  pepper, seeded and

chopped, or pinch
of dried pepper
flakes
1 large clove garlic,
minced
About ¼ cup water

1 recipe Basic Boiled
Grits, hot and
liquid, but not too
runny
2 teaspoons chopped
fresh parsley

Heat the fat in a large skillet over medium-high heat. Mix the flour, salt, and pepper together on a plate. Dip both sides of the cutlets in the mixture and brown quickly on each side. Set aside.

Add the onions, celery, and bell peppers to the skillet and sauté until tender, about 10 minutes. Add the tomatoes, cayenne, and garlic; bring to a simmer. Thin the sauce with water, if desired. Add the sautéed pork and simmer until the meat is tender and cooked through, about 20 minutes.

Divide the grits among 4 warm plates. Top with the grillades and sauce. Sprinkle with the parsley and serve immediately.

SERVES 4

Turn the page for a special excerpt from
Tamar Myers's new wacky and wonderful
Pennsylvania Dutch mystery

Custard's Last Stand

Includes heavenly recipes for
custard and crème brûlée!

A New American Library hardcover
Available in February 2003

After serving us, Miss Anne Thrope retired to the kitchen to rejoin the clucking Freni. Ivan Yetinsky, I was told, would eat his meal up in his room. That left just the very handsome Colonel George C. Custard and me—and my foster daughter, Alison.

Although I am engaged to be married to a wonderful man, it was still fun to pretend that Alison and the colonel and I were a nuclear family. What did one call a colonel's wife anyway? A colonel*less*? I'd certainly settle for Your Ladyship.

"Please pass the fancy-shmancy carrots, dear," I said. The orange roots, which had been doctored up with some incredible seasonings, were midway between Alison and George C. I held my breath to see who would respond to my request.

Alas, it was Alison who picked up the bowl. "These things are hard as rocks. I like Auntie Freni's better."

"Mind your manners," I said, but couldn't suppress a grin. I knew from experience that Freni would be in the kitchen with her ear pressed to a glass. I widened the grin into a friendly smile. "So, Colonel, what brings you to this neck of the woods?"

Before answering, he patted the corners of his mouth with a genuine polyblend napkin. "I'm here on business."

"Really? But Hernia has no businesses—outside of my inn, a small grocery, and a feed store."

"Ah, but soon that's all going to change. And that's why I'm here."

"There's some kind of yucky sauce on this meat," Alison whined.

I gave her a loving glare. "How is it going to change, Colonel?"

"Do you know the Jonas Troyer property at the end of Main Street?"

"Yes, what about it?"

"I purchased it last month."

"Get out of town!" In retrospect, I should have meant that literally. "But I didn't even know the Troyers were in the market to sell."

The Colonel winked. "They weren't. I made them an offer they couldn't refuse. They've decided to retire to Florida."

"And you'll be moving here?" My fiancé is everything I could want in a man, but in the event he turned out to be a bigamist, it would be nice to have a backup.

"Maybe—I haven't decided. Fortunately I have enough good people working for me that I could work out of my home in Louisville."

I will be the first to admit that I am easily distracted. "You said business. What kind of business?"

He dabbed his mouth again and took a sip of ice water. As a faithful Christian, I don't serve my guests wine. The Colonel had brought his own, but I had insisted he keep it in the limousine.

"I plan to build a five-star hotel," he said.

"What?"

"I've been to Lancaster County many times, Miss Yoder. I know what a draw the Amish are for tourists. But in my opinion that area has become overdeveloped. Just too many tourists and urban refugees. I've done very careful market research and concluded that Bedford County contains some of the best Amish ambience in the world. Your charming Hernia, of course, is the epicenter. I think the time has come to capitalize on that, don't you?"

Through the wall I heard the thud of Freni's glass hitting the floor.

"But you can't do that!" I cried. "It will ruin Hernia."

He cocked his silvered head in amusement. Suddenly he didn't seem at all handsome.

"I'm not building another Amish World," he said. "This is a very small, but tasteful, hotel that will cater to the elite. The crème de la crème, so to speak. They know how to comport themselves."

"You mean like *my* hotel?"

"Not quite. My hotel will be a five-star operation."

"But I have Hollywood stars—well, usually."

"Yours is an inn, Miss Yoder. Hotel Hernia will have one hundred well-appointed rooms and all the best amenities, including a spa."

"But you'll be stealing my guests!"

"I don't think so. You draw mostly from the celebrity crowd, don't you?"

"Babs has class. You can't get any more elite than that."

"Yes, but I'm talking about real thoroughbreds. The Cabots, the Vanderbilts—"

"Haufta mischt!"

"I beg your pardon."

"That's Pennsylvania Dutch for horse manure."

He looked taken aback. If only he'd taken himself back to Louisville or wherever he came from.

"Why do you find this so upsetting?" he asked.

"Because you're going to put me out of business, that's why."

"Miss Yoder, I've already explained that we're not

competing for the same customers. Your quaint little inn can just keep chugging along as usual."

"It doesn't chug! Why, I'll have you know I'm booked solid for the next year. You only managed to get in by lying. I doubt if you're even a real colonel," I said.

"I am. I'm a Kentucky colonel."

"Like Colonel Sanders?"

His face hardened. "What about you? Are you a *real* Mennonite, or is this some little charade you put on for the benefit of your guests?"

That shocked me to the toes of my heavy hose. I patted my organza prayer cap.

"Of course I'm a real Mennonite. My family has been either Mennonite or Amish for the last five hundred years."

"Well, you could have fooled me. I thought Mennonites were supposed to be a kind, peaceful people."

"We are."

"Maybe most are. But you, Miss Yoder, have a tongue that could slice Swiss cheese."

Alison, who'd been watching this discourse intently, jabbed the air with her fork. "Hey, you can't say that to my mom."

My heart burst with sinful pride. She may not have sprung from my loins, but she was as faithful as any daughter. At least when the attack came from the outside.

I flashed Alison a smile. "Colonel Custard," I said, "I feel it is only fair to warn you that I fully intend to inform the citizens of this community of your diabolical plan to destroy their way of life."

"I don't intend to destroy anything. But if you think you can stop me from getting a building permit, you're too late. I've already got it."

I gasped. "Melvin Stoltzfus! That miserable, menacing mantis who poses as our mayor."

Colonel Custard nodded. "He was actually a very pleasant man. I think I'll offer him a job in—"

I didn't stay to hear the rest of his sentence.

Hazel Holt

"Sheila Malory is a most appealing heroine."
—*Booklist*

MRS. MALORY AND THE DELAY OF EXECUTION
0-451-20627-4

When a schoolteacher at a prestigious English prep school
dies suddenly, Mrs. Malory is talked gets shanghaied into
being substitute teacher with a little detecting on the side.

MRS. MALORY AND THE FATAL LEGACY
0-451-20002-0

Sheila Malory returns, this time as executor to the estate of
a late, bestselling novelist. And what Malory reads into the
death is a crime.

To order call: 1-800-788-6262